文法俏佳人

English Grammar Power from Legendary Beauties

邱佳翔◎著

三大 Superb 體驗

看俏佳人說什麼，體驗全新文法學習

6週打造你的 A list 英文文法高手路

● 【俏佳人怎麼說】
截取**英美小說**（例如：亂世佳人、傲慢與偏見）中，膾炙人口的俏佳人名句以及作品概述，由此**導入文法學習主題**。

● 【英文文法概述】
收錄共**75組**必考混淆**文法概念**，每組列舉易混淆的字詞，詳解其中的差異，使讀者能釐清常混淆的用法，並能靈活運用於各類考試中。

● 【實作練習與解析】
精選**5-6題**必會題目並搭配文法解析，檢視是否確實吸收文法精華，立即回憶那些曾學過的文法，**無師也能自通**。

Preface 作者序

　　若想要深度了解一種語言，閱讀以該種語言所撰寫的經典文學作品會是個非常好的方法。原因在於這些作品與句法應用上實為上乘，有助於語言學習者建立正確的文法觀念。

　　當選定某個作品開始閱讀時，若留意當中女性角色的話語，更可提高學習之效，原因在於女性性格多較男性細膩，故作者對其刻劃也較為深刻。本書挑選亂世佳人、傲慢與偏見、理性與感性、咆哮山莊、小婦人與簡愛這六本經典名著，以當中女性人物具代表性的話語為題材，除講述其中的文法句型，更羅列具混淆性的用法解析箇中差異，以期讀者未來不在有誤用的情況發生。

　　文法對語言學習很重要，但方法可以很多元，本書希望能以輕鬆的方式，讓讀者理解許多用途廣泛的文法，以提升整體英文能力。

邱佳翔

Editor 編者序

　　在學習文法的過程中，我們大多忽略了，英文文法與主題連結的學習在學習成效上所帶來的幫助。大多時候，課堂上和教科書的文法，限定了我們更靈活地理解外國人的表達，囫圇吞棗地寫了許多試題，卻只是跟英語有了短暫的瞭解而已，隨著大考成績的出爐跟時間的推移漸漸淡忘，每每都在需要它時，又要重新認識它。

　　在學習文法上我們無疑會陷入一種循環：考完指考後認識它最深，直到大學三、四年級遇到校內畢業門檻又得重拾書本，或是工作後某天深覺自己該加強英文時，發現自己已經不認識他了，又或是大學時期某天猛然回頭看著一群新鮮人，卻跟好友們揶揄著，不知道自己現在去報考大學學測英文科會幾分呢？

　　相信許多人都可能曾遇過上述的狀況，而這本文法俏佳人就是你的伴讀好手，從六大經典文學主題中，精選了女主角說過的俏佳人名句，與文法主題作結合，就如同你看了八點檔，隔天腦海中卻還能記住某些角色說過的話一樣，對文法的印象也會因為這些句子讓印象更加深，實力夠的話也可以跳過文法概述直接寫寫題目殺時間，相信能找回你對文法的熱愛，不用老是上演著要重新跟它談戀愛的困擾啦！

編輯部敬上

$\mathcal{C}ontents$ 目次

Part 3 **Week 3 理性與感性**

Part 6 **Week 6 簡愛**

Part 1

Week 1 亂世佳人

Unit 01
亂世佳人

俏佳人怎麼說

Tomorrow is another day—Scarlett O'Hara

明天又是嶄新的一天——郝思嘉

作品概述

　　歷經戰亂洗禮後，女主角郝思嘉才終於恍然大悟自己最愛的人不是衛希禮而是白瑞德，但被傷透了心的白瑞德已選擇離去。此時彷彿失去一切的郝思嘉並未灰心，而是說出此小說中最讓人印象深刻的一句台詞：Tomorrow is another day (明天又是嶄新的一天)。此經典台詞中也出現了一個英文學習者常常會搞混的 another，現在就透過本單元的解析，弄懂 another、others、the other、the others 到底該怎麼用。

文法概述

Another / other / the other / the others

★ Another 另一個

　　若將 Another 拆解 an + other 來理解，意思是「一個 + 一些」。

從這個架構去推演，既然只是剩下的全部中的一部份，代表整個範圍至少分成三部分。此外，由於 an 沒有限定範圍的作用，another 也可用來表示完全獨立的另一個體或集合。

EX Joe orders some dishes. One is fried chicken, another is sandwich, and the other is soup.

喬點了一些菜。其中一道是炸雞，另一道是三明治，另一道是湯。

➡ 從 one, another, the other 這三個代名詞，就可以推知範例中的 some=three。

EX Since I am too hungry, I eat another after having one burger.

我太餓了，所以吃一個漢堡後又吃了另一個。

➡ 由兩個漢堡在範圍上是獨立不重疊的，因此用 another 做為第二個漢堡的代名詞。

★ Others 任何其它的

由於沒有 the 限制範圍，如果沒有特別說明總數，常會用 others 來泛指剩下的所有部分。

EX Some support this act, but others against it.

有些人支持此法案，有些人則表示反對。

➡ 當要表達正反、多少等二元對立的概念時，數量的重要性次之，因此 some…, but others…是很實用的句型。

★ The other 剩下的…

若推敲 the 與 other 的各別語意，the 表達範圍上的限定，由於 other 是單數，代表就只有這個部分，沒有其他。兩者一組合，就表

1 亂世佳人

2 傲慢與偏見

3 理性與感性

4 咆哮山莊

5 小婦人

6 簡愛

達出某一事物分成兩部分，而現在說明的是其中一份。

EX I buy two books. One is about literature, and the other is about travel.

我買了兩本書。一本有關文學，剩下的有關旅遊。

→ 書的總數是兩本，敘述了其中一本，剩下來的當然只剩一本，
因此符合 the other 的使用時機。

★ **The others 剩下全部的…**

此用法與上述用法差別在於 others 是複數，若用在描述共幾項，代表此範圍內，共為三個部分，現在說明的是其中一份。若用在表達二分法，就代表現在描述這個分類的數量不只一個。

EX I buy three pairs of shoes. One is for formal occasion, the others are for sport.

我買了三雙鞋。一雙是正式場合穿，剩下的運動時穿。

實作練習與解析

❶ Three models of smart phone are available. One is Z6, _____ __ is C6 plus, and the other is P6.
(A) another (B) other (C) others (D) the another
Ans: (A)。因為總共有三種，扣除 one 與 the other 後剩下那個應當以 another 表示。

❷ John is too hungry, so he eats _____ piece of pie after having lunch.

(A) other　(B) the others　(C) others　(D) another

Ans: (D)。派跟跟午餐吃的食物範圍不重疊，因此用 another 為正確用法。

❸ Some of the members are professional athletics, while _____
__ are amateur ones.

(A) another　(B) the other　(C) others　(D)the another

Ans: (B)。因為要職業與業餘是二分法，因此要選 the other。

❹ Some of the members are professional athletics, while _____
__ are amateur ones and coaches.

(A) other　(B) the other　(C) the others　(D) the another

Ans: (C)。因為教練與業餘選手是兩個不同分類，故選 the others。

❺ There are four books on the desk. One is blue cover, another
is red cover, and _____ are purple cover.

(A) the others　(B) the another　(C) the other　(D) other

Ans: (A)。四本書扣掉紅色與藍色封面各一本還剩兩本，故選 the others。

❻ Jason buys three jeans this time. One is regular and _____
are boots.

(A) the others　(B) the other　(C) others　(D) the another

Ans: (A)。總共買三件，扣掉一件直筒褲，剩下的兩件都是靴型，因此選 the others。

Unit 02
亂世佳人

俏佳人怎麼說

If I have to lie, steal, cheat or kill,
as god as my witness, I'll never be
hungry again!—Scarlett O'Hara

即使要我撒謊、去偷、去騙、去殺人，
上帝為證，我再也不要挨餓了！——郝思嘉

作品概述

　　亂世佳人的故事開始於美國南北戰爭爆發的前夕。戰爭前，郝思嘉住在無需擔心的莊園中，但戰爭爆發後，郝思嘉一家人只能被迫離開家園。歷經顛沛流離之苦的郝思嘉，由於不想再挨餓了，便說出即便要她幹盡各種壞事，也不要再挨餓的這句台詞。這句台詞中出現了 have to，多數人應該都知道它的意思是必須…，但如果要區分它 must、ought to 之間的差別，就有點不容易，現在就透過本單元的解析，讓你搞懂三種用法到底差在哪。

文法概述

Have to / must / not have to / must not

★ Have to 必須/不得不

Have to 意思是「必須…」，屬於初階的文法，但由於多數人都忽略了「客觀敘述」的作用，因此常與 must、should 等字混用。因此，當要表達某事有必要性，但不參雜說話者個人意見於其中，就該使用 have to。

EX You have to turn right at the next block, or you will miss the restaurant you are looking for.

你必須在下個街區右轉，否則就會錯過你在找的那間餐廳。

→ 由於說話者是在告知對方資訊，因此要使用敘述客觀事實的 have to 來說明必要性。

★ Must 必須/得要

細究修辭上的差異，雖然語意上與 have to 都可以解釋為「必須…」，但 must 帶有主觀意識，也就是訊息傳達者希望接收者可以依照內容行事。因此，只要牽涉某人的期望，就可以使用 must。

EX This meeting is very important, so you must show up.

此次會議很重要，所以你務必要出席。

→ 由於說話者自己覺得此次會議不去不行，因此使用 must 而不是 have to 來強調必要性。

★ Not have to 不必

雖然 have to 與 must 在語意上可以共通，但在否定用法上，兩者就完全不同。Not have to 意思是「不必…」，代表你有選擇權，做或

1 亂世佳人

2 傲慢與偏見

3 理性與感性

4 咆哮山莊

5 小婦人

6 簡愛

不做操之在己。

EX You do not have to wake up early on Sunday morning.
星期天早上你不必早起。

→ 由於星期天早上你要早起當然很好，但睡晚些也無傷大雅，所以用 not have to 恰如其分。

★ Must not 不可

與 not have to 不同，must 意思是「不可…」，代表你有能力做但不該真的去做。因此當要表達提醒或警告時。就可以使用 must not。

EX Unless there are some emergent events, you must not press the emergency button; otherwise, you will get fired.
除非有緊急事件發生，不可按壓緊急按鈕，否則重罰。

→ 由於按下按鈕並沒有操作上的困難度，只是時機恰當與否，因此使用 must not 來表達十分恰當。

實作練習與解析

❶ You _____ compromise in some aspects, or the communication will be in a deadlock.
(A) must (B) have to (C) must not (D) don't have to
Ans: (B)。此句客觀敘述事實，因此選擇 have to。

❷ The retail price could affect sales, so you _____ have compressive researches before the release of the new product.

(A) must not   (B) have to   (C) have not to   (D) must

Ans: (D)。此句中的 could 表現出推測語氣，故選擇帶有個人觀感的
   must。

❸ You _____ wake up early in this Monday morning because that day is Christmas.

(A) don't have to   (B) not must   (C) must not   (D) have not to

Ans: (A)。由於放假早起與否取決於個人，故選擇 don't have to。

❹ This reached consensus in the meeting determines the direction of our annual plan, so you _____ be late.

(A) have to   (B) don't have to   (C) must not   (D) not must

Ans: (C)。由於遲到與否屬於人為可控制範圍，因此選擇 must not。

❺ The traffic downtown is busy all the time in the afternoon, so you _____ leave early or you may be stopped in the traffic jam.

(A) not must   (B) have to not   (C) must   (D) have to

Ans: (D)。由於交通繁忙可以是某地區的常態，因此選擇客觀表述事
   實的 have to。

❻ The structure of the house is seriously damaged after the hurricane, so you _____ repair it soon.

(A) have to   (B) have not to   (C) must   (D) not must

Ans: (A)。房子受損要維修屬於客觀描述，因此選擇 have to。

Unit 03
亂世佳人

俏佳人怎麼說

Now I find myself in a world which for me is worse than death. A world in which there is no place for me.—Scarlett O'Hara

現在我發現我自己活在比死還痛苦的世界，
一個無我容身之處的世界。——郝思嘉

作品概述

在亂世佳人的故事中，當南北戰爭爆發後，原本生活優渥，居住在莊園的郝思嘉除了流離失所外，還身無分文。這樣巨大的變化讓她難以承受，覺得比死亡還痛苦，天地間彷彿無其可容身之處。在這句經典台詞中，出現了大家都知道但卻常常搞混的關係代名詞 which，以及 in which 這樣介系詞 + 關係代名詞的正確使用時機，現在透過本單元的解析，往後就不會在關係代名詞 which 的使用上出現問題了。

文法概述

Which / in which

★ Which

在解釋 which 怎麼用之前，讓我們先搞懂到底關係代名詞的作用為何。若把其拆解成關係+代名詞，關係指的就是與先行詞有關係，而代名詞，意思就是此名詞可以代替指代前述的所有字群。因此，關係代名詞最大的功用就是連接先行詞與修飾部分。

理解了關係代名詞的基本概念後，接下來解釋 which 的用法。由於代名詞可能是代替人或是事物，人的部分會用 who、whom、whose，而事物部分就會 which、 whose。換言之，先行詞+which+不完整句(缺主詞、受詞、限定詞都有可能)就是最基本架構。

在學習英文文法的路上，大家一定都有做過合併句子練習，此種練習的目的就是要練習者理解到底如何透過關係代名詞來連接並修飾句子。接下來透過以下範例，更進一步說明：

EX I write a book.

The book is about how to learn English well.

➔ The book which I write is about how to learn English well.

➔ 由於 a book 與 the book 指的都是同一本書，因此透過 which 連接，以誰是作者為形容詞來修飾。

★ In which

當介系詞+ which，在功用上就等於關係副詞 when、where、why、how。當先行詞是地方時，in which=where。由於 where

是副詞，適用的句構是: 先行詞+where+完整句，這點與 which 接不完整句不同。理解此原理後，往後就可以依此判斷該用 which 還是 in which。以下透過範例再進一步說明:

EX I will go to the arena.

The basketball game is held in the arena.

→ I will go to the arena where the basketball game is held.

→ 比較兩個句子後，第一個會發現主要是敘述地點 arena，符合用 in which 的條件之一。另去掉地點後 the basketball game is held 仍可獨立成句，代表是完整句。兩者皆符合 in which 的使用時機。

實作練習與解析

❶ The car ＿＿＿＿＿ John bought yesterday is blue.
(A) in which　(B) who　(C) which　(D) in that
Ans: (C)。車子屬於物品，因此選 which。

❷ The room ＿＿＿＿＿ Susan has been living for seven years is spacious.
(A) which　(B) in that　(C) who　(D)where
Ans: (D)。房間是地點，加上蘇珊住了七年是完整句，因此選 where。

❸ I buy a book＿＿＿＿＿ is about how to play tennis well
(A) where　(B) which　(C) who　(D) in which
Ans: (B)。書是物品，因此選 which。

❹ I went back to the community _____ I lived during my university days.

(A) in which   (B) on which   (C) which   (D) in where

Ans: (A)。社區是地點，我大學時所居住是完整句，因此選 in which

❺ The police arrived at the room_____ the girl was killed.

(A) which   (B) on which   (C) where   (D) in that

Ans: (C)。房間是地點，女孩被殺是完整句，因此選擇 where。

❻ Ken is looking for the hotel _____ the opening ceremony is held.

(A) where   (B) on that   (C) which   (D) that

Ans: (A)。飯店是地點，舉行開幕儀式是完整句，因此選擇 where。

1 亂世佳人

2 傲慢與偏見

3 理性與感性

4 咆哮山莊

5 小婦人

6 簡愛

Unit 04
亂世佳人

俏佳人怎麼說

You are no gentlemen! —Scarlett O'Hara
先生，你也太不紳士了！──郝斯嘉。

作品概述

　　在故事前段，也就是南北戰爭爆發之前，女主角愛上了男主角衛希禮，但衛希禮卻早已和他表妹訂婚，並於十二橡樹園舉行燒烤宴會，正式宣布此喜訊。在宴會中，郝斯嘉有一小段與衛希禮獨處的時間，卻發現白瑞德偷聽兩人的對話，因此說出這句指責的台詞。此句台詞結構簡單，但也是練習區分 S is/are no N、S is/are not a N 與 S have/had none of N 這三個具否定意思句型的好教材。

文法概述

No + N / Not a N / None of N

★ No N

　　說到 No 這個單字，大家都很熟，意思是「沒有」。當 No 加上 N

時，意思是「並非」或是「一點也不」。因此，當要表達某人名實不符，就可以用 S is/are no N 或是 It is no adj…來表示。以下透過範例進一步說明：

EX You are no honest businessmen.

你並非誠實的商人。

➜ 由於說話者可能原本認為對方童叟無欺，但後來發現並非如此，因此用 S is/are no N 句型來吐槽。

★ Not a N

Not 意思是「並非」，英文中表達否定中極為常見的單字。此語意與上述用法相同。但由於 not 是副詞，用法會有差異，其句型為 S is/are not a N。

以下透過範例做進一步說明：

EX John is not an aggressive sales representative.

約翰並不是一個積極的業務。

➜ 由於說話者認為 John 的工作態度跟他所預期的有落差，因此用 S is/are not a N 來說明他的失望。

★ S have/had none of N

None 是代名詞，通常會與 of 連用，意思是「一點也沒有…」或是「一點也不…」。 當要運用 none 來表達預期與實際的落差，可使用 S have/had none of N。以下透過範例做進一步說明：

EX Leo has none of his older brother's courage.

里歐不像他哥那樣勇敢。

➜ 由於說話者可能先認識里歐的哥哥，以為兄弟應該都同樣勇

1 亂世佳人

2 傲慢與偏見

3 理性與感性

4 咆哮山莊

5 小婦人

6 簡愛

敢,但後來發現並非如此,因此 S have/had none of N 句型來描述這種差異恰如其分。

實作練習與解析

❶ You are _____ careful engineer.
(A) none　(B) none of　(C) no
Ans: (C)。由於說話者可能認為對方凡事謹慎,但實際接觸後才發現並非如此,因此用 S is/are no + (adj) N 句型來點出落差。

❷ John is _____ aggressive learner.
(A) no　(B) none of　(C) not
Ans: (A)。由於說話者可能原本覺得約翰態度應該是積極的,但後來發現其實不然,因此用 S is/are no + (adj) N 句型來點出落差。

❸ Ada is _____ a smart but a hard-working student.
(A) no　(B) none of　(C) not
Ans: (C)。由於有冠詞 a,故用 not 來表達艾達並非天資聰穎,而是努力用功的學生。

❹ Eddie is _____ an insightful leader.
(A) not　(B) none of　(C) no
Ans: (A)。由於有冠詞 an,故用 not 來表達說話者對艾迪的看法。

❺ Mark has _____ of his father's good temper.
(A) no　(B) none　(C) not

Ans: (B)。由於後有 of，故以 none 來表達馬克並不像他爸爸那樣好脾氣。

❻ Lucy has ＿＿＿＿ of her mother's good manner.
(A) none   (B) not   (C) no

Ans: (A)。由於後有 of，故以 none 來表達露西並不像她媽媽那樣有禮貌。

1 亂世佳人

2 傲慢與偏見

3 理性與感性

4 咆哮山莊

5 小婦人

6 簡愛

Unit 05
亂世佳人

🔍 俏佳人怎麼說

I can't let him go. I can't. There must be
some way to bring him back. Oh, I can't think
about this now! I'll go crazy if I do! I'll think
about it tomorrow. But I must think about
it. I must think about it. What is there to do?
What is there that matters? Tara! Home.
I'll go home. —Scarlett O'Hara

我不能讓他離開，我做不到。一定有可以挽回他的方法。
哦，我不能去想這個了！如果現在去想，我一定會發瘋！
我明天一定會想，必須仔細去想，仔細去想到底該怎麼做？
有什麼是重要的？塔拉！我的家，我就回家了！──郝思嘉

作品概述

在故事的末段，郝思嘉雖然選擇接受白瑞德，但他們倆的女兒卻意外身亡，這樣的鉅變埋下兩人最後分手的導火線。但壓倒駱駝的最後一根稻草，是梅拉妮的臨終託付，梅拉妮希望郝思嘉能替她繼續照顧衛希禮，而這樣讓白瑞德在此選擇離去，心慌意亂的郝思嘉便自言自語地說出這段台

詞。在此段台詞中，出現大家常使用的片語 think about，意思是考慮。但在英文中尚有 think of、think over、think out 等用法也有近似語意，透過本單元的解析，將可釐清四種用法的差異。

文法概述

Think of / think about / think over / think out

★ Think of 想到、打算、考慮

若不細究修辭上的差異，本單元的四個片語其實可以互通。如果細分考慮周延的程度，think of 所產生的想法像是雛形，具有可行性但細節可能要多加琢磨。以下透過範例進一步說明：

EX Can you_____ any good place for us to picnic this Saturday?

你有想到任何適合週六去野餐的好地方嗎?

→ 說話者提出此問題是希望對方能根據時間與目的給予一些建議，並不是要馬上決定，因此用 think of 十分恰當。

EX Please think of resources we have now.

請把手邊到底有多少資源列入考慮。

→ 由於資源是個概括性的敘述，用 think of 來表達初步思考下一步計畫相當貼切。

★ Think about 考慮

雖然同樣表達考慮，但 think about 在思考的周延性更高一些，思考的面向架構、細節與可行性高低兼具。以下透過範例進一步說明：

1 亂世佳人

2 傲慢與偏見

3 理性與感性

4 咆哮山莊

5 小婦人

6 簡愛

EX Now I am thinking about shortening the opening hours.

現在我有考慮縮短營業時間。

➜ 由於改變營業時間影響層面大，用 think about 來表達這次經過思考後的決定。

★ Think over 考慮

與 think about 相比，think over 所產生的想法完整性更高，over 表現出此決定是反覆思考後的結果。以下透過範例進一步說明：

EX Please give me few days to think this plan over.

請給我幾天仔細考慮這個計畫。

➜ 由於說話者希望多方考慮後再決定是否執行計畫，因此用 think over 來表達其謹慎態度。

★ Think out 想出、仔細考慮

在這四種考慮中，think out 與 think of 在思考細密度上接近，但很能表現那種終於想出某種方法的意境。以下透過範例做進一步說明：

EX Think out the outline before you write the thesis.

寫論文之前，請仔細構思大綱。

➜ 由於論文如果下筆後才要大修綱要會事倍功半，因此用 think out 來表達仔細思考的重要。

實作練習與解析

❶ Can you _____ any good restaurant for you class reunion?
(A) think over   (B) think about   (C) think of   (D) think out

Ans: (C)。因為只是提出選項來考慮，因此用 think of 最適合。

❷ _____ the rent you can afford and then find the proper place.
(A) think over   (B) think of   (C) think out   (D) think about
Ans: (B)。由於說話者要先粗估租金才去找地段，因此用 think of 來表達只是初步考慮。

❸ _____ the labor, I am considering cutting the position of assistants.
(A) thinking about   (B) thinking of   (C) thinking out   (D) thinking over
Ans: (A)。由於裁員茲事體大，用 think about 較能表現通盤考量的語意。

❹ _____ the total man power you need before you start the plan.
(A) think over   (B) think about   (C) think of   (D) think out
Ans: (B)。由於人力充足與否可以左右計畫的成敗，因此用 think about 來表達思考廣度十分恰當。

❺ Since the investment of this project is huge, please give me few days to _____ it.
(A) think over   (B) think of   (C) think about   (D) think out
Ans: (A)。由於投資與否是很重大的決定，因此用 think over 來表達多方思考的語境。

1 亂世佳人

2 傲慢與偏見

3 理性與感性

4 咆哮山莊

5 小婦人

6 簡愛

Unit 06
亂世佳人

俏佳人怎麼說

Money does help and of course I am fond of you... If I said I was madly in love with you, you'd know I was lying. You always said we had a lot in common... —Scarlett O'Hara

錢總是好的，我當然很喜歡。如果我說我很瘋狂地愛你，那我肯定是在說謊，但你常說我們有許多相同之處。——郝思嘉

作品概述

　　女主角郝斯嘉一開始對白瑞德沒有好感，甚至還很討厭他。但是隨著故事劇情的推移，生活出現巨變的郝思嘉慢慢明白，適合自己的不是衛希禮，而是白瑞德，因此才說出這句表白的台詞。在此段台詞中，出現了大家熟悉的單字 help。雖然 help 可以涵括各類型的協助，但意境尚可能就是稍嫌不足，透過本單元的解析，將可以讓搞懂何時用 help、aid、assist 最洽當。

文法概述

Help / aid / assist

★ Help 幫忙

Help 為本單元所介紹「幫助」中範圍最廣的，可以用來指稱物質或精神上的協助，說話者與訊息接收者並無明顯強弱差異，另在緊急性的表達上也是急迫與非急迫皆可。其句型為: S+ help O (to) V，以下透過範例進一步說明：

EX Can you _____ me to move this chair to the second floor?

可以請你幫我把這張椅子搬到二樓嗎？

→ 由於搬椅子屬於一般性的協助，加上沒有前後文判斷緊急與否，因此使用 help 即可。

★ Aid 幫忙

雖然語意上同為「幫忙，」但 aid 更凸顯以下兩種語境的表達，一是強者協助弱者脫離險境或困難，二是此問題若無法解決，茲事體大。也因為有此差異，aid 給予的幫助通常是實質的而非精神的。其句型為 S aid O in/with…。以下透過範例做進一步說明：

EX I aid him with money to avoid going bankrupt.

我金援他以免他破產。

→ 會有大量資金缺口往往都是生意上出了些問題，因此用 aid 來表達脫險的語意十分貼切。

★ Assist 幫忙

若以幫忙的程度作為區分點，aid 是強者為主，弱者為輔，情況多為

1 亂世佳人

2 傲慢與偏見

3 理性與感性

4 咆哮山莊

5 小婦人

6 簡愛

弱者無法獨立脫困，故強者出手相救。但 assist 的角色互換，強者扮演的角色像是軍師，實際的執行與操作有時候還得靠被幫助者自己。其句型為 S assist O in N/Ving，以下透過範例做進一步說明：

EX ABC Foundation assists the poor student in paying the tuition fee by themselves through part-time work.
ABC 基金會協助貧困學生透過打工自籌學費。

→ 持續有收入才能真的應付學費這筆固定開銷，基金會於此的角色是協助學生找到打工機會，因此用 assist 表協助。

實作練習與解析

❶ Can you _____ to turn off the light?
(A) help   (B) aid   (C) assist
Ans: (A)。由於關燈沒有急迫性，也無所謂強者協助弱者氛圍，因此用 help 來表達幫助之意。

❷ Are you free to _____ me to double check the document?
(A) assist   (B) help   (C) aid
Ans: (B)。由於沒有上下文，檢查文件無法看出急迫與否，加上此舉無明顯主從之分，故使用 help 表幫助即可。

❸ I _____ Ken with money to make up the shortfall in funding.
(A) help   (B) assist   (C) aid
Ans: (C)。若資金如果不能及時補足，後續的影響極大，因此用 aid 來表達需要協助的迫切性。

❹ She tries her best to _____ Lydia to settle down this thorny issue.

(A) aid   (B) help   (C) assist

Ans: (A)。從 thorny issue 可以得知 Lydia 遭遇的問題不好處理，因此用 aid 來表達幫助恰如其分。

❺ Mary _____ her students to find the answer by themselves.

(A) helps   (B) aids   (C) assists

Ans: (C)。從句末可以得知瑪莉老師扮演的是輔助角色，因此用 assist 來表示協助之意。

❻ I can _____ you to outline the project.

(A) assist   (B) aid   (C) help

Ans: (A)。由 outline 一字可以得知說話者可能只幫對方勾勒出大綱，細節就不插手，因此用 assist 來表幫助十分恰當。

1 亂世佳人

2 傲慢與偏見

3 理性與感性

4 咆哮山莊

5 小婦人

6 簡愛

Unit 07
亂世佳人

俏佳人怎麼說

Rhett, if you go, where shall I go?
What shall I do? —Scarlett O'Hara
白瑞德，如果你走了，我將去哪裡？我該做什麼？——郝思嘉

作品概述

　　整部作品中，女主角郝思嘉從一開始對於衛希禮的迷戀，到後來才發現白瑞德才是自己的真命天子。但造化弄人，當郝思嘉選擇接受白瑞德，以為兩人自此可以過著幸福快樂的日子，白瑞德卻故再次離開，郝思嘉為了挽回，才說這句希望他留下的經典台詞。在此句台詞中，出現大家常用的 shall，本單元特將與其容易搞混的 should、would 、willl 並列，解析四者的差異。

文法概述

Shall / should / will / would

★ Shall 將會…

　　若以嚴謹的文法來看，第一人稱表將會用 shall，二、三人稱則用

will。但現代英語已不刻意區分，皆使用 will。以下透過範例作進一步說明：

EX I shall/will be thirty years old next month.
我下個月滿三十歲。

→ 若從嚴謹的文法來看，第一人稱要表現「將會」，應使用多數人所不習慣的 shall。但現在若以 will 表示其實也無妨。

★ Should 將會…

雖然較少人使用，若 should 意為「將會」時，是 shall 的過去式，多用於轉述。但若做「應該」解，S should V/have pp 是大家熟知的句型。以下透過範例做進一步說明：

EX James told me that the interview should be held this Friday.
詹姆士告訴我面試將於本星期五舉行。

→ 由於說話者是在轉述訊息，加上是描述過去，故以 should 來表將會。

EX You should work harder.
你應該更努力工作。

→ 由於對方可能先前比較散漫，故說話者以 should 表達應有改變之意。

★ Will 將會…

由於未來式中會用 will，大家對於 S+ will…「某人將會…」這樣的句型並不陌生。以下透過範例做進一步說明：

1 亂世佳人

2 傲慢與偏見

3 理性與感性

4 咆哮山莊

5 小婦人

6 簡愛

EX I will send you a reply this afternoon.

我下午就會回覆你。

→ 由於説話時下午還沒到，故以 will 表即將做某事的意涵。

★ Would

雖然同樣都表「將會…」，與其他三者不同的是，Would 表達某事物將不會發生或是沒有發生，故多用於條件句。以下透過範例作進一步説明：

EX I would travel in France if I could afford it.

如果夠有錢的話，我就能去法國旅行。

→ 由於説話者就是沒有閒錢可以去旅遊，故以 would 來表達不可能成行。

EX I would have arrived on time if I had taken the bus earlier.

如果有早點搭上公車，我就能即時抵達了。

→ 由於真實情況是説話者晚搭車所以遲到，故用 would 表示提早搭車與即時趕到的狀況其實沒有發生。

實作練習與解析

❶ I _____ be 18 next month.

(A) shall   (B) would   (C) should   (D) ought to

Ans: (A)。由於説話時説話者尚未滿 18 歲，加上是第一人稱，故選 shall。

❷ Ann told me that the interview _____ be held this Monday.

(A) shall　(B) should　(C) would　(D) will

Ans: (B)。由於説話者轉述安所説的話，故用 should 表達將會。

❸ You have good talent, so you_____ work harder.

(A) should　(B) shall　(C) will　(D) would

Ans: (A)。由於説話者覺得對方有天賦卻不努力，因此用 should 來表達「應當…」之意。

❹ When _____ I get your official reply?

(A) should　(B) shall　(C) will　(D) would

Ans: (C)。由於説話時尚未收到正式回覆，因此用 will 來詢問將於何時。

❺ I _____ buy a car if I could afford it.

(A) will　(B) should　(C) shall　(D) would

Ans: (D)。由於説話者根本沒有足夠金錢，故用 would 來表達購車的不可能性。

❻ I _____ have passed the document examination in time if I had sent the package earlier.

(A) should　(B) shall　(C) would　(D) will

Ans: (C)。由於真實情況是晚寄包裹，以至於趕不上書面審查，故以 would 來表示提早寄包裹與趕上審查的情況其實沒有發生。

1 亂世佳人

2 傲慢與偏見

3 理性與感性

4 咆哮山莊

5 小婦人

6 簡愛

Unit 08
亂世佳人

俏佳人怎麼說

Now I didn't come to talk silliness about me, Rhett.
I came 'cause I was so miserable at the thought
of you in trouble. Oh, I know I was mad at
you the night you left me on the road to Tara,
and I still haven't forgiven you!—Scarlett O'Hara

現在我並不是來跟你說我有多糊塗，瑞德。我來是因為當想到你身陷麻煩，我就感到痛苦。那晚你把我丟在回塔拉的路上，我非常生氣，到現在我也還不打算原諒你。——郝思嘉

作品概述

　　郝思嘉與白瑞德的感情糾葛是亂世佳人故事架構中非常重要的部分。思嘉雖然多次拒絕瑞德，但卻也有迫於現實，而向瑞德請求協助的時候。此段看似對瑞德的真情告白，事實上思嘉卻是另有目的。在此段話語中，出現了表達氣憤的句型 S be mad at…，但由於生氣也有程度之分，本單元特將此句型與常用來表示憤怒的 S be angry…、S is annoyed…與 S is irritated…做比較，說明四者的差異。

文法概述

❧ *S be mad at / S be angry / S annoyed / irritated* ❧

★ S be mad at

就氣憤的程度來看，mad 是四者中最高的。因此當情緒強度大，但還沒到憤憤難平的程度，就可以用 S be mad at.. 句型來表示。以下透過範例作進一步說明：

EX The fans are mad at the baseball team for losing the important game.

球迷對於棒球隊輸掉重要比賽大為不滿。

➔ 正所謂愛之深責之切，球迷支持球隊，因此當球隊輸球，其氣憤程度自然高，故用 mad 表示實為恰當。

★ S be angry at…

同樣表達生氣，使用 angry 時，通常肇因於不佳或不平等的對待，因此，若所遭遇的事由符合上述情況，就可以用 S be angry at…表示。以下透過範例進一步說明：

EX All clients should be treated equal, so I am angry at your bad attitude.

所有顧客都應受到平等對待，你態度不佳讓我很不高興。

★ S be annoyed…

讓人生氣的原因有很多，若是因為失去耐性，或是對方讓你感到心煩，則可用 S is annoyed by…/if…句型來表示。以下透過範例作進一步說明：

1 亂世佳人

2 傲慢與偏見

3 理性與感性

4 咆哮山莊

5 小婦人

6 簡愛

EX I am annoyed by his negative attitude

他的消極態度使我大為火光。

EX Mr. Huang will be annoyed if we can't finish the project today.

如果我們無法今天完成報告，黃經理會不高興。

★ S be irritated...

在本單元的四種生氣中，irritated 與 annoyed 程度相當，肇因也相近，差別前者表現出那種本來不想大動肝火，但最後還是被惹毛的語境。其句型為 S be irritated by⋯。以下透過範例做進一步說明：

EX I am totally irritated by his irresponsible attitude to this project.

他對此專案的不認真態度徹底地激怒我了。

→ 由於說話者原本可能沒這樣介意工作態度，但對方真的太沒責任感，故可使用 irritated 表達被惹火的感受。

實作練習與解析

❶ I am_____ at the poor performance of basketball team I support.

(A) annoyed　(B) mad　(C) angry　(D) irritated

Ans: (B)。即使是球迷，所支持球隊如果表現太差，還是會很生氣，因此可用 mad 來表達憤怒。

❷ I am _____at the unreasonable charge of repair.

(A) angry　(B) annoyed　(C) irritate　(D) mad

Ans: (A)。由於不合理的收費可歸類於不平等待遇，故可使用 angry 來表達憤怒。

❸ My boss will be ＿＿＿＿＿＿ if I can't finish the report today.
(A) mad　(B) irritated　(C) annoyed　(D) angry

Ans: (C)。由於報告須於今日完成，若做不到，説話者老闆的怒氣可用 annoyed 表示。

❹ In the meeting, I am ＿＿＿＿＿＿ by Ken's ridiculous behavior.
(A) angry　(B) irritated　(C) mad　(D) annoyed

Ans: (D)。由於離譜行徑很容易讓人失去耐性，因此 annoyed 來表達惱怒十分恰當。

❺ Kevin is ＿＿＿＿＿＿ by the negative attitude of his partner.
(A) irritated　(B) annoyed　(C) mad　(D) angry

Ans: (A)。凱文一開始也許還可以接受不積極，但後來無法忍受，故可以用 irritated 表達被激怒的語境。

❺ The teacher is ＿＿＿＿＿＿ by the dishonest behaviors of his students.
(A) annoyed　(B) angry　(C) irritated　(D) mad

Ans: (C)。由於老師無法忍受學生説謊，故可用 irritated 那種忍無可忍，憤怒終於爆發出來的感受。

1 亂世佳人

2 傲慢與偏見

3 理性與感性

4 咆哮山莊

5 小婦人

6 簡愛

Unit 09
亂世佳人

俏佳人怎麼說

I don't care what you expect or what
they think. I'm gonna dance and dance.
Tonight I wouldn't mind dancing with Abe
Lincoln himself. —Scarlett O'Hara

我不管你想得到什麼，或者他們怎麼想，我要跳舞，跳舞。
今晚就是和亞伯拉罕·林肯跳也不要緊。——郝思嘉

作品概述

　　女主角的第一次婚姻才沒幾個月，丈夫就戰死。梅拉妮邀請郝思嘉與之同住，思嘉也因此與瑞德在一場募款會中再次相逢，由於瑞德立下戰功，思嘉已對其改觀。但瑞德也坦承說他是為了私利而戰。由於募款會由男性以競標方式邀請女性與之共舞，將得標金捐出。瑞德邀請思嘉共舞，使其在開心之餘說出段話語。在這段內容中，出現 mind 這個大家常用卻又常將其與 care about 搞混用法的單字，故本單元特針對三者的句型做解析，說明其差異與適用時機。

 **文法概述**

❦ *Mind / care about* ❦

★ **Mind 介意**

Mind 若做「介意」解，通常用於否定句與疑問句中，若其後分成加 Ving，其實是變相地請對方幫我們做某事，若接 if 子句，則詢問對方自己是可以做某事。兩種用法的主從關係完全相反，請務必注意。另外許多人掛在嘴邊的 no mind 其實是錯誤用法，由於 no 做副詞用時，並無「不要」的語意，故 never mind 才是正確語法。以下透過範例做進一步說明：

EX Would you mind switching the TV to channel 32?

可以幫我把電視頻道切換到 32 台嗎？

➡ 說話者可能因為某些原因無法自己轉台，因此 would you mind Ving 句型用於請對方給予協助。

EX Would you mind if I turn off the fan?

我可以關掉電扇嗎？

➡ 說話者可能覺得冷，故以 Would you mind if… 句型來徵詢對方意見，希望可以答應。

EX Never mind. We still have time to revise the project.

別在意，我們還有時間修改計畫書。

➡ 由於對方也許對於自己的疏失耿耿於懷，因此說話者要其放寬心，大家一起再努力即可。

★ **Care (about) 在乎、介意**

在語意上，Care 本身或是 care about 也可表「介意」，因此在廣

1 亂世佳人

2 傲慢與偏見

3 理性與感性

4 咆哮山莊

5 小婦人

6 簡愛

義而言可以與 mind 相互替換。其用法相對簡單，S care about N/子句表達就是說話者的態度。以下透過範例做進一步說明：

EX I don't care much about the matter of fashion.

我不在乎這個流行趨勢。

→ 由於說話者不追流行，因此用 don't care about 可表明其態度。

EX I don't care what happened to the singers and actors.

我不在乎歌手與演員所發生的大小事。

→ 由於說話者可能對娛樂動態沒有興趣，因此可用 S don't care 加上子句表達其立場。

實作練習與解析

❶ Would you mind_____ the table for me before lunch?

(A) setting   (B) to set   (C) have set   (D) set

Ans: (A)。由於 mind 後接動名詞或子句，故選擇 setting。

❷ Would you mind if _____ the light?

(A) turn on   (B) turning on   (C) I turn on   (D) I have turn on

Ans: (C)。由於 mind 其後也可加子句，故選擇 I turn on 使其句構完整。

❸ _____mind the budget. Just try until you find the solution of the bug.

(A) No   (B) Never   (C) Not   (D) None

Ans: (B)。選項只有 never 可以表達出「千萬不要…」的語境,故選
其與 mind 連用形成「別在意」的語意。

❹ I don't _____ the privacy of the celebrity.
(A) care about (B) care of (C) mind knowing (D) mind
Ans: (A)。由於説話者沒興趣知道名人的私生活是怎樣,故可以用
don't care about 表達不在乎。

❺ Don't waste your time telling me the details because what I
_____ is the outcome.
(A) concerned (B) care about (C) mind (D) care of
Ans: (B)。由於説話者重結果不重過程,故可用 care about 來描述
其行事作風。

❻ Let me alone, because I don't _____ what happens to me
next.
(A) mind (B) care of (C) concern (D) care about
Ans: (D)。由於説話者已不在意事情的後續發展,故用 S don't care
about 來説明其消極態度。

1 亂世佳人

2 傲慢與偏見

3 理性與感性

4 咆哮山莊

5 小婦人

6 簡愛

Unit 10
亂世佳人

🔍 俏佳人怎麼說

You'd rather live with that silly little
fool who can't open her mouth except
to say "yes" or "no" and raise a passel of
mealy-mouthed brats just like her.
—Scarlett O'Hara

你幹嘛不說出來，你這個膽小鬼！你不敢跟我結婚！你倒情願和那個傻丫頭過日子，她只會唯唯諾諾，別的什麼都不會說，過幾天養出一窩小鬼來也和她一樣百依百順！。——郝思嘉

作品概述

　　在整個故事中，郝思嘉一共成為寡婦兩次，在一段她、衛希禮與白瑞德的談話中，當時已成寡婦的郝思嘉，對於希禮仍不願接受她感到不悅，因而說出這段對於梅拉妮的批評。這樣具攻擊性的言論當然引起希禮的不滿，從而回嘴反擊。在這段簡短的話語中，出現了大家常用的 S would rather…句型，由於當其與後接原形動詞、完成式與句子時，可表達不同心中想法實際情況的落差，故本單元特對此作分析說明。

文法概述

S would rather / S would rather have + p.p /
S would rather S V / V-ed / have + p.p

★ S would rather…

S would rather…的運用很廣泛,當其後所接分別為 V、have pp 與
句子時,分別可以表達出不同「寧願」語氣。以下個別說明:

1.1. S would rather V

S would rather V 表現出的「寧願」最直觀,因此當要表達中文
的「與其…,不如…」。就可以用此句型來表達。以下透過範例做
進一步說明:

EX If you invite me to watch a movie with you, I would rather
stay at home.

如果你邀請我一起看電影,我還寧願待在家。

→ 對說話者來說,他不喜歡看電影,因此用 would rather 來說
明自己的偏好。

1.2. S would rather have pp

當 would rather 與 have pp 連用,表達的就是過去想做某事,
但最後卻沒做,中文的「本來想…」與其意涵相當貼近。以下透過
範例做進一步說明:

EX We get there by bus, but I would rather have gone by air.

我們最後搭巴士去,但我本來是想搭飛機的。

→ 由於說話者的交通工具首選並非巴士而是飛機,因此用 S
would rather have pp 句型來說明心中真正的想法。

1 亂世佳人

2 傲慢與偏見

3 理性與感性

4 咆哮山莊

5 小婦人

6 簡愛

1.3. S would rather S V/ Ved /have pp

若 would rather 其後接的是句子，不論現在式、過去式或是完成式，在語意的理解上都很直觀，可由其時間點作切入。以下透過範例做進一步說明：

EX I would rather you didn't know what is going on now.
我寧可你不知道現在的狀況為何。

→ 由於當下可能正遭遇某些問題，故說話者寧可希望對方一無所知，以免淌渾水。

EX I would rather you haven't told me the truth.
我寧可你沒有跟我說實話。

→ 由於說話者可能寧願選對方沒講出真實情況，讓其蒙在鼓裡，故用完成式來表達心聲。

實作練習與解析

❶ If you want me to surrender to you, I would rather _____ suicide.

(A) committing　(B) to commit　(C) commit　(D) committed

Ans: (C)。由於說話者可能與對方勢不兩立，與其投降，不如自我了斷，故選擇原形動詞

❷ We get there by bus, but I would rather _____ the high speed railway

(A) have taken　(B) take　(C) to take　(D) taking

Ans: (A)。由於說話者本來想搭高鐵最後卻只能屈就搭巴士，故可用

完成式來表達那種本來想的感受。

❸ When I was young, I would rather _____ an artist rather than a security guard.

(A) being   (B) have been   (C) is   (D) to be

Ans: (B)。由於說話者年輕時可能迫於現實無法當藝術家，只能改當保全，故可用完成式來表達當時的理想為何。

❹ This company has no future, so I would rather you _____ a business.

(A) run   (B) to run   (C) running   (D) have run

Ans: (A)。由於說話者覺得對方任職的公司前景堪慮，想勸對方自己創業比較好，故選擇原形動詞以符合文法。

❺ I would rather Joe _____ the price.

(A) didn't mention   (B) haven't mention   (C) not to mention
(D) not mentioning

Ans: (A)。由於講出價錢可能會壞事，但 Joe 卻做了，因此說話者用過去式來表達此一已發生的事件的遺憾。

❻ I would rather she _____ me before borrowing the van.
(A) has asked   (B) asking   (C) ask   (D) to ask

Ans: (A)。由於對方肯定是沒問就先用使用車輛，因此說話者可用完成式來發牢騷。

1 亂世佳人

2 傲慢與偏見

3 理性與感性

4 咆哮山莊

5 小婦人

6 簡愛

Unit 11
亂世佳人

俏佳人怎麼說

Oh, I could never hate you! And...
and I know you must care about me,
because... Oh, you do care, don't you?
—Scarlett O'Hara

哦!我決不會恨你!而且我知道你肯定喜歡我,因為…
哦,你確實喜歡我,不是嗎?——郝思嘉

作品概述

　　在故事的前段,女主角發現自己深深迷戀衛希禮,也覺得對方也被自己深深吸引。但希禮卻早已和郝思嘉的表妹梅拉妮訂婚。在希禮與梅拉妮宣布訂婚的燒烤聚會中,郝思嘉找到空檔向希禮告白,卻慘遭拒絕。不甘心的思嘉因而說出了這段連續追問的話語。在這些反問句中,出現了表達恨的單字 hate。但恨總是有等級之分的,因此本單元特別將其與 dislike、recent 這兩個語意相近的詞彙做比較,說明到底三者的差異為何。

文法概述

✑ *Hate / dislike / resent* ✐

★ Hate

本單元的三個單字雖然都表「恨」，但在程度與原因上各有不同。會以 hate 表達感受，通常起因於對某人不滿或不想做某事，因此在情緒強度上未達引爆點。常用句型有 S hate sb / to V。以下透過範例做進一步說明：

EX I hate my older brother because he always plays tricks on me.

我討厭我哥，因為他老是捉弄我。

➜ 說話者並非真的對哥哥懷有恨意，而是因為不想被捉弄，因此用 hate 來表達心中的感受。

EX I hate to bother you all the time.

我討厭一直麻煩你。

➜ 由於說話者其實不想麻煩別人，因此用 hate 來表示自己的不好意思。

★ Dislike

Dislike 是 like 的反義詞，通常用於沒有意願做某事，或是不喜歡某種事物。故在三種「恨」當中程度最輕微。若以句型為: S dislike Ving /S have N for/of⋯。以下透過範例做進一步說明：

EX I dislike asking for help before trying.

我不喜歡沒自己試過就求救。

➜ 由於說話者認為要嘗試過後才求救，因此用 dislike 來表達他對

1 亂世佳人

2 傲慢與偏見

3 理性與感性

4 咆哮山莊

5 小婦人

6 簡愛

不這樣做的人的不滿。

EX I have a dislike of raining day.

我不喜歡下雨天。

→ 雨天可能造成說話者的某些不便，故說話者用 dislike 來表達其好惡。

★ Resent

若 hate 是恨的「標準版」，resent 就是「加強版」，原因在於 resent 多了憤怒的成分。因不喜歡而恨，不與之往來或不要做即可。但因憤怒而恨，可能會有想報復或是擺爛的衝動。其常用句型為: S resent N for···/ Ving。以下透過範例做進一步說明:

EX I resent Joe for being so tough to me.

我恨喬對我如此苛刻。

→ 說話者對於喬的苛薄深感不滿，因此用 resent 表達恰如其分。

EX I resent explaining why I quit the high-paid job.

我懶得解釋為何我要放棄這份高薪的工作。

→ 由於可能已經解釋無數次辭職的原因，以致於如果還有人問，他已不想多做說明，故用 resnet 來表達內心的抗議。

實作練習與解析

❶ I _____ my young sister because she likes to scare me.
(A) hate (B) dislike (C) resent

Ans: (A)。說話者並非真的對自己的妹妹恨之入骨，而是討厭被她嚇，故應使用 hate 來表達。

❷ Jason ___ to work with Mary because she often neglects his opinion.

(A) dislikes (B) resents (C) hates

Ans: (C)。由於意見總是遭到瑪莉忽視，因此傑森對她的不滿可以用 hate 來表示。

❸ Amy has a _____ for eating vegetables.

(A) hate (B) dislike (C) resent

Ans: (B)。對食物的好惡關乎個人，故應以 dislike 來表達說話者的好惡。

❹ Peter _____ having to get up early in the weekend.

(A) dislikes (B) hates (C) resents

Ans: (A)。由於假日不想早起屬個人好惡，故應用 dislike 來表達自身偏好。

❺ My younger brother _____ his boss for being picky to him

(A) dislikes (B) hates (C) resents

Ans: (C)。由於說話者的弟弟對於他老闆的挑三揀四積怨已深，這樣的不滿可用 resent 來表示。

❻ Lisa _____ explaining why he moves in a rush.

(A) hates (B) resents (C) dislikes

Ans: (B)。由於可能太多人問麗莎為何從忙搬家，因此她懶得一一給予回應，故用 resent 表達不滿。

1 亂世佳人

2 傲慢與偏見

3 理性與感性

4 咆哮山莊

5 小婦人

6 簡愛

Unit 12
亂世佳人

俏佳人怎麼說

Oh, Mammy, this house won't seem the same without Bonnie. How's Miss Scarlett bearing up?—Melanie Hamilton

喔!媽咪,這間房子少了邦妮就不可能一如往昔了。
郝思嘉要如何承受呢?——梅拉妮

作品概述

　　當郝思嘉選擇嫁給白瑞德,並順利產下一女後,似乎終於可以過著幸福快樂的日子,怎料愛女竟意外墜馬身亡。聞此噩耗,女主角的表妹梅拉妮也深感不捨,不禁向思嘉的兒時褓姆表達感慨之意。在這段充滿哀傷的話語中,出現了 bear up 這個表達「承受」的片語,但英文中根據依照所承擔的事物不同,適用的單字或片語就不同,故本單元特針對易和 bear up 混淆的 undertake 、endure 與 withstand 進行解析。

文法概述

Bear up / undertake / endure / suffer

★ **Bear up**

由於 bear 本身有「負載」、「承擔」之意,因此當心理或是生理上有負擔,但仍須保持勇敢堅強,就可以用 bear up 來表達「承受得了」、「不氣餒」的語意,其句型為: S bear up…under…。以下透過範例作進一步說明:

EX I don't bear up well under the problem with my family.

與家人的問題讓我感到氣餒。

→ 由於說話者與家人相處出現問題,且問題無法得到解決,故以 can't bear up well 表達沮喪。

★ **Undertake**

由於 undertake 的語意之一為「著手…」。由於參與其中,當其表「承擔」、「接受」時,其客體多為工作或是責任,其常用句型為: … is/are undertook by…,以下透過範例做進一步說明:

EX The design of the new logo is undertaken by Ken's team.

肯的團隊接下新商標的設計工作。

→ 設計商標為一項工作,故以 undertake 來表達承接的意願。

★ **Endure**

同樣表「承受」,但由於 endure 常與 cannot 跟其他否定詞連用,多用於表達看不下去的不捨感或撐不下去的無力感。其常見句型有: S can't endure to V/Ving…,以下透過範例作進一步說明:

亂世佳人 *1*

傲慢與偏見 *2*

理性與感性 *3*

咆哮山莊 *4*

小婦人 *5*

簡愛 *6*

EX I cannot endure to see John so disappointed.

我不捨看到約翰如此失望。

→ 由於説話者不希望約翰持續處於負面情緒，故用 can't endure 來表達心中的不捨。

★ Withstand

與 endure 的負面傾向不同，withstand 多用來説明那種已經熬過磨難，現在一切豁然開朗的放鬆。其常見句型有: S can't have/to…，以下透過範例作進一步説明:

EX Pioneers have to withstand the loneliness.

先驅者要能耐得住寂寞。

→ 先知的想法總是難以為一般人所了解，因此寂寞在所難免，故用 withstand 來表達他們已有此覺悟。

實作練習與解析

❶ I _____ well under the problem with my classmates
(A) endure   (B) undertake   (C) bear up   (D) withstand
Ans: (C)。由於説話者雖與同學相處出現問題，但未因此喪氣，故可用 bear up well 來表達自己將持續努力解決。

❷ I don't _____ under the problem with my colleagues
(A) withstand   (B) bear up   (C) endure   (D) undertake
Ans: (B)。説話者與同事相處出現狀況，且對於找不出解決之道感到沮喪，故以 don't bear up 來表示。

❸ The design and production of the new uniform is _____ by ABC Clothing.

(A) undertaken   (B) endured   (C) bore up   (D) withstood

Ans: (A)。制服的設計與生產為一項業務，故應使用 undertook 表示承接意願。

❹ Coach Jason _____ the responsibility of losing the important game.

(A) withstands   (B) undertakes   (C) endures   (D) bears up

Ans: (B)。由於輸球讓人沮喪，若有人願意對此負責，應以 undertake 表達其承擔的意願。

❺ I can't _____ seeing my children so sad.

(A) bear up   (B) undertake   (C) endure   (D) withstand

Ans: (C)。由於前有否定詞，後有動名詞，故應以 endure 表達難以承受的強烈情緒。

❻ The Marine have to _____ a cruel torture if caught by the enemy.

(A) withstand   (B) endure   (C) bear up   (D) undertake

Ans: (A)。海軍陸戰隊受過特別訓練，故應以 withstand 表達他們經得起拷問而不投降。

1 亂世佳人

2 傲慢與偏見

3 理性與感性

4 咆哮山莊

5 小婦人

6 簡愛

Part **2**

Week 2 傲慢與偏見

Unit 13
傲慢與偏見

 **俏佳人怎麼說**

Mr. Darcy is not so well worth listening
to as his friend, is he? -- Poor Eliza!
-- to be only just tolerable. —Charlotte Lucas

達西先生的話沒有他朋友的話中聽，可不是嗎？

可憐的伊麗莎！他不過認為她還可以！——夏綠蒂・盧卡斯

作品概述

　　傲慢與偏見的故事圍繞在 18 到 19 世紀間英國鄉紳貴族間的情感與婚姻，女主角伊麗莎一家由於家族中沒有男性繼承人，若父親過世，家產最後可能為親戚所接手。母親怕女兒們最後會無家可歸，於是積極物色女婿。在某次聚會中，伊麗莎白與男主角達西相遇，但當時達西極其高傲，女主角好友夏綠蒂也才有機會聽到達西輕率的言語，並將其轉述給伊麗莎白。在這句台詞中，出現了大家常會與 worthy 及 worthwhile 搞混的 worth。透過本單元的解析，將可釐清三者差異。

文法概述

Worth / worthy / value

★ **Worth 有…的價值/值得…**

若作為形容詞，Worth 可以用來表示某個事物的價值，用法就是很直觀的 something is worth 金額，若表示某事有去實行的價值，則是 something worth +Ving/N。以下透過範例來做進一步說明

EX This sport watch is worth 1000 USD.

這隻運動錶值 1000 美金。

→ 由於是在說明手錶的價值，因此使用 worth。

EX This program is worth investing.

這項計畫值得投資。

→ 由於是在敘述計畫具有實行的價值，因此使用 something is worth Ving 句型

EX The tourist attraction is worth a visit

這個旅遊景點值得一去。

→ 由於是在敘述此地點有實地參訪的價值，故也可以用採用 something is worth N 的句型。

★ **Worthy 值得的**

由於 worth 與 worthy 都是形容詞，因此很容易會搞混，做「值得的」，常使用的句型是 something is worthy of Ving/N 或是 something is worthy to V。以下透過例句再進一步說明：

EX The book is worthy of reading.

1 亂世佳人

2 傲慢與偏見

3 理性與感性

4 咆哮山莊

5 小婦人

6 簡愛

這本書值得一讀。

➔ 由於是要表現這本書有被閱讀的價值，因此使用 something is worthy of Ving 句型。

EX This book is worthy to read.

這本書值得一讀。

➔ 與例 1 相同，此範例也是要呈現書的閱讀價值，但由於是與 to V 連用，因此記得將 of 去掉。

★ Worthwhile 值得的

光是 worth 區分 worthy 就已經讓人頭大，偏偏英文中還有一個類似的字 worthwhile。這個字有點像另外兩個單字的綜合版，常用的句構是: something is worthwhile to V。為了有效區分三者的不同，可以選擇盡量不使用 worthy to V 這個用法，將接 to V 視為 worthwhile 專用，這樣就可以大大降低誤用的機會。

EX This place is really worthwhile to visit.

這個地方值得一去。

➔ 由於是要表現此地點有拜訪的價值，因此使用 worthwhile to V 句型。

實作練習與解析

❶ This jacket is _____ 100 USD.

(A) worth of　(B) worthwhile　(C) worthy　(D) worth

Ans: (D)。由於是在敘述夾克的價值，因此選擇 worth。

❷ The article that Professor Wong writes is _____ reading

(A) worth　(B) worthy　(C) worthwhile　(D) wroth of

Ans: (A)。由於是在描述文章有閱讀的價值，加上後接 Ving，因此選擇 Worth。

❸ John's method is _____ a try.

(A) worthy　(B) worth of　(C) worth　(D) worthwhile

Ans: (C)。由於是在描述方法有嘗試的價值，加上後接 N，因此選擇 worth。

❹ The new collection this season is _____ of buying.

(A) worth of　(B) worthy　(C) worthwhile　(D) worth

Ans: (B)。由於是在敘述新商品值得買，加上後接 of Ving，因此選 worthy。

❺ The movie released last Friday is _____ to watch.

(A) worth　(B) worthy　(C) worthy of　(D) worthwhile

Ans: (D)。由於是在敘述電影值得一看，加上其後接 to V，因此選 worthy。

❻ Such cuisine is really _____ to try.

(A) worth　(B) worthy of　(C) worthwhile　(D) worth of

Ans: (C)。由於是在描述菜餚值得一吃，加上其後接 to V，因此選 worthwhile。

1 亂世佳人

2 傲慢與偏見

3 理性與感性

4 咆哮山莊

5 小婦人

6 簡愛

Unit 14
傲慢與偏見

俏佳人怎麼說

I could easily forgive his pride,
if he had not mortified mine — Elizabeth

要是他沒有觸犯我的驕傲，我也很容易原諒他的驕傲。——伊麗莎白

作品概述

　　首次與男主角達西接觸後，女主角伊麗莎白對他的印象是驕傲自大。甚至還口出：「她還沒有漂亮到可以打動我的地步」這種輕率言論。但到後來她才發現他只是因為較不擅言詞，且飽受流言毀謗，才會給人如此負面印象。從誤解到了解，伊麗莎白也娓娓道來，如果達西一開始不要如此自命不凡，她對他印象也就不會如此糟糕了。在此台詞中，出現了用來描述原諒的單字 forgive。在英文中，常用來表達此類語意的尚有 pardon、excuse，接下來透過單元的解析，可以讓你更了解這三個單字到底如何同中有異。

文法概述

Forgive / excuse / pardon

★ Forgive 原諒、寬恕

就語氣的強弱來看，forgive 在本單元的三種「原諒」中位居中間，且說話者的主觀意識較強。但 forgive 同時也最能表現那種自此一筆勾銷的意境，常用的句型有: S forgive O for Ving 或是 S forgive O N，以下透過範例進一步說明：

EX I forgive Jason's carelessness. / I forgive Jason for being careless.

我原諒傑森的粗心大意。

→ 雖然粗心實屬不該，但由於說話者願意表現氣度，不予追究，因此使用 forgive。

★ Excuse 原諒

Excuse 做名詞用時，意思是「理由」，但做動詞表「原諒」用，大家最熟悉的用法大概就是 excuse me 了，意思可以是「請原諒我」、「借過」等。仔細思考其使用時機，大多是因為犯了一些小錯誤，有時甚至只是為了社交上的禮貌，因此語氣也為三者中最輕。句型為 S excuse O for Ving。以下透過範例做進一步說明：

EX Excuse me occupying your seat?

抱歉坐到你的位置了？

→ 由於坐錯位置只要起身讓座問題就解決了，並不是多嚴重的錯誤，因此用 excuse me 來表示歉意恰如其分。

1 亂世佳人

2 傲慢與偏見

3 理性與感性

4 咆哮山莊

5 小婦人

6 簡愛

★ Pardon 原諒

本單元所介紹的三種道歉中，pardon 的語氣最重，目的是希望對方不要再追究，法律用語上更將其解釋為赦免。常用的句型是 S pardon O for Ving 或是 S forgive O N。以下透過範例進一步說明：

EX Pardon me for interrupting you. /Pardon me my interrupting.

抱歉打擾你

→ 當說話者覺得打擾到對方的是很嚴重的事，使用 pardon 來請求原諒就是恰當用法。

補充說明：

閱讀完上述三種的原諒的解析後，會發現只有 excuse 沒有 S excuse O N 的用法。就文法規則而言，其實結構是對的，但由於在實務上甚少人使用，因此不建議使用。

實作練習與解析

❶ Lucy _____ Mary for her rudeness.
   (A) forgives (B) excuses (C) pardons
   Ans: (A)。由於魯莽可能是無心的，因此當要敘述露西很大氣地不去計較，就應選擇 forgive。

❷ I _____ Nick for his impolite behavior.
   (A) pardon (B) forgive (C) excuse
   Ans: (B)。雖然不禮貌的行為可能讓人難以忍受，但如果說話者覺得何需計較，就可以用 forgive 來表現氣度。

❸ _____ me using your pen by accident.
(A) Pardon　(B) forgive　(C) Excuse
Ans: (C)。由於不小心用到別人的筆並不是多嚴重的事，因此用
excuse 來請求原諒十分恰當。

❹ _____ me, can you explain it with more details?
(A) Excuse　(B) Pardon　(C) Forgive
Ans: (A)。由於說話者可能沒弄懂對方說明的內容，而這也說不上做
錯事，因此用 excuse 來請求對方講得更清楚些。

❺ Please _____ me for breaking you mug.
(A) excuse　(B) pardon　(C) forgive
Ans: (B)。打破別人馬克杯這件事，若說話者認為是件嚴重的事，請
求原諒時用 pardon 就非常適合。

❻ _____ me messing up your desk.
(A) Forgive　(B) Excuse　(C) Pardon
Ans: (C)。雖然說桌面擺設亂了再整理好就好，但如果說話者覺得這
會讓對方很困擾，用 pardon 請求原諒並無不妥。

1 亂世佳人

2 傲慢與偏見

3 理性與感性

4 咆哮山莊

5 小婦人

6 簡愛

Unit 15
傲慢與偏見

俏佳人怎麼說

And those are the words of a gentleman. From the first moment I met you, your arrogance and conceit, your selfish disdain for the feelings of others made me realize that you were the last man in the world I could ever be prevailed upon to marry. —Elizabeth Bennet

這些為紳士才會說的話。從第一次與你相遇，你的傲慢自大，你對其他人的鄙視態度，讓我明白你是這個世界上我最不想嫁的人。——伊麗莎白

作品概述

女主角伊麗莎白與男主角達西的第一次相遇並不是當公主遇上王子那樣詩情畫意，相反地，由於達西表現一副自命不凡的樣子，讓女主角對他不只沒有好印象，還說出我絕不會選擇他當我老公的這句台詞。在此段台詞中，出現了大家容易與 understand、know 搞混的 realize，透過本單元的解析，將可理解這三種「理解」到底差別在哪。

文法概述

Realize / understand / know

★ Realize

雖然在語意上都可以解釋為「了解」，但 realize 與其他兩者最大的差異在於那種「恍然大悟」的感覺。即使沒有上下文可供參考，當使用 realize 時，就可以表現出過去的疑惑或是未曾留意的事物，此刻突然得以釐清與清楚呈現。正因為有一定的程序性，當某些事物只需短時間就可理解，或是無需反覆斟酌，就不宜用 realize 來表達理解之意。以下透過範例做進一步說明：

EX The failure makes me realize the importance of risk management.

此次失敗讓我了解風險管理的重要性。

→ 由於說話者在過去並不覺得風險管理是件要緊的事，但現在知道了，因此用 realize 來表達親身體悟的那種了解。

★ Understand

若從內容理解程度來區分，由於不需要反覆思考或是花費長時間去體悟，因此 understand 所表現出的理解程度不如 realize，但仍可呈現對事物有一定認知，根據此特性，此單字可以用來表達是否懂得某些知識，或是聽懂某種語言這類情況。以下透過範例進一步說明：

EX Do you understand this formula?

這個公式你懂嗎？

→ 由於公式一定有其依據，因此用 understand 來詢問對方理解與否十分合理。

1 亂世佳人

2 傲慢與偏見

3 理性與感性

4 咆哮山莊

5 小婦人

6 簡愛

EX Do you understand English vocabulary I just used?

你懂我剛用的英文單字嗎？

→ 有些英文單字雖然不常見，但透過上下文的輔助，應不至於艱澀到無法理解，因此用 understand 來詢問並無不妥。

★ Know

在本單元的三種理解中，know 比較偏向粗淺的了解。因此，如果是原則性的詢問，以 know 表示十分恰當。但如果對語言的理解，know 表現出的就是「精通」而非「略懂」。常用的句型為:S know about/of…或是 S know that…。以下透過範做進一步說明：

EX I know that Mary is against this proposal.

我知道瑪莉對此提案表示反對。

→ 由於沒有敘明反對的原因，因此用 know 來表達大方向的理解十分恰當。

EX Jason knows at least six languages.

傑森至少精通六國語言。

→ 當以 know 來表達對語言的理解時，語意就不再是略知一二，而是信手拈來。

實作練習與解析

❶ John's betrayal makes me _____ overly trusting business partners can sometimes cause troubles.

(A) realize (B) know (C) understand

Ans: (A)。由於說話者過去可能非常相信他的合作夥伴，因此才會用

realize 來表達遭背叛後的這種深刻體悟。

❷ Do you_____ what I am saying?

(A) know　(B) understand　(C) realize

Ans: (B)。由於說話者是要確定對方是否理解自己的說話內容，因此用 understand 表基本的理解即可。

❸ Can you _____ the instruction that the engineer provide?

(A) know　(B) realize　(C) understand

Ans: (C)。由於要解決問題，對於指示要有一定認知，因此選擇 understand 來表示理解最為恰當。

❹ The change in the past few months is what I want to _____ about.

(A) know　(B) understand　(C) realize

Ans: (A)。由於說話者主要是要知道來龍去脈，加上其後有介系詞 about，因此選擇 know 表了解。

❺ I _____ that our crossover products do hit the market

(A) understand　(B) know　(C) realize

Ans: (B)。由於字裡行間並未表達出要研究轟動市場的原因，因此用 know 來表達對此現象的理解即可。

❻ Vicky _____ three languages, so she wins this job.

(A) knows　(B) understands　(C) realizes

Ans: (A)。從薇琪贏得這份工作的語意，可以推敲出他是精通三種語言，因此要選 know。

1 亂世佳人

2 傲慢與偏見

3 理性與感性

4 咆哮山莊

5 小婦人

6 簡愛

Unit 16
傲慢與偏見

俏佳人怎麼說

His pride does not offend me so much as pride
often does, because there is an excuse for it.
One cannot wonder that so very fine a
young man, with family, fortune, everything
in his favour, should think highly of himself.
If I may so express it, he has a right
to be proud.—Charlotte Lucas

他驕傲，但與一般人相比，沒那麼令我反感，皆因有其理由。如斯優
秀男子，名門之後，大富大貴，萬事順心，理當自視很高，不足為
奇。容我說，他有權驕傲。——夏綠蒂・盧卡斯

作品概述

　　雖為女主角的好友，夏綠蒂在性格上與伊麗莎白迥異，對於男主角的
性格，也不免有一番評論。她認為達西的高傲其來有自，因為達西出身名
門，自然會以達官顯貴的態度來待人處事。在夏綠蒂這段台詞中，出現了
大家很熟悉的 because。Because 可以用來解釋因果關係，但也常與
because of 及 due to 有所混淆，透過本單元的解析，將可有效釐清三

1 亂世佳人

2 傲慢與偏見

3 理性與感性

4 咆哮山莊

5 小婦人

6 簡愛

種用法的適當使用時機。

文法概述

Because / because of / due to

★ **Because 因為…**

雖然本單元的三個用法都可解釋為「因為」，但其適用時機各有不同。由於 Because 為從屬連接詞，若要以此說明因果，because 之前為因，為句子的主要部份，之後則為果，為附屬的補充或修飾，兩者是完整的句子。以下透過範例做進一步說明：

EX The concert is cancelled because the weather is bad.

音樂會因天候不佳而取消。

→ 由於音樂會取消與天候不佳都可獨立成句，故可以用 because 以後者為因，前者為果。

★ **Because of**

會將 because of 與 because 混用，最大癥結點往往在於沒有弄懂詞性。Because 是連接詞，但 Because of 卻帶有「副詞」特性，因此它修飾的是其前的「動作」，其後接名詞，因此可透過文法結構上的這個差異來加以判斷。以下透過範例做進一步說明：

EX Joe can't show up because of his sickness.

喬沒有出席是因為生病。

→ 若用 can't show up 來表達缺席某場合，符合動作的條件，以 sickness 說明身體不適，此為名詞，故使用 because of 來闡明因果關係。

★ Due to

由於 due to 後也接名詞，無法像 because of 與 because 那樣從語構立即判斷出差異，而這也是許多人混用 due to 與 because of 的原因。但 Due to 具有「形容詞」特性，修飾的是「狀態」，因此可以由此區分該用 because of 還是 due to 。以下透過範例做進一步說明：

EX The flight is delayed due to bad weather.
班機由於天候不佳而延誤。

→ 班機延誤是一種狀態，bad weather 是以名詞方式表達天氣不好，因此使用 due to 來表達因果。

實作練習與解析

❶ I missed the bus _____ I got up late this morning.
(A) because   (B) because of   (C) due to
Ans: (A)。由於空格前後都可獨立成句，因此用 because 來說明因果關係。

❷ James wins the singing competition _____ he knows how to attract audience's attention.
(A) due to   (B) because   (C) because of
Ans: (B)。由於空格前後都可獨立成句，因此用 because 來說明因果關係。

❸ Alice quits the job _____ her poor health.
(A) because   (B) due to   (C) because of

Ans: (C)。由於辭職屬於動作，health 可做名詞用，故使用
because of 來說明因果關係。

❹ John fails to hand in the report in time _____ his poor time management.
(A) due to   (B) because of   (C) because
Ans: (B)。無法如期交出報告是動作，time management 是名詞，
故以 because of 來說明因果關係。

❺ All the flights are cancelled _____ the typhoon.
(A) due to   (B) because   (C) because of
Ans: (A)。班機取消是在說明狀態，typoon 是名詞，因此用 due to
來說明因果關係。

❻ My travel schedule is delayed _____ the unexpected malfunction of my car.
(A) because of   (B) because   (C) due to
Ans: (C)。由於行程耽擱是在說明狀態，malfunction 是名詞，故以
due to 來解釋因果。

Unit 17
傲慢與偏見

俏佳人怎麼說

Married life is happiness, completely is
a chance to question. — Charlotte Lucas.
婚姻生活是否幸福，完全是機會問題。——夏綠蒂

作品概述

　　由於夏綠蒂在個性上與女主角南轅北轍，對於婚姻的看法也是大不相同。夏綠蒂不憧憬夢幻的愛情，希冀穩定的生活，但最後也在現實的考量下嫁給柯林斯。夏綠蒂對於婚姻的看法，也在 Married life is happiness, completely is a chance to question 這句話中表露無遺。在這個句子中，出現了 chance 這個表「機會」的單字，但由於英文中 opportunity、possibility、probability 也有相近語意，本單元特對其適用時機與差異解析說明。

 文法概述

Chance to / opportunity to / possibility of / probability of

★ Chance to

　若從數學的角度看 Chance，意思是機率，可用來說明某事發生的可能性。也因為帶有不確定性，當用來表示機會時，通常帶有僥倖的成分。其常見句型為: S have/has the chance to⋯。以下透過範例做進一步說明：

EX Spend one hundred dollars to join the lucky draw, and you will have the chance to win the jackpot.
花個一百塊參加抽獎，就有機會把大獎帶回家。

→ 由於中獎靠的是機率，帶有運氣成分，故用 chance 表達機會。

★ opportunity to

　若 chance 是意料之外，opportunity 就為意料之中。當用 opportunity 表機會時，有利條件與環境多已成形，差的是臨門一腳，因此多用於表達發展性或其他正面效益。其常用句型為: S has opportunity to⋯，以下透過範做進一步說明：

EX Since experience is the priority in this interview, I have the opportunity to win this job.
由於本次面試首重經驗，我很有機會得到這份工作。

→ 選定某職務尋求面試機會，代表自己有符合該職缺的條件，故用 opportunity 方為適當。

右側標籤：
1 亂世佳人
2 傲慢與偏見
3 理性與感性
4 咆哮山莊
5 小婦人
6 簡愛

★ possibility of

possibility 是 possible 的名詞，因此這樣的機會以機率為依歸，著眼在於某事是否會發生，其常用句型有 There is a possibility of…。以下透過範例作進一步說明：

EX There is a good possibility of rain tonight.

今晚下雨的可能性很高。

➜ 由於說話者強調是下雨的可能性，因此用 possibility 來說明有機會出現此天氣變化。

★ probability of

雖然都以機率為出發，但與 possibilty 不同之處在於 probability 著眼於事情發生可能性的高低。其常用句型有: The probability of … when…。以下透過範例做進一步說明：

EX The probability of making mistakes will increase when you do it in a rush.

越是想搶快，出錯機會就會高。

實作練習與解析

❶ Since only few consumers join the lucky draw, the winning __ _____ is high for me to win the prize I want.

(A) chance　(B) opportunity　(C) possibility　(D) probability

Ans: (A)。抽獎憑的是運氣，因此用 chance 來表達有此機會。

❷ It is a good_____ for you to get promoted.

(A) opportunity   (B) chance   (C) probability   (D) possibility.

Ans: (A)。有機會晉升代表自己有某些條件為長官所賞識，此種機會應以 opportunity 表示。

❸ There is a good _____ of snow this weekend.

(A) chance   (B) opportunity   (C) possibility   (D) probability

Ans: (C)。由於是在描述天氣變化的可能性，故應使用 possibility。

❹ The _____ of breakage is high if you don't follow the instruction.

(A) possibility   (B) probability   (C) chance   (D) opportunity

Ans: (B)。由於是在描述發生損壞的機率高低，故應使用 probability。

❺ The crossover product hit the market, so it is a(n) _____ for us to put more resource in.

(A) chance   (B) opportunity   (C) probability   (D) possibility

Ans: (B)。要市場反應良好，資方才可能繼續投入資源，故應以 opportunity 表達這種可乘勝追擊的機會。

❻ My performance is awful, so the _____ is high for me to lose the competition.

(A) possibility   (B) probability   (C) opportunity   (D) chance

Ans: (D)。由於輸掉比賽屬於不好的事情，故應以 chance 來表達有此機會。

1 亂世佳人

2 傲慢與偏見

3 理性與感性

4 咆哮山莊

5 小婦人

6 簡愛

Unit 18
傲慢與偏見

俏佳人怎麼說

Oh! that my dear mother had more command
over herself; she can have no idea of the pain
she gives me by her continual reflections on him.
But I will not repine. It cannot last long. He will be forgot,
and we shall all be as we were before.—Jane

但願媽媽多控制她自己一些吧！她沒曉得她這樣時時刻刻提起他，叫我多麼痛苦。不過我絕不怨誰。這局面不會長久的。他馬上就會被我們忘掉，我們還是會和往常一樣。——珍

作品概述

　　班內特一家沒有男性繼承人，大部分財產未來將由其表兄柯林斯繼承。為避免女兒們將來生活慘淡，當得知柯林斯有意取珍為妻時，女主角的母親大表贊同。無奈珍愛的是賓利先生，柯林斯把目標移轉至女主角，母親同樣極力撮合。面對母親只顧現實不顧女兒感受的市儈心態，珍娓娓道出內心的無奈。在這段話語中，command 一字可表「控制」之意，但該字不論在語意或用法皆與 control 相近，故本單元特將其並列加以解析說明。

文法概述

✦ *Command / control* ✦

★ **Command**

除了多數人所熟知的表「命令」外，Command 也可表「控制」。就要求程度來看，command 高過 control。更準確地說，若 control 為有能力控制，command 就是收放自如。當 command 後接為說話者本人，或是轉述對某人的要求時，就能表達自我約束的意涵，其常見句型有: S have command N/over oneself。若要表達某人的管理的團隊總人數，則可採用 S have a…under one's command …，以下透過範例做進一步說明:

EX James has a 100 people team under his command.

詹姆士管轄 100 名員工。

➔ 由於詹姆士為主管職，故以 has … under his command 來說明其團隊成員數。

EX Kevin is told to command his temper.

凱文被告知要控制脾氣。

➔ Command 可用於表達自我約束，故其後加上 one's temper 意即做好情緒控管。

★ **Control**

若要以一個單字表達「控制」之意，不少人應該會先直覺想到 control。此單字之所以廣泛使用，原因在於使用者可根據語句需求，來決定要採動詞還是名詞。若採名詞，其常見句型有:S have the/no control over/of…。若採動詞，其常見句型有: S is/isn't … enough to control…。以下透過範例做進一步說明:

EX The assistant coach has no control over John, so he asks the manager for help.

助理教練管不住約翰。

→ 由於助理教練無法讓約翰聽從其指揮，故以 has no control over...來表達其無能為力的窘狀。

EX Mary's skill is not mature enough to control the machine on her own.

瑪莉的技術還沒有純熟到可以獨立操作機器。

→ 瑪莉懂得技巧，但未達嫻熟，故以 is not mature enough to control 來表達控制度的不足。

實作練習與解析

❶ Amanda has a four-designer team under her ＿＿＿＿
(A) control (B) command (C) master

Ans: (B)。由於是在敘述所管理團隊之人數，故使用 command 表控制之意。

❷ Brown is warmed to ＿＿＿＿ his temper, or he will pay the price for it.
(A) master (B) control (C) command

Ans: (C)。由於不收斂脾氣就得付出代價，故應以 command 表達努力控制。

❸ You can have a better performance in the basketball court if you can have more ＿＿＿＿ over yourself in emotion control.

(A) master　(B) command　(C) control

Ans: (B)。由於情緒管理不佳真的會影響球場表現，故應以 command 表達高度的自我要求。

❹ Thompson is not skillful enough to _____ this machine.

(A) control　(B) command　(C) master

Ans: (A)。由於操控機器講求的是熟練度，故以 control 表達控制之意。

❺ The new manager has a good _____ over Joe.

(A) command　(B) control　(C) master

Ans: (B)。由於過去喬可能是個很難管理的員工，故以 a good control 來表達新任經理管理上的獨到之處。

❻ Now my older brother learned to _____ her temper.

(A) master　(B) command　(C) control

Ans: (C)。由於説話者的哥哥過去情緒管理很差，故以 control 來表現「控管」的語意。

1 亂世佳人

2 傲慢與偏見

3 理性與感性

4 咆哮山莊

5 小婦人

6 簡愛

Unit 19
傲慢與偏見

🔍 俏佳人怎麼說

"I have this comfort immediately,
that it has not been more than an error of fancy
on my side, and that it has done no harm to any one but myself.
— Jane

我立刻就可以安慰自己說：這只怪我自己瞎想，
好在並沒有損害別人，只損害了我自己。——珍

作品概述

　　在一場公共舞會中，賓利與珍互見傾心，但由於珍天性害羞，讓人難以捉摸，讓這段可能萌芽的愛情暫時無疾而終。後來從達西交給伊麗莎白的信中得知，原來賓利是因為珍始終沒給正面回應，才選擇放棄。知道真相後，珍只好自我解嘲，慶幸自己的胡思亂想沒傷害到其他人。由於在這段自嘲的話語中所出現的 error 一字，很容易與 mistake、fault、wrong 混用，因此本單元特別將其並列，説明四者的相似與相異之處。

文法概述

Mistake / error / fault / wrong

★ **Mistake**

廣義而言，本單元所介紹的四個單字表達錯誤。但若根據其成因來區隔差異，mistake 用於想法上的偏差或判斷上的失準。其常見句型為: S mistake.../S by mistake。以下透過範例做進一步說明：

EX I mistake the address, so I can't find the hotel I ordered online.

我記錯地址，所以找不到網路上訂的那間飯店在哪。

→ 由於記錯地址屬於判斷失準，故應以 mistake 來說明自己的失誤。

EX I open your mail instead of mine by mistake.

我不小心打開你的信件。

→ 説話者原本要開自己的信卻開到別人的，故應 by mistake 來表達此種粗心大意。

★ **Error**

Error 與 mistake 最大不同之處在於前者所違反的是較為明確的標準。例如公式、法規等等。因此若有違反規定之虞，即可以用 error 表示。另 error 只有名詞型態，故沒有 S error…這樣的句型，其用法多為: S feel…for the error of…。以下透過範例做進一步說明：

EX Tim feels regretful for the error of youth.

提姆對於年少時的過錯感到後悔。

→ 由於説話者可能年少時曾做了嚴重的錯事，至今仍耿耿於懷，

1 亂世佳人

2 傲慢與偏見

3 理性與感性

4 咆哮山莊

5 小婦人

6 簡愛

故應以 error 表達這類的錯誤。

★ Fault

由於 Fault 強調性格上的缺點、道德上的瑕疵與過失責任的歸屬，故可傳達這樣的失誤有時不見得是違反規定，而是基於道義而有意一肩扛起，其常見句型有: It is my fault that…。以下透過範例做進一步說明：

EX It is all my fault that we lost the game.

輸掉比賽都是我的錯。

➔ 比賽的勝負或許並非說話者一個人可左右，但他選擇承擔，故應以 fault 表達這種過錯。

★ Wrong

同樣是違反規範，由於 wrong 做形容詞時可表示是非中的「非」，改名詞使用時，所指稱的錯誤多為違法或是不道德行為。其常見句型有 It is wrong of sb to…。以下透過範例做進一步說明：

EX It is wrong of you to use drug.

你吸毒是不對的。

➔ 吸毒違反法律，故應以 wrong 表達此種錯誤。

實作練習與解析

❶ I _____ the series number and order the wrong product.
(A) mistook   (B) error   (C) faulted   (D) wronged

Ans: (A)。由弄錯序號屬於判斷上的失誤，故應以 mistake 來表達錯誤。

❷ Don't be so angry Frank used your pen by_____.

(A) fault　(B) wrong　(C) mistake　(D) error

Ans: (C)。由於用到別人的筆多出自於沒有多加留意，故應使用 by mistake 來表達。

❸ I feel regretful for the _____ I have made in my school days.

(A) wrong　(B) error　(C) fault　(D) mistake

Ans: (B)。由於求學時期可能就是說話者最荒唐的歲月，故可用 error 來表達當時所犯的錯。

❹ It is my _____ to lose this order.

(A) error　(B) mistake　(C) wrong　(D) fault

Ans: (D)。失去訂單的責任歸屬或許不全然在說話者身上，但若有勇氣承擔，則可用 fault 來說明此為自己的疏失。

❺ It is _____ to drive a car before you are 18.

(A) wrong　(B) fault　(C) mistake　(D) error

Ans: (A)。由於駕照取得有法定年齡限制，故未達此年齡前開車皆為違法，應以 wrong 來表達其錯誤。

1 亂世佳人

2 傲慢與偏見

3 理性與感性

4 咆哮山莊

5 小婦人

6 簡愛

Unit 20
傲慢與偏見

俏佳人怎麼說

You are too good. Your sweetness and
disinterestedness are really angelic;
I do not know what to say to you.
I feel as if I had never done you justice,
or loved you as you deserve.—Elizabeth

親愛的珍，你太善良了。你那樣好心，那樣處處為別人著想，
真像天使一般；我不知道應該怎麼同你說才好。
我覺得我從前待你還不夠好，愛你還不夠深。──伊麗莎白

作品概述

　　珍和伊麗莎白對於自己的愛情各有想法。珍所愛的是賓利先生，但母親卻只想將她與柯林斯先生送作堆。但由於珍生性害羞，讓兩人的感情暫時破局。事後得知原來賓利先生打從首次相遇就對她動心，不禁向妹妹伊麗莎白大吐苦水。為了安慰姐姐，伊麗莎白說出了這段語帶自責的真情告白。在這段感性的話語中，出現了表公平的片語 do sb justice，但英文中根據立基點的不同，尚有 be fair to 與 be equal to 等表達法，故本單元特將其並列，解析三者之差異。

文法概述

Do justice to / be fair to / be equal to

★ **Do justice to…**

雖然語意同為「公平對待…」，但本單元的三個片語其出發點各有不同。Do justice to 的出發點就是 justice，換句話說，就是受到怎樣的對待，就給予適切的回應。但會使用本片語，往往也都是知道該如此，但卻做不到，故其常見句型有:S can't do justice to one's N，以下透過範例做進一步說明：

EX I really can't do justice to Frank's kindness.
我真的無法答謝法蘭克對我的好意。

→ 法蘭克給予諸多協助，故說話者深覺自己很難償還此人情，故以 can't do justice to 來表示。

★ **Be fair to**

Be fair to 的出發點是 fair，也就是「公正合理」與「無差別待遇」。根據此原則，若某一情況或事件符合公平原則，可使所有人受到應有的對待，即為 be fair to 的適用時機。其常見句型有: It is fair on sb to…，以下透過範例做進一步說明：

EX It is fair on Ken to get bonus as the reward of his hard working.
肯相當努力工作，由他獲得獎金十分公平。

→ 努力的人應當到鼓勵，故應以 be fair to 表達此公平性。

★ **Be equal to**

Be equal to 的出發點是 equal，數學上表示「等於」，故可以之表

示「所有人都相同」。本單元其他二者強調立足點平等，也就是在公平的規則下，使每個人得到符合自身的對待，be equal to 則強調齊頭式平等，也就是無論身分，所有人一體適用一套規則。其常見句型有: The… of… should be equal to…，以下透過範例做進一步說明：

EX The pay of women should be equal to that of men if they are in the same position.
如職位相同，男女的薪水也應當相同
➜ 由於是在說明同工不應不同酬，故應以 be equal to 來表現此齊頭式平等。

實作練習與解析

❶ Cathy really helps me a lot, so I can't _____ her kindness.
(A) be fair to　(B) do justice to　(C) be equal to
Ans: (B)。由於說話者自認受凱西太多恩惠，因此用 can't do justice to 來表達自己無論怎麼回報都顯不足 。

❷ Don't feel worried, and _____ what you are treated.
(A) be equal to　(B) be fair to　(C) do justice to
Ans: (C)。說話者想傳達的概念是直來直往。故應以 do justice to 來表達。

❸ It _____ on Linda to get the promotion.
(A) is fair　(B) is equal　(C) do justice
Ans: (A)。由於說話者認為琳達具備升官的客觀條件，故應以 be fair to 表達此事具公平性。

❹ Sam is new here, so it is not _____ to ask him to finish the duties in such a short time.

(A) fair   (B) equal   (C) justice

Ans: (A)。由於新人業務熟悉度相對不足，要求他快速完成工作有失公平，故應以 fair 來表達，

❺ The welfare should _____ all workers.

(A) be fair to   (B) do justice to   (C) be equal to

Ans: (C)。勞工不應受到差別待遇，故以 be equal to 來表達齊頭式平等。

❻ If the salary of the experienced _____ that of the freshmen, no job seekers will send their resume to your company

(A) is equal to   (B) do justice to   (C) be fair to

Ans: (A)。若無視工作經驗，起薪一律相同，此為假齊頭式平等，故應以 is equal to 來表達此種謬論。

1 亂世佳人

2 傲慢與偏見

3 理性與感性

4 咆哮山莊

5 小婦人

6 簡愛

俏佳人怎麼說

They have known her much longer than
they have known me; no wonder if they
love her better. But, whatever may be their
own wishes, it is very unlikely they should
have opposed their brother's.—Jane

她們認識她比認識我早得多，難怪她們更喜歡她。可是不管她們自己
願望如何，她們總不至於違背她們兄弟的願望吧。──珍

作品概述

　　聽到夏綠蒂選擇嫁給柯林斯先生，伊麗莎白將其數落的一無是處，但珍提出較為中庸的見解，認為女性對愛情有時也會不切實際。面對她自己的愛情，珍深信是賓利的姊妹出的主意，因為她們不知道賓利先生喜歡自己。其屬意的人選與他相識較久。在這段珍替賓利先生辯護的內容中，出現了常用來表期待的單字 hope，但由於此字極易與 wish 混用，而使語意表達出現誤差，甚至完全相反，因此本單元特將其並列作解析說明。

 **文法概述**

✎ *Wish / hope / want* ✎

★ Wish

就發生的可能性高低來看，wish 為本單元三種「希望」中最低的一個。原因在於使用 wish 時，代表某事尚未發生，或是幾乎不可能發生。而即使某事已經發生，也與原本的期待完全相反。據此特性。其常見句型有: S wish O N /S wish that O were/ have pp。以下透過範例做進一步說明：

EX We wish you a merry Christmas.

祝你聖誕快樂。

➔ 由於此祝福語會在聖誕節前說，故應以 wish 表達希望對方佳節愉快。

EX I wish that I were a billionaire.

我希望自己是億萬富翁。

➔ 由於說話者知道自己擁有如此巨額財富的可能性甚低，故可用 wish 來表達有夢最美的無奈。

EX I wish you have submitted the report in time.

我多希望你有及時交出報告。

➔ 由於對方當時沒有及時交出報告，所以說話者才會用 wish 來表達事與願違的感受。

★ Hope

與 wish 相反，當使用 hope 表「希望」時，代表說話者所期待的事有成真的可能性，在語言邏輯上相對直觀。其常見句型有 S hope to

亂世佳人 **1**

傲慢與偏見 **2**

理性與感性 **3**

咆哮山莊 **4**

小婦人 **5**

簡愛 **6**

V… / S hope that…。以下透過範例做進一步說明:

EX I hope to see you soon.

我希望很快就能與你見面。

→ 説話者認為未來很有機會與對方見面,以 hope 來説明此可能性。

EX I hope that my younger brother can pass the exam.

我希望我弟可以通過考試。

→ 由於説話者覺得自己的弟弟有可能通過測驗,故以 hope 表達自己的祝福之意。

★ Expect

Expect 與 hope 的差異在於前者表達出的希望,是從想法面出發,後者從情感面出發。更具體地來説,就是 expect 除了腦中這樣想之外,還可以提出理由來佐證。其常見句型有: S expect to V / sth,以下透過範例做進一步説明:

EX I expect a phone call from you today.

我覺得你今天會打電話給我。

→ 由於説話者覺得對方今天會因為某種需求而來電,故以 expect 來表達此可能性。

實作練習與解析

❶ I _____ you good luck.

(A) wish (B) hope (C) expect

Ans: (A)。由於此鼓勵話語通常用於某人做某事之前，故應以 wish
表達希望好運真的降臨。

❷ Kevin _____ that he could have a sport car.
(A) expected   (B) wished   (C) wanted

Ans: (B)。由於凱文實際上未擁有跑車，故以 wish 表達此一未實現
的夢想。

❸ As your tutor, I _____ you have passed the examination.
(A) expect   (B) hope   (C) wish

Ans: (C)。由於說話者的學生當時未通過考試，故說話者以 wish 表
達他的惋惜之意。

❹ I _____ to hear from you soon.
(A) wish   (B) hope   (C) expect

Ans: (B)。由於說話者覺得對方不會拖延，故以 hope 來表達此快速
獲得回覆的可能性。

❺ My mother do _____ that I can find a job soon after her
graduation.
(A) hope   (B) wish   (C) expect

Ans: (A)。由於說話者的媽媽希望說話者有機會一畢業就找到工作，
故以 hope 表示她的殷殷期盼。

❻ I _____ to leave this team within one year.
(A) hope   (B) expect   (C) wish

Ans: (B)。由於說話者有預感自己無法在此團隊久待，故以 expect
來表達此事有發生的可能性。

1 亂世佳人

2 傲慢與偏見

3 理性與感性

4 咆哮山莊

5 小婦人

6 簡愛

Unit 22
傲慢與偏見

🔍 俏佳人怎麼說

I am far from attributing any part of Mr. Bingley's conduct to design, but without scheming to do wrong, or to make others unhappy, there may be error, and there may be misery. —Elizabeth

我絕不是說賓利先生的行為是事先預謀的。可是即使沒有存心做壞事,或者說,沒有存心叫別人傷心,事實上仍然會做錯事情,引起不幸的後果。——伊麗莎白

作品概述

　　即使發現賓利的家人試圖阻撓自己與賓利先生的愛情,珍仍試圖將整個事件合理化。但身為妹妹的伊麗莎白並不認同,認為即使本人無此意圖,但如果身邊的人推波助瀾,一樣可能造成傷害。在此段語帶些許諷刺的話語中,出現了表計畫的單字 scheme,但英文針對規劃的程度與目的不同,尚有 plan、schedule 等單字可表相似語意,故本單元特將其並列,說明其相異之處。

文法概述

Scheme / plan / schedule

★ **Scheme**

雖然語意上都可以解釋為「計畫」，但由於 scheme 可表系統性的籌劃，故其內容較為縝密，可做為未來行動的指南。其句型有: S scheme out…。此外，當 scheme 後接 to V 時，可用來表達「秘密籌畫…」的意思。以下透過範例做進一步說明：

EX We are scheming out a new method to shorten the waiting time of the customized product.
我們正在計畫一個可以縮短客製化商品等待時間的方法。

➔ 由於說話者可能已經找出如何提升效率，但尚需一些時間將其系統化，故可使用 scheme out 來表達此一發想過程。

EX I scheme to give John a surprise at his birthday.
我計畫在約翰生日時給他驚喜。

➔ 由於說話者想讓約翰有料想不到的感受，故用 scheme to V 來表達祕密籌畫的語境。

★ **Plan**

不像 scheme 已包含清楚的細項，當以 plan 表計畫時，其內容可能只是架構，有時還包含像未整理的雜項。也因為 plan 較無章法，往後只要記得 scheme 就是系統化的 plan，plan 就是未系統化的 scheme，就不會產生混淆。其常見句型有: S plan to V/S plan on Ving，以下透過範例做進一步說明：

EX Peter plans to visit his high school teacher this weekend.

彼得想在本週末去拜訪他的高中老師

→ 由於彼得可能心裡有此想法，但相關細節還沒確定，故以 plan
　來表示計畫尚未成形。

EX Mary is planning on the trip to France.

瑪莉正在計畫她的巴黎行。

→ 由於瑪莉可能只是有出遊計畫，但尚未規畫內容，故以 plan
　on…表示。

★ Schedule

由於 schedule 有行程表的意思，當做動詞表「計畫」時，常以被動
式表示，來說明先後順序或是時間安排，其常見句型有：S is
scheduled to V，以下透過範例做進一步說明：

EX The flight is scheduled to land San Francisco one hour
later.

本班機預計一小時後降落舊金山。

→ 由於是要說明航班資訊，故 schedule 採被動語法，且後接 to
　V。

實作練習與解析

❶ Tom is ＿＿＿＿ out a method to improve the working
efficiency.

(A) scheduling　(B) scheming　(C) planning

Ans: (B)。由於湯姆可能已經找出問題癥結點，故以 scheme 表達其
　　　計畫已成形。

98

❷ Though my brother_____ to surprise me, his weird attitude let me find his intent.

(A) planned　(B) schedules　(C) schemes

Ans: (C)。說話者的兄弟想秘密策畫驚喜，故應以 scheme 來表示。

❸ Sandy is _____ to go to the national park next month.

(A) planning　(B) scheduling　(C) scheming

Ans: (A)。由於一個月才後會動身，故應以 plan 來表達姍蒂的初步計畫。

❹ I _____ to visit one of my old friends in Sydney this summer vacation.

(A) schedule　(B) plan　(C) scheme

Ans: (B)。由於說話者只先訂出時間，細節尚未確定，故應以 plan 表示整體規劃未完成。

❺ I have to get the airport by 8:30 AM because the flight is _____ to take off at 9:00 AM.

(A) scheduled　(B) planed　(C) schemed

Ans: (A)。由於是在說明起飛時間，故應以 scheduled 來表時間安排。

❻ The train is _____ to arrive on 19:30.

(A) planned　(B) scheduled　(C) schemed

Ans: (B)。由於是在說明抵達時間，故應選擇 scheduled 來表時間安排。

1 亂世佳人

2 傲慢與偏見

3 理性與感性

4 咆哮山莊

5 小婦人

6 簡愛

Unit 23
傲慢與偏見

🔍 俏佳人怎麼說

Your first position is false. They may wish many things besides his happiness; they may wish his increase of wealth and consequence; they may wish him to marry a girl who has all the importance of money, great connections, and pride.—Elizabeth

你頭一個想法就錯了。她們除了希望他幸福以外，還有許多別的打算；她們會希望他更有錢有勢；她們會希望他跟一個出身高貴、親朋顯赫的闊女人結婚。——伊麗莎白

作品概述

　　由於姊姊珍相信人性本善，如果自己的親人已有喜歡的對象，兄弟姊妹會衷心祝福，而不是出手干預。但伊麗莎白並不這樣想，她認為貴族還是考量門當戶對，因此說出這段有關權貴聯姻現實面的評論。在這段評論中，出現了表「地位」的單字 consequence，但由於許多人不知有此用法，故本單元特別將其與常見的 position、status 並列做解析說明。

文法概述

Consequence / position / status / hierarchy

1 亂世佳人

2 傲慢與偏見

3 理性與感性

4 咆哮山莊

5 小婦人

6 簡愛

★ Consequence

除多數人所熟知的「結果」的用語以外，consequence 尚可表「重要性」。當一個人的重要性高，其地位高或低其實不言可喻，故 consequence 也可引申為「地位」。其常見句型有: S is a N of great consequence to…，以下透過範例做進一步說明：

EX Helen is a woman of great consequence to this club.

海倫是本社團很重要的人物。

→ 由於海倫是社團很重要的成員，故可用 great consequence 來彰顯其崇高地位。

★ Position

在用法上與 consequence 相似，position 做「地位」解時，通常用於指稱高社會經濟族群。其常見句型為 S have a adj position in…，以下透過範例做進一步說明：

EX Mr. James has a high position in the society.

詹姆士先生擁有高社會地位。

→ 由於說話者欲說明詹姆士先生的身分位居金字塔頂端，故可使用 position 來表示。

★ Status

雖然同表「地位」，但 status 是四者中最能強調此身分的「定位」或「狀態」的。依此特性，status 常與 social 或 economic 等字連用，說明個人或是群體的地位變化。其常見句型有: The status of…

has/have pp，以下透過範例做進一步說明：

EX Women's social status has changed much over the past few decades.

女性的社會地位在過去幾十年大幅提升。

★ Hierarchy

不同於其他三者，若以 hierarchy 表「地位」，凸顯的是「階級差異」與「原則導向」。hierarchy 所表現的地位，是在一個固定架構下，依照各成員的重要程度加以排序。其常見句型有:S have a … hierarchy in…，以下透過範例做進一步說明：

EX Some companies have complex hierarchies in their organization.

有些公司的架構階級複雜。

→ 由於說話者想表達有些公司組織階級森嚴，故應以 hierarchy 表示身分的不易流動型。

實作練習與解析

❶ Josh is a man of great_____ to this company.
(A) position　(B) consequence　(C) status　(D) hierarchy
Ans: (B)。由於說話者想表達賈許在公司的重要性，故應以 consequence 表達其身分。

❷ Mark has a high _____ in this region.
(A) hierarchy　(B) position　(C) consequence　(D) status

Ans: (B)。由於說話者想表達馬克在此區域深具影響力,故應以 position 表達其社會地位。

❸ The social _____ of technicians has been overturned in the past few years.

(A) status   (B) hierarchy   (C) consequence   (D) position

Ans: (A)。由於說話者主要是在描述某族群地位的改變,故應以 status 表現此一變化情況。

❹ The fixed _____ hinders the development of this company.

(A) position   (B) consequence   (C) status   (D) hierarchy

Ans: (D)。由於說話者是在描述階級劃分成為進步的阻力,故應以 hierarchy 來說明身分的區分。

❺ Though Kelly is young, she is a woman of great _____ to ABC Company.

(A) status   (B) consequence   (C) position   (D) hierarchy

Ans: (B)。凱莉雖然年輕,但影響力舉足輕重,故應以 consequence 顯示其身分之重要性。

❻ The income of workers is better now, but their social _____ remains in the bottom of the pyramid.

(A) status   (B) hierarchy   (C) consequence   (D) position

Ans: (A)。說話者想表達的是勞工階級雖收入增加,但社會地位未見改善,故應以 status 來強調階級仍未改變。

Unit 24
傲慢與偏見

🔍 俏佳人怎麼說

It is very often nothing but our own
vanity that deceives us. Women fancy
admiration means more than it does. —Jane

我們往往會因為我們自己的虛榮心，而給弄迷了心竅。女人們往往會把愛情這種東西幻想得太不切合實際。——珍

作品概述

　　雖然與賓利先生的愛情受到阻撓，但珍不想就此怪罪賓利先生的家人，強調人都會自我膨脹，導致於判斷失準。面對愛情，女性都會有所憧憬，但這些美好幻想卻往往不可能實現。在這段珍深刻自省的話語中，出現常用來表「驕傲」的單字 vanity。但由於此字易與 pride、conceit 混淆，故本單元特將其並列做解析說明。

文法概述

❧ *Vanity / pride / conceit* ❧

★ Vanity

廣義來看，本單元所解析的三個單字都表「驕傲」，但其動機各有不同。達到某事後的耀武揚威是 vanity 的核心。當能詔告天下，證明自己有此能力，做此事的必要與否對當事人來說無關痛癢。其常見句型有: S… out of vanity，以下透過範例作進一步說明：

EX Ben buys this heavy motor out of vanity.
班買這部重機是出於虛榮心。

→ 班可能無力負擔購買重機的高額開銷，但還是逞強購買，故可用 out of vanity 來表現其愛慕虛榮。

★ Pride

不同於 vanity 的單純炫耀，Pride 起因於對自己或是自己有關的人的好表現感到滿意，反感程度相對較低。因此，若完成某事後自覺很值得大肆宣揚，就可以用 S feels the sense of pride when… 的句型來表示，以下透過範例做進一步說明：

EX I feel the sense of pride when I get the prize from the chief judge.
當從裁判長手中接過獎座時，我深感自豪。

→ 說話者對於得獎感到滿意，故可用 pride 來呈現他想與人分享的感受。

★ Conceit

同樣是四處宣揚自己達成某一成就，pride 給人的感受還勉強算得上

1 亂世佳人

2 傲慢與偏見

3 理性與感性

4 咆哮山莊

5 小婦人

6 簡愛

105

恰如其分，也就是做三分但渲染至五分。但如果是 conceit，就是做了三分但卻誇大到十分，極易令人反感。其常見句型有: The conceit of …is… ，以下透過範例作進一步說明：

EX The conceit of John is incredible, so he always despises other colleagues.

約翰極其自大，所以他鄙視其他同事。

→ 由於約翰非常驕傲，故可以用 conceit 描述他的自我膨脹。

實作練習與解析

❶ I bought this luxury watch out of _____ last week, and now I feel regret.

(A) vanity (B) pride (C) conceit

Ans: (A)。說話者可能上週因為礙於面子而逞強購買昂貴錶款，故應以 vanity 表現其愛慕虛榮。

❷ Parker buys this expensive bag to gratify his girlfriend's _____.

(A) conceit (B) vanity (C) pride

Ans: (B)。帕克的女友不見得真的需要這個包包，但出於與人比較的心態，還是要求帕克買給她，故應以 vanity 來顯現其貪戀物質。

❸ Benny feels the sense of _____ when he gets the trophy.

(A) vanity (B) pride (C) conceit

Ans: (B)。由於拿到獎盃是光榮的事，故可用 pride 來描述班尼此時的心境。

❹ When I know that I am the only one who gets the scholarship, I feel the sense of _____

(A) conceit   (B) vanity   (C) pride

Ans: (C)。由於只有說話者拿到獎學金,故可用 pride 來表現他心中的驕傲。

❺ The _____ of my roommate is the reason why I move.

(A) conceit   (B) vanity   (C) pride

Ans: (A)。由於說話者覺得他的室友非常自大,故可用 conceit 來表現那種自命不凡。

❻ Lisa's _____ is the reason why she almost has no friend.

(A) vanity   (B) conceit   (C) pride

Ans: (B)。自負會讓人不想與之親近,故可用 conceit 來凸顯自大的程度。

1 亂世佳人

2 傲慢與偏見

3 理性與感性

4 咆哮山莊

5 小婦人

6 簡愛

Unit 25
傲慢與偏見

俏佳人怎麼說

> *My dear Lizzy, do not give way to such feelings as these. They will ruin your happiness. You do not make allowance enough for difference of situation and temper. Consider Mr. Collins's respectability, and Charlotte's prudent, steady character. —Jane*

親愛的麗姿，不要這樣胡思亂想吧。那會毀了你的幸福的。你對於各人處境的不同和脾氣的不同，體諒得不夠。你且想一想柯林斯先生的身份地位和夏綠蒂的謹慎穩重吧。——珍

作品概述

伊麗莎白非常討厭柯林斯先生，但偏偏自己的好友夏綠蒂卻選擇嫁給他。面對這樣的衝擊，伊麗莎白毫不留情地把兩人狠狠地批評一遍。此時個性溫和的珍勸她凡事給人留點餘地，因為如果去想，柯林斯先生好歹出身算是優渥，夏綠蒂的務實性格也是會答應求婚的主因。在這段珍給妹妹的忠告中出現了表「性格」的單字 character，但此字與 personality、individuality、temperament 容易產生混淆，故本單元特將四者並列做解析說明。

文法概述

Character / personality / individuality / temperament

★ Character

本單元的三種「性格」所著重的面向各有不同，character 為四種中最為內斂的一個，所描述的特性偏向道德觀與心理層面。其常見句型有: N is part of the personality of…，以下透過範例做進一步說明：

EX Always being humble is a part of the character of my younger brother.

虛懷若谷是我弟性格中的一環。

→ 謙虛是心理層面的描述，故應以 character 來說明說話者弟弟的特質。

★ Personality

不同於 character 的內斂，personality 所表現的特質相對外顯，通常與外貌、行為有關。一般來說，personality 會被視為一系列特質的組合，而這樣的組合讓每個人都是獨一無二的個體。其常見句型有:S have/has a… personality，以下透過範例做進一步說明：

EX Helen has a warm personality, so she often helps the weak.

海倫古道熱腸，所以她經常協助弱勢族群。

→ 熱心助人屬於外顯行為，故應以 personality 來表示。

★ Individuality

Individuality 是由 individual 衍生而來。Individual 強調個體的獨

1 亂世佳人

2 傲慢與偏見

3 理性與感性

4 咆哮山莊

5 小婦人

6 簡愛

立性，因此 Individuality 也多用於凸顯性格上的獨樹一幟。其常見句型有:S is/are a N of individuality，以下透過範例做進一步說明：

EX Wendy is a women of weird individuality, so it is hard to predict her next step.

溫蒂是個性格古怪的女人，很難預測她的下一步。

→ 之所以無法預測溫蒂接下來的行動，原因在於她性格上的特異，故可用 individuality 來表示。

★ Temperament

Temperament 是由 temper 衍生而來，故其描述重點自然與脾氣有關。若以 temperament 表性格，通常用於說明當中會影響情緒與行為的部分，概念上就是中文所說的氣質。其常見句型有: S have/has adj temperament，以下透過範例作進一步說明：

EX Hank has a romantic temperament.

漢克生性浪漫。

→ 由於浪漫可透過情緒與行為來表現，形成一種其他人所能感受到的氣質，故應以 temperament 來表示。

實作練習與解析

❶ Aggressive is part of the ＿＿＿＿＿ of Jason.
(A) individuality (B) temperament (C) personality (D) character

Ans: (C)。積極進取偏向心理層面的描述，故應以 character 表示。

❷ Sally has cold _____, so she prefers to work alone.

(A) temperament   (B) individuality   (C) character   (D) personality

Ans: (D)。獨立作業屬於外顯行為，故應以 personality 說明此特點。

❸ Alice is a women of strange _____, making me feel difficult to cooperate with her.

(A) personality   (B) temperament   (C) individuality   (D) character

Ans: (C)。怪異也是一種獨特性，故應以 individuality 表示。

❹ Lulu has an adventurous _____.

(A) character   (B) personality   (C) temperament   (D) individuality

Ans: (C)。愛冒險可歸類為一種氣質，故應以 temperament 表示。

❺ Negative is part of the _____Ray, so she often worries too much.

(A) temperament   (B) character   (C) individuality   (D) personality.

Ans: (B)。負面思考偏向心理傾向，故應以 character 來表示此種特性。

❻ Jill has a romantic _____, so she paints her room in pink.

(A) personality   (B) individuality   (C) temperament   (D) character

Ans: (B)。浪漫可透過空間佈置具體呈現，故應以 individuality 說明此一特性。

1 亂世佳人

2 傲慢與偏見

3 理性與感性

4 咆哮山莊

5 小婦人

6 簡愛

Part 3

Week 3 理性與感性

俏佳人怎麼說

What do you know of my heart? What do you know of anything but your own suffering? For weeks, Marianne, I've had this pressing on me without being at liberty to speak of it to a single creature. It was forced on me by the very person whose prior claims ruined all my hope. I have endured her exaltation again and again whilst knowing myself to be divided from Edward forever. —Elinor

妳知道我在想什麼嗎?除了妳自己的煩惱外,妳還知道甚麼呢?幾個星期以來,無法自由地與人交談讓我倍感壓力。就是那個人所提出的要求毀了我所有的希望。當我知道將永遠與艾德華先生分開時,我早已一次又一次地忍受她的耀武揚威。——愛蓮娜

作品概述

　　不同於妹妹瑪麗安的衝動個性,姐姐愛蓮娜的思考較為理性。因此當妹妹批評她凡事只懂得逆來順受,連面對愛情都不極力爭取時,愛蓮娜才大吐心中的委屈,直言得知遭人從中作梗被迫和愛德華分開時,自己也是

內心百般煎熬。在這段宣洩情緒的話語中，出現了表「破壞」的單字 ruin。但由於此字極易與 destroy 跟 damage 混淆，故本單元特根據肇因的不同與損壞程度的差異來進行解析說明。

文法概述

Ruin / destroy / damage

★ ruin

雖然同樣意指「損壞」，但本單元的三種用法其肇因各不相同。Ruin 通常是因為自然現象、人為疏失而產生破壞，且其損害程度達到「無法修復」。若用於比喻手法，則可表達「搞砸…」的語意。其句型有:S ruin…，以下透過範例做進一步說明：

EX The unexpected heavy rain ruins my trip.

意料之外的大雨毀了我的這趟旅行。

→ 由於說話者並不認為他出遊時會下雨，故可用 ruin 來表達天氣搞砸旅程的無奈感。

EX The war ruined this city.

戰爭摧毀了這座城市。

→ 戰火足以使一座城市毀壞致無法重建，故可使用 ruin 來表達。

★ Damage

不同於 ruin 與 destroy 可表「非實體」受損， damage 通常用於表達「實體」的「部分」損壞。由於此破壞不至於到無法復原，故所傳達出的訊息是在效能、價值、功用等方面已因此降低。其常見句型有:S is/are damaged by…，以下透過範例做進一步說明：

右側邊欄：1 亂世佳人　2 傲慢與偏見　3 理性與感性　4 咆哮山莊　5 小婦人　6 簡愛

EX The dam is seriously damaged by the earthquake.

水壩在地震中嚴重損壞。

➔ 地震的破壞力雖大，但要到摧毀水庫也並不常見，故以 damage 表達損壞的嚴重性已相當足夠。

★ Destroy

就損壞程度來看，destroy 通常會是到「難以修復」的程度，可說是 damage 的強化版。若將其應用於比喻中，在語意強度上與 ruin 不相上下，皆可表現出「徹底」摧毀或抹滅的意涵。其常見句型有:S destroy…，以下透過範例做進一步說明：

EX The fire destroyed the library.

大火燒毀了圖書館。

➔ 火災足以讓建物毀損至無法修復，故可用 destroy 來說明其嚴重程度。

實作練習與解析

❶ The delay of the flight almost _____ my trip.
(A) ruins   (B) destroys   (C) damages

Ans: (A)。由於班機延誤讓說話者無法準時開始旅程，故應 ruin 來表達搞砸之義。

❷ The hurricane almost_____ the whole city, making the residents start to consider the feasibility of relocation.
(A) destroys   (B) damages   (C) ruins

Ans: (C)。由於颶風對城市造成的損害可能是無法復原的，故應以 ruin 來表達其嚴重程度。

❸ The main bridges are _____ in the flood, blocking the access to the road network around the city temporarily.

(A) destroyed   (B) damaged   (C) ruined

Ans: (B)。除非是整座橋樑沖毀，否則搶通所耗費的時間理論上都不會太久，故應使用 damage 來描述此種破壞。

❹ The spilled milk _____ my cell phone.

(A) ruins   (B) destroys   (C) damages

Ans: (C)。濺到牛奶手機功能會受損，故應以 damage 來表示。

❺ The flood _____ the most part of the road, so the polite set the warning sign to remind us not to enter this area.

(A) damages   (B) ruins   (C) destroys

Ans: (C)。洪水可使道路嚴重損壞，但不直於到無法修復，故應以 destroy 表示。

❻ I have a good mood at the very beginning, but Andy's impolite behaviors soon _____ it.

(A) destroy   (B) ruin   (C) damage

Ans: (A)。説話者一開始心情很好，但沒多久就因為安迪的不禮貌行為而深受影響，故應以 destroy 來表達被惹毛的感受。

1 亂世佳人

2 傲慢與偏見

3 理性與感性

4 咆哮山莊

5 小婦人

6 簡愛

Unit 27
理性與感性

俏佳人怎麼說

But time alone does not determine intimacy.
Seven year would insufficient to make some people
acquainted with each other and seven days are
more than enough for others.—Marianne

**但親密感不是單憑時間就能建立起來的。有些人用七年的時間還無法
認識彼此;而對有些人來講,七天都還嫌多呢!——瑪麗安**

作品概述

　　在與魏勒比先生碰面後的隔天,愛蓮娜與瑪麗安姊妹倆仍繼續討論這
位男士。瑪麗安表示她與魏勒比的關係已經相當密切,但愛蓮娜卻不這樣
認為。瑪麗安不甘示弱,提出只要彼此投緣,即使相識的時間很短,一樣
可以一見如故。在這段表明想法的話語中,出現了表「決定」的單字
determine,但由於英文中尚有 decide 與 resolve 有相近語意,若未
釐清差異極易誤用,故本單元特將三者並列做解析説明。

118

文法概述

~ *Determine / decide / resolute* ~

★ **Determine**

雖然同表「決定」，若描述控制或是影響某項因素使最終結果一如預期，此時 determine 強調的是有效掌控。其常見句型有:S is determined by…，若表做出選擇，語意上強調「下定決心」，其常見句型有：S determine to V/ that，以下透過範例做進一步說明：

EX The durability is determined by the material you use.

選材決定了耐用度的高低。

→ 使用特定材料可使成品的耐耗損程度如製造前所預期，故應以 determine 來表達。

EX John determines to go abroad to have further study. .

約翰畢決心要出國進修。

→ 約翰打算在自我充實，故應以 determine 來表達已經下定決心。

★ **Decide**

不同於 determine 技巧性地將事物導向預期達到的目標，Decide 所傳達的是經過仔細思考多種可能性之後，從多個可能選項中所做出的選擇。其常見句型有：S decide to V，以下透過範例做進一步說明：

EX In the end, we decide to use plan A.

最後我們決定採用 A 計畫。

→ 說話者一開始有多個計畫可供選擇，但幾經思考後選擇 A 計畫，故應以 decide 表達此決策過程。

1 亂世佳人

2 傲慢與偏見

3 理性與感性

4 咆哮山莊

5 小婦人

6 簡愛

★ Resolve

不同於 determine 的要素掌控與 decide 的項目選擇，Resolve 主要用於表達做出決定這個「動作」本身。其常見句型有:S resolve to V，以下透過範例做進一步說明：

EX They resolve to visit this national park at least once every year

他們決定每年至少前往此國家公園一次。

→ 由於說話者是在轉述對方所做出的決議，故應以 resolve 來表示。

實作練習與解析

❶ The size of the office we are going to rent is _____ by the number of staff.

(A) determined   (B) decided   (C) resolved

Ans: (A)。員工的多寡左右辦公室大小的選擇，故應以 determine 來表達此要素的影響力。

❷ The weather will _____ whether the baseball game will be held or not

(A) resolute   (B) decide   (C) determine

Ans: (C)。天候不佳球賽就無法如期舉行，故應以 determine 來表達此要素的影響力。

❸ After this meeting, we _____ to postpone the release date of our new product.

(A) decide　(B) determine　(C) resolute

Ans: (A)。說話者可能有意改變新產品的上市時間，最後選擇延後，故應以 decide 表達此決策過程。

❹ Considering the budget, we ＿＿＿＿ to take the bus instead of high speed railway.

(A) determine　(B) decide　(C) resolve

Ans: (B)。說話者有不只一種交通工具可供選擇，但最後選了巴士，故可用 decide 來表達此決策過程。

❺ Helen ＿＿＿＿ to leave early today, but the heavy rain stops her from going.

(A) resolves　(B) determines　(C) decides

Ans: (A)。海倫原本已經安排好行程，但因為天候因素而被迫延遲，故應以 resolve 表達此決策。

❻ I ＿＿＿＿ to visit the place next year because of its beautiful scenery.

(A) determine　(B) resolve　(C) decide

Ans: (B)。說話者覺得此處風景美到值得往後在此造訪，故應以 resolve 來表述此決策。

亂世佳人 1
傲慢與偏見 2
理性與感性 3
咆哮山莊 4
小婦人 5
簡愛 6

Unit 28
理性與感性

俏佳人怎麼說

Good work, Marianne, you have cover all forms
of poetry; another meeting will ascertain
his view on nature and romantic attachments
and then you will have nothing left to
talk about and the acquaintanceship will be over.—Elinor

你表現真好啊，和他談遍了各種詩歌。下次見面必會談到他對大自然
與愛情的想法，然後你們的話題將終結，連同這段情誼也告吹。
——愛蓮娜

作品概述

　　妹妹瑪麗安個性活潑外向，當有第一次機會與心儀的魏勒比先生交談時，瑪麗安話匣子大開，一直向他介紹自己喜歡的文學作品。由於魏勒比對於瑪麗安的看法也表認同，兩人熟稔程度快速提升。看到妹妹聊到欲罷不能，姊姊挪揄她說第一次就用掉如此多話題，往後見面很快就會無話可聊了。在這段提到了表「友誼」的單字 acquaintanceship，但跟友好程度不同，英文中所對應的用語也跟這不同，因此本單元特別將 acquaintanceship 中的 acquaintance 獨立出來，將其與 friend、 companion、buddy 等相似單字做解析説明。

文法概述

Acquaintance / friend / companion / buddy

★ Acquaintance

就熟稔程度而言，acquaintance 指的是你認識但沒有很熟的人。未與此類友人深交的原因又可在細分為不應或無須深交，例如生意往來的客戶與夥伴。或是只有幾面之緣，尚無法決定是否要進一步認識的新朋友。其常見句型有: S have some acquaintance with…以下透過範例做進一步説明：

EX I have some acquaintance with Jason.
我與傑森不是很熟。

→ 由於説話者可能只見過傑森幾次，故可用 acquaintance 來表達這種與某人認識但不熟的情況 。

★ Friend

同樣以熟稔程度來分級，friend 指的是你很了解且喜歡與其來往的人，但通常不會將家人歸在此類。其常見句型有 S is/are a adj friend with sb，以下透過範例做進一步説明：

EX I am a good friend with Ken, so we meet four days a week.
我和肯是好朋友，所以我們一週碰面四次。

→ 好朋友才會頻繁見面，故可用 friend 來表達説話者與肯的友好程度。

1 亂世佳人
2 傲慢與偏見
3 理性與感性
4 咆哮山莊
5 小婦人
6 簡愛

★ Companion

若以 companion 來表達與某人的情誼，其重點落在兩人有很長的相處時間。一般來說，此情況會發生在朋友之間，但在於若兩人因旅遊而一起行動，也可以用此單字表示。其常見句型有: S has been one's companion for…，以下透過範例做進一步說明：

EX I have been Peterson's companion for ten years, so I like to play him practical jokes.

我和彼得森成為好友已經十年了，所以我愛對他惡作劇。

→ 對彼此夠熟才敢對對方惡作劇，因此可用 companion 來表達兩人的情誼。

★ Buddy

就熟稔程度來看，buddy 是本單元四者中最高。一般來說，好友才會以此相稱。但倘若你覺得某位男性的舉動讓你很反感，也可以使用 buddy 稱呼他，但此時的語意就轉變為「老兄」，其後接續的內容通常帶有警告意味。其常見句型有：sb and I have been buddy for…，以下透過範例做進一步說明：

EX Nick and I have been buddies for several years, so I know all of his bad habits.

尼克與我是多年好友，所以我知道他所有的壞習慣。

→ 好兄弟不只知道對方的好，也知道對方的壞，故可用 buddy 相稱。

實作練習與解析

❶ I only have some _____ with Helen, so I don't know her preference in food.

(A) acquaintance (B) friend (C) buddy (D) companion

Ans: (A)。若與對方不熟，自然對飲食習慣了解有限，故可用 acquaintance 説明兩人的情誼。

❷ I am the _____ with Josh, so we meet very often.

(A) companion (B) acquaintance (C) friend (D) buddy

Ans: (C)。朋友才可能常見面，故應以 friend 來表現兩人的熟識程度。

❸ Nico has been Mary's _____ for ten years, so she knows her temper very well.

(A) buddy (B) friend (C) acquaintance (D) companion

Ans: (D)。一個人的脾氣要透過長時間相處才可摸透，故可用 companion 來描述兩人的熟稔。

❹ Bob and I have been _____ for a long time, so I always play joke on him.

(A) companions (B) buddies (C) friends (D) acquaintances

Ans: (B)。好友才會互開玩笑，故應使用 buddies 來表達説話者與鮑伯的友誼

1 亂世佳人

2 傲慢與偏見

3 理性與感性

4 咆哮山莊

5 小婦人

6 簡愛

Unit 29
理性與感性

俏佳人怎麼說

Love is not love which alters when it
alteration finds, or bends with the remover to
remove. Oh no! It is an ever fixed mark that
looks on tempests and is never shaken."
Willoughby. Willoughby. Willoughby.— Marianne

愛非真愛，若遭逢更改時即刻更改，或屈就於離去者而離開：哦，
不！愛是恆定的航海指標，俯望暴風雨，絕不動搖。魏勒比、魏勒
比、魏勒比。──瑪麗安

作品概述

　　瑪麗安個性外向，且對於文學充滿熱情，當有機會與心儀的魏勒比先生討論彼此對愛情的想法時，她引用了莎士比亞十四行詩第 116 首的內容，認為愛應當經得起考驗。在這段描述真愛定義的文字中，出現了表「離開」的單字 remove，但由於此字與 depart、leave 等字在相關文法有些相似而容易混用，故本單元特將其並列做解析說明。

文法概述

➤ *Remove / depart / leave* ➤

★ Remove

若將 remove 拆解為 re(表再次…的字首)與 move(移動)，就很容易理解其語意重點為何。因此當我們將某事物改變位置或是讓某人離開某地，就可以用 remove 來說明。其常見句型有: S is removed from …，以下透過範例做進一步說明:

EX The rubbish is removed from the backyard by my father.

我爸把垃圾從後院中清走。

➔ 由於說話者正在描述垃圾位置的改變，故應以 remove 表示。

EX Jessica is removed from this school by her parents.

潔西卡的父母將潔西卡從這間學校轉走。

➔ 由於是在描述某人離開某地，故應以 remove 表示。

★ Depart

雖然同樣表離開，depart 特別強調從此地動身前往另一處的語意，因此經常用於描述旅行時各地點的移動順序。其常見句型有: S will depart from…to …，以下透過範例做進一步說明:

EX The plane departs from Taiwan to London at 6:00 PM.

本班機於下午六點從台灣飛往倫敦。

➔ 此公告旨在說明班機的交通資訊，故應以 depart 來描述起飛與降落地點。

1 亂世佳人

2 傲慢與偏見

3 理性與感性

4 咆哮山莊

5 小婦人

6 簡愛

★ leave

若就離開的時間長短來看，leave 是三者中最常用於描述「短時間」或「暫時」遠離的一個。若強調從「何處」離開，其常見句型有: S leave… by….，若強調「何時」離開，其常見句型有: S will leave in…，以下透過範例做進一步說明:

EX Steve left the classroom by the back door.

史蒂夫從教室的後門離開。

→ 由於說話者強調對方從哪邊離開，故應以 leave…by…來表示。

EX The train will leave in ten minute

本班火車將於十分鐘後發車。

→ 由於此公告旨在說明車班離開的時間，故應以 leave…in…來表示

實作練習與解析

❶ The barrier is ＿＿＿＿ from the entrance.

(A) left (B) departed (C) removed

Ans: (C)。由於是在說明物體位置的移動，故應以 remove 來表示。

❷ Mary is ＿＿＿＿ from the marketing team by her boss.

(A) left (B) removed (C) departed

Ans: (B)。由於是在描述人員業務單位的轉變，故應以 remove 表示。

❸ The flight _____ from New York to Paris.
  (A) departs   (B) removes   (C) leaves
  Ans: (A)。由於是在描述班機的起降資訊，故應以 depart 來表達離開之意。

❹ Helen _____ the lab from Exit 2.
  (A) removes   (B) leaves   (C) departs
  Ans: (B)。由於說話者主要表達海倫暫時不會在實驗室，故應以 leave 來表達離開之意。

❺ The shuttle bus will _____ in ten minutes.
  (A) depart   (B) remove   (C) leave
  Ans: (C)。由於說話者是在說明車班駛離時間，故應以 leave 來表達離開之意。

❻ The train _____ from Rome to Venice at 7:00 AM.
  (A) leaves   (B) departs   (C) removes
  Ans: (B)。由於是在描述火車車班資訊，故應以 depart 來表達離開之意。

1 亂世佳人

2 傲慢與偏見

3 理性與感性

4 咆哮山莊

5 小婦人

6 簡愛

Unit 30
理性與感性

俏佳人怎麼說

*Can he really love her? Can the soul really be satisfied
with such polite affections? To love is to burn,
to be on fire, all made of full of passion,
of adoration, or sacrifice. —Marianne*

**他真的能夠愛她嗎?熱切的靈魂怎能滿足於溫吞掩飾的愛情呢?愛是燃
燒的火焰,是完全的熱情、崇拜及犧牲。——瑪麗安**

作品概述

　　相較於姊姊的逆來順受,當面對這個社會加諸在她身上的種種限制,
瑪莉安會不惜起身對抗。當從母親口中得知愛蓮娜與愛德華的戀情受到愛
德華姊姊芬妮的阻擾時,瑪麗安認為姊姊不會也不敢為愛奮戰。而她自己
認為愛往往是得付出代價的。在這情緒激昂的話語中,出現了表「滿意」
的單字 satisfied,但由於 pleased 與 content 在語意與用法上皆與之
相似,容易產生誤用,故本單元特將其並列做解析說明。

文法概述

✄ *Satisfied / pleased / content* ✄

★ Satisfied

本單元的三個單字都可以表達「滿意」，但其原因各有不同。Satisfied 是因為獲得自己所想要的事物，或是事情的進展一如我們所預期。但要特別注意的是，雖然 satisfied 表達出一切似乎都在掌控之中，其實它也隱含事情的發展有機會可以更好。其常見句型有: S is/are satisfied with…，以下透過範例做進一步說明:

EX My supervisor is satisfied with my performance.
長官對我的表現感到滿意。

→ 說話者做出的成果是長官所想要的，故應以 satisfied 表示。

★ Pleased

就滿意度而言，pleased 又比 satisfied 更高一級，原因在於前者表現出現在的狀態已經是最好，不可能發生更好的情況。其常見句型有: S is pleased with...，以下透過範例做進一步說明:

EX I am greatly pleased with our new kitchen.
我對新廚房十分滿意。

→ 說話者覺得廚房整修過後已達最佳配置，故可用 pleased 來表達心滿意足的感受。

★ Content

不像 satisfied 與 please 還需區分是否可能更好，Content 所表現出的滿意是對現狀感到滿足，不希望再有改變與進展。其常見句型有:S is content to V/with，以下透過範例做進一步說明:

1 亂世佳人

2 傲慢與偏見

3 理性與感性

4 咆哮山莊

5 小婦人

6 簡愛

EX I am content to live in the apartment I rent now.

我非常滿意現在所租的公寓。

→ 說話者覺得目前的居住地點非常好，不打算再搬家，故應以 content 來表現其滿意程度。

EX David is content with his job, so he is always having a good mood while at work.

大衛對他的工作感到十分滿意，因此上工時心情都很好。

→ 大衛對於工作沒有不滿，故應使用 content 來說明他「樂在其中」的感受。

實作練習與解析

❶ My mom is _____ with my performance in the entrance test.

(A) satisfied　(B) pleased　(C) content

Ans: (A)。說話者的媽媽覺得他入學考試的成績很不錯，故應用 satisfied 來呈現她的滿意程度。

❷ I am great _____ with your design, so I will recommend your studio to my friend.

(A) content　(B) pleased　(C) satisfied

Ans: (B)。說話者覺得對方的設計完全符合他的要求，故可用 pleased 來表達其滿意程度。

❸ Ricky is _____ with the office he rent now, so he want to sign a long-term contract with the land owner to ask for discount in rent.

(A) pleased　(B) satisfied　(C) content

Ans: (C)。目前所租用辦公室很符合瑞奇的需求,他也想延長租約故應以 content 來說明他的滿意程度。

❹ James is ＿＿＿＿ to live in the dormitory which his company provides, so he won't move in the coming few years .

(A) content　(B) satisfied　(C) pleased

Ans: (A)。詹姆士覺得公司配給的宿舍很不錯,短期內不會搬家,故應以 content 來表達他的滿意程度。

❺ I am ＿＿＿＿ with the presentation which Walker just made, so I recommend him to be the host of the product release next month.

(A) content　(B) pleased　(C) satisfied

Ans: (C)。說話者覺得華克的報告很精采,很適合擔任產品發表的主持人,故應以 satisfied 來表達他的滿意程度。

❻ My boss is ＿＿＿＿ with my performance in the trade show, so I get his authorization to be the leader of the special marketing team.

(A) satisfied　(B) content　(C) pleased

Ans: (C)。老闆因為說話者的好表現而授權他成為特別小組的組長,故可用 please 來表達老闆的滿意程度。

1 亂世佳人

2 傲慢與偏見

3 理性與感性

4 咆哮山莊

5 小婦人

6 簡愛

Unit 31
理性與感性

俏佳人怎麼說

Believe me, Marianne, had I not
been bound to silence I could have provided
proof enough of a broken heart, even for you." — Elinor

瑪麗安我跟妳說，如果我沒有一直保持沉默的話，即使是對妳，我也能證明我已心碎。——愛蓮娜

作品概述

　　在得知自己無法與愛德華長相廝守後，愛蓮娜滿腹的委屈卻無處可以傾訴，所幸後來有機會跟妹妹大吐苦水，她才說出她其實痛苦到心碎。在這段姐妹的真情告白中，出現了表「應當⋯」的片語 be bound to，但由於英文中尚有 be obligate to 與 ought to 在用法上與之相似，差別在各字所強調的重點不同，故本單元特將三者並列做解析說明。

文法概述

Be bound to / be obligated to / be sure to

1 亂世佳人

2 傲慢與偏見

3 理性與感性

4 咆哮山莊

5 小婦人

6 簡愛

★ Be bound to

雖然在語意上本單元三種用法都可解釋為「應當」，但其強調的重點各有不同。單看 Bound 一字，除做「綑綁」解釋外，也可表達「受…約束」之意。故 be bound to 的重點放在讓某人信守承諾。其常見句型有: S is/are bound to N，以下透過範例做進一步說明：

EX We are all bound to the contract.

我們都需遵守合約。

➔ 由於說話者主要是在強調合約所帶來的限制，故應以 be bound to 來說明其約束力。

★ Be obligated to

相較於 bound 是從大架構來說明限制，由於 obligate 一字，意為「有義務…」，故 be obligated to 是強調如何在規範下「履行義務」。其常見句型有: S is/are obligated to V…，以下透過範例做進一步說明：

EX The seller is obligated to pay the freight according to the contract.

根據合約內容，賣方需支付運費。

➔ 由於說話者是在表達依約賣方所需盡的義務，故應以 be obligated to 來表達。

★ ought to

若從法律的角度來說明行事的準則，obligated 與 bound 實為貼切

的用語。但若只想單純表達某事有執行的「必要性」，或是做了某事會有「益處」，則可用 ought to 來表示，其常見句型有: S ought to V⋯，以下透過範例做進一步說明：

EX We ought to think twice before we take actions.
凡事都應三思而行。

→ 由於說話者要表達的是做之前多想想對自己是有好處的，故應以 ought to 來表示。

實作練習與解析

❶ All members in the alliance are_____ to the regulation.
(A) bound　(B) obligate　(C) sure
Ans: (A)。加入聯盟的成員自然應遵守其相關規範，故應以 be bound to 來說明所受的限制。

❷ Since the special team has been dismissed, you are not ____ ___ to the related regulation.
(A) sure　(B) obligated　(C) bound
Ans: (C)。由於該團隊已經解散，同屬其成員的對方自然不再受其規範所約束，故應以 be bound to 來表示。

❸ The buyer is _____ to cover the insurance according to the agreement.
(A) bound　(B) obligated　(C) sure
Ans: (B)。說話者是在合約所規定買方應進的義務，故應以 be obligated to 來表示。

❹ Since the maintenance fee is the not included in the contract, I am not _____ to pay it for you.

(A) obligated　(B) bound　(C) sure

Ans: (A)。若未於合約中載明，被要求履行額外事項的一方有權不予執行，故應以 be not obligate to 來表達拒絕之意。

❺ Even if you are experienced baseball player, you _____ get familiar with the field in advance.

(A) are obligated to　(B) are bound to　(C) ought to

Ans: (C)。事先熟悉場地有百利而無一害，故說話者特別用 ought to 來表達職業球員也應做到此點。

❻ Though you are an experienced speaker, you _____ rehearsal your speech for several times to make sure everything goes well.

(A) ought to　(B) are obligated to　(C) are bound to

Ans: (A)。即使是有經驗的講者，沒有事先演練過內容，實際上場還是有可能會出錯，故說話者使用 ought to 來說明預演的必要性。

Unit 32
理性與感性

 **俏佳人怎麼說**

They're all exceedingly spoiled, I find.
Miss Margaret spends all her time up trees
and under furniture, and I've barely had a
word from Marianne.—Fanny

我發現她們真的被寵壞了。瑪格莉特小姐不是爬到樹上就是躲到傢具底下，所以我很少聽到瑪麗安小姐客氣地說話。──芬妮

作品概述

　　生性自私勢利的芬妮，在得知丈夫約翰受父親之託協助照顧後母與姐妹時，極力表示反對。也因心存成見，她對於約翰姐妹的行為更是以放大鏡檢視，認為小妹成天亂跑沒有規矩，二妹說話不得體。在這段批評的話語中，出現了表「幾乎沒有」的副詞 barely，但由於此字與 scarcely 與 hardly 在語意與用法上都容易使人混淆，故本單元特將其並列作解析說明。

文法概述

✿ *Barely / scarcely / hardly* ✿

★ **Barely**

雖然本單元的三個副詞在語意上相近，都可以廣義解釋為「幾乎沒有」或「幾乎不」，但在用法上卻有明顯差異。Barely 強調的事物處於最低底限的邊緣，低於此限將可能有不良影響。其常用句型有：S have/has enough N to…，以下透過範例做進一步說明：

EX I barely have enough money to pay the rent this month.
我這個月差一點付不出房租。
→ 說話者本月可動用的金錢就只比房租再多一點而已，故應使用 barely 來表達此種介在最低底限的情況。

★ **Scarcely**

若單看 Scarce 一字，意為「缺乏的」。以此做語意推演，其副詞 scarcely 也會是在表達某種不足。而此種不足就是做到某事的容易度。更簡單來說，若要表達快做不了某事，就可以用 scarcely 來修飾後方的動作。其常見句型有：S can scarcely V…，以下透過範例做進一步說明：

EX I can scarcely walk after I twist my ankle.
扭到腳後我幾乎無法行走。
→ 腳扭傷會是原本毫無難度的走路突然難度大增，故應以 scarcely 來表達說話者的受傷情況。

★ **Hardly**

雖然在用法上與 scarcely、barely 有諸多相似，但此副詞與其他二

者的最大差異在於文法上習慣只以 hardly 描述「頻率」。因此若要表達某人很少做某事，就可以用 hardly 來表示。其常見句型有: S hardly V …，以下透過範例做進一步說明:

EX I hardly watch movie.

我很少去看電影。

→ 說話者主要是說明看電影的頻率，故應以 hardly 來表示次數很少。

實作練習與解析

❶ Johnson _____ has enough money to pay the rent of his shop this month.

(A) scarcely (B) hardly (C) barely

Ans: (C)。強森本月可動用的金錢就只比房租再多一些，故應以 barely 來表示其經濟拮据。

❷ Sandy _____ has enough time to sleep in this business trip.

(A) scarcely (B) barely (C) hardly

Ans: (B)。本次出差的行程非常滿，故可用 barely 來表達除了睡覺外幾乎沒有多餘的休息時間。

❸ Chris can _____ believe that he wins the first prize in the design competition.

(A) scarcely (B) barely (C) hardly

Ans: (A)。克里斯並未預期自己會奪冠，故可用 scarcely 來表達他所表現出的那種驚訝感。

❹ I can_____ move my left arm after I fall from the stairs.

(A) hardly   (B) barely   (C) scarcely

Ans: (C)。摔傷會使動手臂變成一件困難的事情，故應以 scarcely 來描述說話者的情況。

❺ Jenny _____ goes to the concert, so I suggest you find other potential buyer for the spared ticket.

(A) scarcely   (B) hardly   (C) barely

Ans: (B)。真的有興趣的人才會買票看演場會，因此說話者用 hardly 來提醒對方甚少參與此類活動的珍妮並非好人選。

❻ Green _____ eat beef , so I suggest you not to invite him to have dinner in a steakhouse.

(A) scarcely   (B) barely   (C) hardly

Ans: (C)。邀請人一同用餐要考慮其飲食習慣，故說話者以 hardly 提醒對方別選擇去牛排館吃飯。

1 亂世佳人

2 傲慢與偏見

3 理性與感性

4 咆哮山莊

5 小婦人

6 簡愛

Unit 33
理性與感性

 **俏佳人怎麼說**

I am by no means assured of his regard,
and even were he to feel such a preference,
I think we should be foolish to assume that there
would not be many obstacles to his marrying a... a
woman of no rank who cannot afford to buy sugar. —Elinor

我無法確定他對我是否有情，但即使他對我有好感，願意選擇我這樣
沒社會地位，連糖也買不起的女人，我們也不該蠢到以為這樣的選擇
不會遇到重重的障礙。──愛蓮娜

作品概述

　　在與芬妮的弟弟愛德華相識後，愛蓮娜被其紳士風度所吸引，兩人的愛苗似乎也開始悄悄滋長。但此時愛蓮娜一家因為家產將為其同父異母的兄弟約翰所繼承，全家被掃地出門，加上芬妮也希望弟弟能娶個有權有勢的大家閨秀，愛蓮娜只好把這份愛放在心中，說出此段無奈的自白。這段話語中提到了表「阻礙」的單字 obstacle，但由於 barrier 及 hindrance 在用法上雖有相似之處，所表現的阻擋特性卻有所差異，故本單元特將其並列做解析說明。

文法概述

Obstacle / barrier / hindrance

★ Obstacle

雖然同表「障礙」，obstacle 不僅可用於有形的阻擋，也可用於表達某一狀況會使事情無法或是難以進行，來表現無形的阻擋。其常見句型有: S is the obstacle to….，以下透過範例做進一步說明：

EX The biggest obstacle in the road expansion is the old abandoned house.

道路拓寬所遭遇的最大阻礙是路旁的廢棄老舊房舍。

→ 若老舊房舍沒有拆除，道路的範圍難以擴大，故應以 obstacle 來表達此一有形的阻擋。

EX The opposition from the Accounting Department is the obstacle to her new project.

會計部門的反對是她新專案的最大阻礙

→ 如果會計部門不撥款，新專案自然無法執行，故應以 obstacle 來說明此一無形的阻擋。

★ Barrier

不像 obstacle 同時涵蓋有形無形的阻擋，barrier 僅限於描述阻擋人們通過有形的阻礙，此種阻礙可以是人工架設，例如圍籬或拒馬，抑或是天然屏障，例如高山、河流等。其常見句型有: S is the barrier to….，以下透過範例做進一步說明：

EX The mountains act as the greatest natural barrier to the spread of this disease.

1 亂世佳人

2 傲慢與偏見

3 理性與感性

4 咆哮山莊

5 小婦人

6 簡愛

群山成為阻擋此疾病傳播的最佳天然屏障。

→ 由於山屬於天然屏障，故應以 barrier 來凸顯其有形阻擋的特性。

★ Hindrance

Hindrance 是由 hinder 所衍生而來。由於 hinder 多用於表達某條件或是狀況會嚴重影響事情的發展，故 hindrance 也多用於描述非實物的阻擋。其常見句型有: S is the hindrance to…，以下透過範例做進一步說明：

EX Her disability is the greatest hindrance in job seeking.
身障成為她求職時的最大阻礙。

→ 由於身體的殘缺對於求職造成阻礙，故應以 hindrance 來表示。

實作練習與解析

❶ The greatest _____ in the new city planning is abandoned factories.

(A) barrier (B) obstacle (C) hindrance

Ans: (B)。工廠的佔地通常不小，廢棄之後如無規劃再利用，對都市再造影響甚鉅，故應以 obstacle 來表示。

❷ The lack of capital is the _____ we are facing in this program.

(A) obstacle (B) barrier (C) hindrance

Ans: (A)。由於資金缺乏計畫就無法順利執行，故應以 obstacle 描述此一無形阻礙。

❸ The mountains is the best _____ to the invasion of the enemy.

(A) hindrance　(B) obstacle　(C) barrier

Ans: (C)。由於山脈屬於自然屏障，故應以 barrier 表示。

❹ The fence is the _____ to stop the stranger from entering the farm.

(A) obstacle　(B) hindrance　(C) barrier

Ans: (C)。圍籬屬於人工架設的阻擋物，故應以 barrier 表示。

❺ The lack of experience is the _____ to his job seeking.

(A) hindrance　(B) barrier　(C) obstacle

Ans: (A)。有些職缺會要求相關經驗，因此可用 hindrance 來描述
新手應徵時所遭遇的阻礙。

❻ The fog is the greatest _____ to mountain climbers in this season.

(A) obstacle　(B) hindrance　(C) barrier

Ans: (B)。濃霧會降低能見度，使登山增加危險性，故應以 hindrance
描述此種阻礙。

1 亂世佳人

2 傲慢與偏見

3 理性與感性

4 咆哮山莊

5 小婦人

6 簡愛

Unit 34
理性與感性

 俏佳人怎麼說

> *But does it follow that, had he chosen me, he would have been content? He would have had a wife he loved, but no money, and might soon have learned to rank the demands of his pocketbook far above the demands of his heart. If his present regrets are half as painful as mine, he will suffer enough.—Marianne*

但是，這是否表示，如果他選擇了我，就會因此滿足？他可以有一個愛他但沒有錢的妻子，而且他可能很快就會領悟到滿足物質需求遠比心理需求重要。如果他表現出的懊悔有我的一半，就夠他吃盡苦頭。——瑪麗安

作品概述

　　瑪麗安雖然很愛魏勒比，但也深知兩人身分地位的差距會是一大阻礙。若真的交往，一開始愛或許可以戰勝一切，但時間一久一定會被現實的經濟條件給壓垮。到那時魏勒比的懊悔有我一半的程度，就夠他受了。在這段理性分析中出現了表「需求」的單字 demand，但由於英文中尚有 require、request 二字在語意與用法上與之相似，故本單元特將其並

列做解析說明。

🐚 文法概述

∽ *Demand / need / requirement / request* ∾

★ Demand

雖然同表「需求」，但本單元四個單字的重點與用法各有不同。若做動詞用，Demand 代表有正當理由來要求對方，且不讓對方有拒絕的機會。做名詞用時，常與 supply 成對使用，以強調供需原則。其常見句型有：S demand to V/that…與 S have the demand for…，以下透過範例做進一步說明：

EX The family of the victims demands the explanation from the related authorities.

受難者家屬要求有關當局給予解釋

→ 家屬有權知道災難的來龍去脈，故應以 demand 來表達提出此要求的正當性。

EX Working overtime for the whole night, I have a demand for sleeping now.

熬夜加班一整晚，我現在很需要好好睡一覺。

→ 原本睡覺的時間說話者需要工作，所以現在要求補眠有其正當性。

★ Require

除同樣與 demand 可表現正當性外，require 強調的是此要求是根據法律、規定或是其他客觀條件所提出。當以被動式表示時，更能突

1 亂世佳人

2 傲慢與偏見

3 理性與感性

4 咆哮山莊

5 小婦人

6 簡愛

147

顯此曾意涵。其常見句型有: S is required by… to V 與 S require Ving/N，以下透過範例做進一步說明:

EX All participants are required by the regulation to return the equipment after the activity.
所有參與者依照規定應於活動後歸還設備。

→ 參與活動就得遵守其規章，故應以 require 來表達於法有據。

EX The house requires repairing after the typhoon.
颱風過後房子需要整修。

→ 災後房子肯定受損，故應以 require 表現出需要修理的客觀條件。

★ Request

相較於 demand、require 強調合理性，request 表現的需求較為客氣，通常用於表示有權獲得自己所要求的事物。若作動詞用，其常見句型有: S request O to V，若做名詞用，則常使用 S make the request for…，以下透過範例做進一步說明:

EX I request my employees to have a meeting at ten this morning.
我要求我員工早上十點開會。

→ 說話者可能是主管或是老闆，故應以 request 來表達自己有權要員工來開會

EX I make the request for more information about this machine.
我要求更多此台機器的資訊。

→ 説話者想更了解這台機器，故應以 request 表現禮貌性的請求。

實作練習與解析

❶ The participants _____ that the event holder should give them a reasonable saying about the cancellation of the free gift delivery.
(A) demand (B) request (C) require
Ans: (A)。主辦單位原本會發送免費禮物，但後來因故取消，故説話者用 demand 來表達參與者有權請主辦單位給予解釋。

❷ Exercising for hours, I have the _____ for water supply now.
(A) request (B) require (C) demand
Ans: (C)。運動會流失大量水分，故可用 demand 來表達補充適時水分的正當性。

❸ The members are _____ by the regulation to pay the membership dues before the end of this month.
(A) requested (B) required (C) demanded
Ans: (B)。社團規章有載明繳會費的最後期限，故應以 require 來表達此條文對成員的約束力。

❹ The facilities _____ repairing after long term usage.
(A) require (B) demand (C) request
Ans: (A)。任何設施歷經長時間使用都會耗損，故應以 require 來表達需要維修的客觀條件。

1 亂世佳人

2 傲慢與偏見

3 理性與感性

4 咆哮山莊

5 小婦人

6 簡愛

Unit 35
理性與感性

俏佳人怎麼說

It is a very great secret. I've told nobody in the world for fear of discovery.—Lucy Steele

這是個天大的秘密，我不會告訴人以免被發現。——露西・斯特

作品概述

　　露西是很有心機的女生。表面上說自己心中藏有天大的祕密，但她不會告訴任何人，事實上卻是要刻意散播。因此當愛德華的姐姐芬妮聞訊後表示自己會守口如瓶時，她就全盤托出。在這段充滿虛情假意的話語中，出現了表以免的片語 for fear of…，但由於英文中尚有 lest、等字在用法上與其有相似之處，故本單元特將其並列做解析說明。

文法概述

For fear of / for fear that / lest / worry

★ For fear of/ that

　　若以 for fear of/that 表達「以免」，代表說話者認為某一特定的事情

「可能會」發生。其常見句型有: S V for fear of Ving/N 與 S V for fear that + S + might/ should/ may V，以下透過範例做進一步說明：。

EX I lower the volume for fear of waking my older brother up.
我降低音量以免吵醒我哥。

→ 說話者覺得如果現在不降低音量就會吵醒他哥，故應用 for fear of 來表達此事發生的可能性。

EX We close the window for fear that the little baby may get a cold.
我們關窗戶以免小嬰兒感冒。

→ 說話者認為小嬰兒會因為氣溫變化而感冒，故以 for fear that 來表達不關窗此一情況就可能成真。

★ Lest

雖然同樣表達「以免」之意，若以 lest 表示則代表說話者極力避免某事發生。從預防的積極度來看，又比 for fear of/that 在更高一級。其常見句型有:S1 V lest S2/N should…. ，以下透過範例做進一步說明：

EX I dare not play a joke on Ben lest he should become angry.
我不敢開班玩笑，因為怕他真的會生氣。

→ 說話者知道班是個嚴肅且應該開不起玩笑的人，故應以 lest 表達他不會真的這樣做。

★ In case

In case 與上述兩種用法最大的不同在於說話者認為某事不太可能發

1 亂世佳人

2 傲慢與偏見

3 理性與感性

4 咆哮山莊

5 小婦人

6 簡愛

生，但還是預作了準備，以防真的發生時會措手不及。由於包含「還是…」的意味，故經常會與 just 連用。其常見句型有: S1 V just in case S2/N should V…，以下透過範例做進一步說明:

EX I bring my umbrella just in case it should rain.
我還是帶了傘以免真的碰上下雨。

→ 說話者認為幾乎不可能下雨，但還是帶了傘以防萬一，故應以 in case 來表達這種有備無患的感覺。

實作練習與解析

❶ I buy one more piece of pizza _____ getting hungry later.
(A) in case   (B) for fear of   (C) lest
Ans: (B)。由於說話者覺得自己等下肯定還會肚子餓，故應以 for fear of 來表達多買一片披薩的必要性。

❷ Kevin chose to take the taxi to ABC Company_____ he might miss the important meeting.
(A) lest   (B) in case   (C) for fear that
Ans: (C)。凱文覺得只有計程車不會讓他遲到，故應以 for fear that 來表達他做出此選擇的必要性

❸ I dare not complain_____ he should become angry.
(A) lest   (B) in case   (C) for fear that
Ans: (A)。對方可能一被抱怨就會發火，故說話者以 lest 表示自己不會明知故犯。

❹ I shorten the presentation time _____ my boss should become impatient.

(A) for fear that   (B) in case   (C) lest

Ans: (C)。簡報太冗長說話者老闆真的會表現出不耐煩，故應以 lest 表現出說話絕對會長話短說。

❺ He buys some spared parts just _____ the machine may have some problems after the expiration of the warranty.

(A) for fear that   (B) lest   (C) in case

Ans: (C)。雖然說話者覺得機器即使過了保固期都還是不會有損壞，但還是買了備品零件做準備，故應以 in case 來表現他的防患未然。

❻ The celebrity wears a mask just _____ she should be recognized by the paparazzi in the movie theater.

(A) in case   (B) for fear that   (C) lest

Ans: (A)。這位公眾人物覺得去看電影應該不會碰到狗仔隊，但還是戴上了口罩做點偽裝，故應以 in case 來表現她的防患未然。

1 亂世佳人

2 傲慢與偏見

3 理性與感性

4 咆哮山莊

5 小婦人

6 簡愛

Unit 36
理性與感性

🔍 俏佳人怎麼說

You talk of feeling idle and useless.
❧ Imagine how that is compounded when one has ❧
no hope and no choice of any occupation whatsoever.—Elinor

你談到沒有目的與無用的感受，請試想當一個人從此以後對於居所沒有著落也沒得選擇，那兩種感受混合起來的感覺會是如何。

──愛蓮娜

作品概述

　　愛蓮娜與愛德華德這段愛情可說是阻礙重重。愛蓮娜一家因為家產為同父異母的兄長所繼承，即將流落街頭。在與愛德華一同閱讀時，愛蓮娜將此壞消息告訴他。在這段表達無奈情緒的話語中，出現了表混合的單字 compound，但由於英文中尚有 mix、mingle、blend 在語意上與之相似，故本單元特將其並列做解析說明。

文法概述

❧ *Compound / mix / mingle / blend* ❧

1 亂世佳人

2 傲慢與偏見

3 理性與感性

4 咆哮山莊

5 小婦人

6 簡愛

★ Compound

在化學領域中，compound 指的是「化合物」，是由兩種以上物質所組成，其特性可能與原物質不同，但可透過科學方法再次將其還原。若將 compound 作動詞用，傳達的意思就是將事物混合，但仍可以看出原來的特性。其常見句型有：N1 and N2 are compounded… into ….，以下透過範例做進一步說明：

EX The lack of tool and the shortage of one key part are compounded into a great challenge to me to assemble the machine by today.

沒有工具加上少了一個重要零件讓今天完成機器組裝成為我的一大挑戰。

→ 沒工具與少零件是兩個獨立的問題，但同時遇到就會更加棘手，故說話者應用 compound 來表達遭遇此種重大挑戰的感受。

★ Mix

若就混合均勻度來看，mix 是本單元四種混合中最高的，要在將各元素分離相當困難，但還是看出各元素些許的原始特性。其常見句型有: S mix N1 with N2 to…，以下透過範例做進一步說明：

EX I mix milk and flour to make bread.

我混合牛奶與麵粉來做麵包。

→ 當牛奶與麵粉混合成為麵糰後，要再分離就很困難，故應以 mix 來表達其混合均勻。

★ Mingle

若以 mingle 表混合，強調是將來源、特性不同的元素加以組合，但若要刻意區分，還是有辦法分辨原來的特性。較為特別的是，當多種情緒混雜時，多會以此單字做表示。其常見句型有: It is a N that mingle N1 and N2，以下透過範例做進一步說明：

EX It is a tear that mingles happiness and gratitude.

這是充滿開心與感激的淚水。

➔ 由於說話者流淚的原因不只一個，故應以 mingle 來表達此時心中複雜的情緒。

★ Blend

同樣是混合，blend 通常用於強調特定比例可使混合物產生特殊的風味或是效果，故經常用於描述食物或飲品的製作。其常見句型有: S have to blend N1 with N2 before/after… ，以下透過範例做進一步說明：

EX You have to blend soda with vodka with the proportion of 3 to 1 before you make a cup of cocktail.

你要把汽水與伏特加以三比一的比例混合才能做出雞尾酒。

➔ 碳酸飲料與酒類按特定比例的混合會產生新風味，故可以用 blend 來說明其製作手法的特殊性。

實作練習與解析

51 The lack of preparation time and the unfamiliarity with the new system are ________ into an acid test to have a good

presentation to my boss this Friday.

(A) compounded   (B) blended   (C) mingled   (D) mixed

Ans: (A)。準備時間不足加上對新系統不熟，讓說話者覺得對老闆做
簡報變成嚴酷的考驗，故應以 compound 來表現此種難上加難
的感受。

❷ I _____ olive oil, black pepper and, sliced garlic to make
source of the boiled vegetable.

(A) mingle   (B) mix   (C) blend   (D) compound

Ans: (B)。要將蒜片、黑楜椒與橄欖油完全分離並不容易，故應以
mix 來表達三種材料得均勻混合。

❸ It is the smile that _____ satisfaction and encouragement.

(A) compounds   (B) blends   (C) mingles   (D) mixes

Ans: (C)。由於說話者微笑的原因不只一個，故應以 mingle 來表達
他心中多重的情緒。

❹ You have to _____ garlic oil with the black pepper with the
proportion of 4 to 1 before you make barbecue source.

(A) mingle   (B) compound   (C) blend   (D) mix

Ans: (C)。由於說話者是在說明透過特定比例調製可使兩種原料產生
新風味，故應以 blend 來表達此種特殊混合。

❺ I _____ egg with flour to make egg roll.

(A) mingle   (B) compound   (C) mix   (D) blend

Ans: (C)。當蛋與麵粉混合成為蛋捲的半成品後，要再分離就很困
難，故應以 mix 來表達其混合均勻。

1 亂世佳人
2 傲慢與偏見
3 理性與感性
4 咆哮山莊
5 小婦人
6 簡愛

Unit 37
理性與感性

俏佳人怎麼說

Love is all very well, but unfortunately
we cannot always rely on the heart to lead
us in the most suitable directions.—Fanny

選其所愛很好，但很不幸地我們無法總是依照內心來選擇最適合自己的方向。——芬妮

作品概述

　　秉持凡是向「錢」看的原則，芬妮對於自己手足的婚事也覺得要門當戶對，因此當達斯伍太太提出婚姻應以愛為基礎時，她便提出因愛而婚很好，但偏偏現實生活中這樣也許不是最適合我們的。在這段表現婚姻觀念的言論中，出現了表「合適」的單字 suitable，但由於此字在用法上容易與 appropriate 及 applicable 二字產生混淆，故本單元特將其並列做解析說明。

文法概述

Suitable / appropriate / applicable

★ **Suitable**

雖然同表「適合」，suitable 所表現的是某種特性足以符合某種目的或任務要求。換句話説，若要使用 suitable，就要先知道欲達成的目標為何。其常見句型有 N is suitable for⋯，以下透過範例做進一步説明：

EX This watch is suitable for mountain climbers.

這隻手錶適合登山者使用。

→ 説話者已經知道登山鞋所應具備的特性，故可用 suitable 來表示現在説明的款式有符合需求。

★ **Appropriate**

Appropriate 與 suitable 的相似之處在於兩者都已事先知道目的，才去找尋符合要求的事物，但後者多了「專程找出」的意涵。其常見句型有: N is appropriate to/for⋯，以下透過範例做進一步説明：

EX I pick up a shirt appropriate for the formal occasion.

我拿了件適合正式場合的襯衫來穿。

→ 説話者可能有很多件襯衫，但這次特地選一件適合正式場合的，故應以 appropriate 來表達精心選擇之意。

★ **Applicable**

由於是從 apply 衍生而來，故 Applicable 與上述兩者最大的不同在於強調「侷限性」。換句話説，若要表達只有某些特定身分或是條件才適用，就可使用 applicable 來表示。其常見句型有 N is

1 亂世佳人
2 傲慢與偏見
3 理性與感性
4 咆哮山莊
5 小婦人
6 簡愛

applicable to…，以下透過範例做進一步說明：

EX The subsidy is only applicable to new applicants.
此補助僅限於首次申請者。

→ 由於此項補助不是所有申請者都適用，故應以 applicable 來
  表達身分上的限制。

實作練習與解析

❶ The jacket is _____ for advanced runner.
(A) suitable   (B) appropriate   (C) applicable
Ans: (A)。說話者了解進階跑者對於外套有哪些需求，故可用
     suitable 來表達此款式有符合要求。

❷ This tight is _____ for the beginner like me, so I buy it
without hesitation.
(A) applicable   (B) suitable   (C) appropriate
Ans: (B)。說話者知道初學者的緊身裝備應注意哪些要點，故應以
     suitable 來表達此款式有符合需求。

❸ I pick up a long pants _____ for outdoor activity.
(A) suitable   (B) applicable   (C) appropriate
Ans: (C)。說話者有很多長褲，但這次特別選一件適合戶外活動的，
     故應以 appropriate 來表達精心挑選之意。

❹ To draw people's attention, she picks up a dress _____ for
party.

(A) suitable　(B) appropriate　(C) applicable

Ans: (B)。說話者有很多洋裝，但這次為了要引人注目特別選了一件
適合派對的，故應以 appropriate 來表達精心挑選之意。

❺ The discount is only _____ to the consumers who buy more
than three items at once.
(A) suitable　(B) appropriate　(C) applicable

Ans: (C)。不是所有有消費的顧客都可享折扣，故應以 applicable
來表達折扣有最低消費額的限制。

❻ The free gift is _____ for new car buyer this year.
(A) applicable　(B) appropriate　(C) suitable

Ans: (A)。由於免費禮物僅限今年買車的顧客才有，故應以 applicable
來表達身分的限制。

Unit 38
理性與感性

俏佳人怎麼說

You see, my dear Mrs. Dashwood, Edward is entirely the kind of compassionate person upon whom penniless women can prey. And having entered into any understanding, he would never go back on his word. He's simply incapable of doing so, but it would lead to his ruin.—Fanny

我親愛的達斯伍太太，愛德華完全是那種會富有同情心，而容易被身無分文女性所欺騙的人。從各方面去想，他從不會食言。他只是不能這樣做，但這樣做卻會毀了他。——芬妮

作品概述

　　與達斯伍太太各自表述對於婚姻的看法後，芬妮表示愛德華就是太容易同情別人，在與異性交往時，很容易因為對方經濟困頓，就失去對方可能是騙財的警戒心。此外，由於愛德華又是個言出必行的人，這樣耿直的個性反而容易成為毀掉他前途的不定時炸彈。在這段探討個性的言論中，出現了表「同情」的單字 companionate，由於其名詞 companion 與 sympathy、pity 與 empathy 在語意表達上容易與之混淆，故本單元

特將其並列做解析說明。

文法概述

Compassion / sympathy / pity

★ Compassion

雖然同表「同情」,但 compassion 強調在表達憐憫之後,會給予後續的協助。換句話說,若要表達有實際行動的同情,就可以 compassion 來表示。其常見句型有:S show compassion for⋯,以下透過範例做進一步說明:

EX We can show compassion for those in need by being the volunteer in charity.

我們可以透過在慈善機構當志工來協助有需要幫忙的人。

→ 做志工除了心理上表達憐憫外,更透過實際行動來給予幫助,故應以 compassion 來表達此種關懷。

★ Sympathy

若以 sympathy 來表示同情,通常是因為發現對方受傷或是正遭受痛苦,因而表現出自己的關心之意,但不會像 compassion 一樣給予實質幫助。其常見句型有:S show/have sympathy for⋯。以下透過範例做進一步說明:

EX I show sympathy for beggars.

我對乞丐表示同情。

→ 說話者覺得乞丐很可憐,但其憐憫也只有心理層面,不會有實質協助,故應以 sympathy 來表達此種同情。

1 亂世佳人

2 傲慢與偏見

3 理性與感性

4 咆哮山莊

5 小婦人

6 簡愛

★ Pity

雖然同樣與 compassion 會給予實質協助，但 pity 強調的重點是覺得對方的處境很可憐，才決定伸出援手。其常見句型有:S take pity on…，以下透過範例做進一步說明:

EX I take pity on an old beggar and give him some food.
我同情一位老乞丐並給他些食物吃。

→ 說話者覺得老乞丐很可憐，所以給予食物做為實質協助，故應用 pity 來表達此同情之意。

★ Empathy

不同於其他三者以自己的看法為看法來表達憐憫或幫助，Empathy 強調的是站在對方的立場來想，然後才給予關心與協助。其常見句型有:S feel empathy with…，以下透過範例做進一步說明:

EX Having the similar growing background, I feel empathy with the hardship you are experiencing now.
由於成長背景相仿，我對你現在所遭遇的困難深感同情。

→ 由於說話者與對方有相似的成長背景，故可用 empathy 來表達以對方立場為出發點的同情。

實作練習與解析

❶ I show_____ for the children enjoying limited education resource, so I work as a volunteer in the charity which provides free after class consulting to this group.
(A) sympathy (B) empathy (C) pity (D) compassion
Ans: (D)。說話者同情無法享有足夠教育資源的學童，所以去慈善機構擔任課輔老師，故應以 compassion 來表達其憐憫。

❷ I have _____ for homeless people.

(A) compassion　(B) sympathy　(C) pity　(D) empathy

Ans: (B)。說話者覺得遊民會因無家可歸而感到痛苦，故應以 sympathy 表示其同情。

❸ I take _____ on the elderly who live alone and spend some of my free time accompanying with him.

(A) empathy　(B) compassion　(C) sympathy　(D) pity

Ans: (D)。說話者覺得獨居老人非常可憐，所以在旁陪伴給予協助，故應以 pity 來表達其關心之情。

❹ Having the similar working environment, I feel _____ with the dilemma he is facing now.

(A) empathy　(B) sympathy　(C) pity　(D) compassion

Ans: (A)。說話者與對方的工作環境相仿，故對於其所遭受的困境感同身受，故應以 empathy 來表達同情之意。

❺ My mom takes _____ on the hungry beggar and gives him some bread.

(A) empathy　(B) sympathy　(C) pity　(D) compassion

Ans: (C)。說話者的母親覺得乞丐挨餓很可憐，所以給他些麵包充饑，故應以 pity 來表達其憐憫。

❻ Having the similar experience in the past, I feel _____ with the difficulty she is facing now.

(A) sympathy　(B) empathy　(C) compassion　(D) pity

Ans: (B)。說話者過去有與對方相似的經驗，所以很能體會她現在所面臨的困境，故應以 empathy 來說明其關心。

1 亂世佳人

2 傲慢與偏見

3 理性與感性

4 咆哮山莊

5 小婦人

6 簡愛

Part 4
Week 4 咆哮山莊

Unit 39
咆哮山莊

俏佳人怎麼說

You're so handsome when you smile...
Don't you know that you're handsome?
Do you know what I've always told Ellen?
That you're a prince in disguise...I said your
father was the Emperor of China. Your mother an
Indian queen. And it's true Heathcliff.—Catherine Earnshaw

你笑的時候很帥,難道你自己不知道嗎?我跟你說,我常常這樣告訴艾
倫,你是喬裝的王子。你的父親是中國皇帝,而你的母親是印度皇
后,且這一切都是真的,希斯克里夫。——凱薩琳・恩肖

作品概述

　　咆哮山莊的老主人在前往利物浦辦事後,帶回一名吉普賽男孩,並將
其取名為希斯克里夫。男孩很快獲得寵愛,且老主人女兒凱薩琳與這名男
孩日久生情。由於出身不明,凱薩琳對其身分也有諸多幻想,覺得他是王
子,父親為中國皇族,母親來自印度王室。在這段帶有幻想色彩的盛讚
中,出現了表「偽裝」的單字 disguise,但由於英文中尚有 hide、
conceal 在語意上與之相似,故本單元特將其並列做解析說明。

文法概述

✤ *Disguise / hide / conceal* ✤

★ Disguise

若以 disguise 來表達「隱藏」之意，其重點在於透過外加新元素的方式讓事物原始的樣貌不易顯現。若作動詞用，其常見句型有：S disguise oneself as⋯/ by Ving⋯，若做名詞用，則常以 S V in disguise 表示，以下透過範例做進一步說明：

EX The super star disguises himself as a taxi driver to leave the hotel.

這位巨星把自己喬裝成計程車司機以便離開旅館。

→ 大明星若沒有偽裝很容易被認出來，他選擇假扮司機掩人耳目，故可用 disguise 來表達此類型的隱藏。

EX A blessing in disguise.

塞翁失馬，焉知非福。

→ 若某件壞事最後卻意外產生好的結果，本質上其實就是件好事，故可用 disguise 來描述此種轉折。

★ Hide

相較於 disguise 是透過偽裝讓人「看到」但「認不出來」，Hide 所表現的隱藏是透過躲藏的方式讓人「找不到」某事物。其常見句型有：S hide sth under/inside/behind⋯，以下透過範例做進一步說明：

EX My younger brother hid the spared door key under the mats.

我弟把門的備用鑰匙藏在地墊下。

1 亂世佳人
2 傲慢與偏見
3 理性與感性
4 咆哮山莊
5 小婦人
6 簡愛

➔ 除非刻意打開，否則不會發現地墊下方有鑰匙，故可以用 hide 此種藏匿物品的方式。

★ Conceal

同樣是隱藏，conceal 是本單元三者中最能表現出「不能被發現」語意的一個。若以之說明某人將物體藏於隱密之處，常見句型有: Sth is/ are conceal under/inside/behind⋯，若用於某人刻意不揭露某些資訊或是感受，則常以 S conceal sth from sb 表示，以下透過範例做進一步說明:

EX The secret document is concealed inside safe.
秘密文件被藏在保險箱裡。

➔ 機密文件不可輕易被發現，放在保險箱相對安全，故應以 conceal 來表達此類型的隱藏

EX It seems that you are concealing something from me.
我覺得你似乎有事刻意隱瞞我。

➔ 說話者覺得對方似乎有刻意不透露某些消息給他，故可以用 conceal 來表達資訊的不公布。

實作練習與解析

❶ The famous actor _____ herself as the hotel staff to check in without getting much attention.
(A) disguises   (B) hides   (C) conceals
Ans: (A)。由於不想引人注目，這位演員透過喬裝低調入住飯店，故可用 disguise 來表身分的隱藏。

❷ The singer _____ himself by wearing a cap and a mask.
(A) conceals　(B) hides　(C) disguises
Ans: (C)。明星戴上鴨舌帽與口罩後，較不容易被認出，故應以
disguise 來達此類型的身分隱藏。

❸ Since my older sister has a poor performance in the test, so she tries to _____ her score sheet.
(A) disguise　(B) hide　(C) conceal
Ans: (B)。說話者的姐姐因為考試考不好，怕媽媽先看到成績單，故
應用 hide 來描述她試圖藏匿某物的行為。

❹ The recipe of this secret source is _____ in the place which only the chef knows.
(A) concealed　(B) hided　(C) disguised
Ans: (A)。特殊配方是一間餐廳吸引客人最重要的東西，故應用
conceal 來表達須將其存放於高安全性地點的必要性。

❺ I feel sad because one of my best men tries to _____ something from me.
(A) disguise　(B) hide　(C) conceal
Ans: (C)。說話者對於好友有刻意不透露某些消息給他感到不開心，
故可以用 conceal 來表達此種選擇性的資訊揭露。

❻ Though Sam _____ the bill of the credit card, his wife still finds it.
(A) hides　(B) conceals　(C) disguises
Ans: (A)。山姆可能刷卡花了很多錢不想讓老婆知道，因此試圖想把賬
單藏起來，故可用 hide 來描述此種藏匿某物的行為。

1 亂世佳人

2 傲慢與偏見

3 理性與感性

4 咆哮山莊

5 小婦人

6 簡愛

Unit 40
咆哮山莊

俏佳人怎麼說

You were kidnapped by wicked sailors
and brought to England. But I'm glad they did.
Because I've always wanted to know somebody of noble birth.
— Catherine Earnshow

你是被壞水手綁架帶到英國,但我很高興他們這麼做。
——凱薩琳・恩肖

作品概述

　　對於自己所愛的希斯克里夫,凱薩琳除了想像其出身外,還替他為何來到英國編了個故事,說他是受到士兵的挾持,才會出現於利物浦,被自己的父親帶回。凱薩琳認為這樣的安排很棒,因為她自己很想認識出身貴族的人。在這段天馬行空的想像中,出現了表高興的單字 glad,但由於英文中尚有 happy、delighted 與其語意相近,但其背後的意涵卻各有不同,故本單元特將其並列做解析說明。

文法概述

❧ *Glad / happy / delighted* ❧

1 亂世佳人

2 傲慢與偏見

3 理性與感性

4 咆哮山莊

5 小婦人

6 簡愛

★ Glad

同樣是表達高興，由於 Glad 所表現的喜悅強度相對較低，且時間也較短，故經常用於與人碰面時的客套話，或是慶幸某事有發生。其常見句型有：S be glad that S V/about one's N，以下透過範例做進一步說明：

EX I am glad that you come today.

我很高興今天您能撥空前來。

➜ 兩人碰面時往往會寒暄，故可用 glad 來表達此種禮貌性用語。

EX We are glad about your success in this project.

我們很高興你的專案圓滿成功。

➜ 說話者可能覺得專案有失敗的可能性，所幸最後成功了，故應用 glad 來表達心中那種鬆了口氣的喜悅。

★ Happy

若以 happy 表達高興，通常是因為以下兩種原因，一是某人的內心得到滿足，進而表現出愉悅的情緒。二是發自內心願意做某事，因而表現極其友善的態度。其常見句型有: S be happy to…，以下透過範例做進一步說明：

EX I am happy to see you again.

很高興能再見上你一面。

➜ 說話者認為要再與對方見面並不容易，故可用 happy 來表達真的碰面時的喜悅之情。

173

★ Delighted

Delighted 與 Happy 最大不同在於前者需要理由，後者則不見得。換句話說，某人因為某事發生而感到開心，才能以 delighted 表示。其常見句型有：S be delighted that S V/ to V 與 S be delighted with…，以下透過範例做進一步說明：

EX I am delighted that you can come today.

我很高興今天你能來。

→ 說話者開心是因為對方今天有來，故應以 delighted 來表達此種喜悅。

EX I am delighted with this result.

有此結果我很開心。

→ 事情的發展可能一如說話者的預期，故可用 delighted 來表達他心中的愉悅。

實作練習與解析

❶ I am _____ that you can spare you time to participate in our event.

(A) glad   (B) happy   (C) delighted

Ans: (A)。說話者可能覺得對方應該不會參加自己的活動，但對方卻真的來，故應以 glad 來表達帶有客套意味的喜悅。

❷ We are _____ about your success in the sales of new fragrance.

(A) delighted   (B) happy   (C) glad

Ans: (C)。説話者可能覺得新款香氛市場反應可能會不好，但所幸此狀況未發生，故應以 glad 來表達終於鬆了口氣。

❸ I am _____ to help you if needed.

(A) glad　(B) happy　(C) delighted

Ans: (B)。説話者很願意給予對方協助，故應以 happy 來表達他的友善態度。

❹ Tom is _____ that I squeeze some time to join his birthday party.

(A) happy　(B) glad　(C) delighted

Ans: (C)。湯姆因為説話者努力空出時間參加他的生日派對而感到高興，故應以 delighted 來表達此種喜悦。

❺ Since I only have few time to prepare the test this time, I am _____ with the result that I get, the score of 61.

(A) delighted　(B) glad　(C) happy

Ans: (A)。由於説話者準備考試的時間有限，考試還有及格已很滿意，故應以 delighted 來表達他心中的確幸。

❻ I am _____ to hear that you get the permission of the graduate school.

(A) glad　(B) happy　(C) delighted

Ans: (B)。説話者可能很希望對方可以獲得研究所的入學許可，現在真的成真了，故應以 happy 來表達他心中的喜悦。

1 亂世佳人

2 傲慢與偏見

3 理性與感性

4 咆哮山莊

5 小婦人

6 簡愛

Unit 41
咆哮山莊

俏佳人怎麼說

Rough as a saw-edge, and hard as whinstone!
The less you meddle with him the better.—Nelly Dean

粗糙如鋸齒邊緣，堅硬如岩石一般，
能不跟他打交道最好。——奈莉‧丁

作品概述

當希斯克里夫再次回到咆哮山莊時，身分地位已不可同日而語，女僕奈莉發現雖然他現在看似謙和有禮，但這一切只是他暫時把兒時所造成的扭曲人格壓抑下來的結果。他在個性上仍然不圓滑，會與人衝突。在這段描述性格的話語中，出現了表「干預」的單字 meddle，但由於英文中根據干涉手法的不同，尚有 interfere 與 interrupt 在語意上與其相似，故本單元特將其並列做解析說明。

文法概述

Meddle / interference / interrupt

★ **Meddle**

若以 meddle 表干涉，通常這件事並非自己的責任，但卻試圖想要影響或是更進一步想改變其發展，且會採用負面的手段，例如批評、破壞或是激怒等等。其常見句型有 S meddle with…與 S meddle in one's N，以下透過範例作進一步說明：

EX My younger brother always meddles in other colleagues' affairs.

我弟愛管同事的閒事。

➜ 同事的私事說話者的弟弟其實無權插手，因此應以 meddle 來描述他企圖干預的行為。

EX Mary always meddles with the thing she doesn't understand.

瑪莉老愛不懂裝懂。

➜ 瑪莉明明對於某事不甚熟悉但卻大放厥詞，故應以 meddle 來表達她的自以為是。

★ **Interfere**

若以 interfere 表干涉，代表你想插手某事，但對方明顯地不希望你介入，或是覺得即使有來幫忙也無濟於事。其常見句型有:S interfere with in…，以下透過範例做進一步說明：

EX We have no right to interfere their family affairs.

我們無權插手他們的家務事。

1 亂世佳人

2 傲慢與偏見

3 理性與感性

4 咆哮山莊

5 小婦人

6 簡愛

→ 家務事就應該由其家庭成員自己處理，若外人企圖插手，應以 interfere 來表達。

★ Interrupt

若以 Interrupt 表干涉，手法上是以言語或是行為來短暫打斷對方説話或是動作，亦或是暫時阻止某事的發生。其常見句型有:S1 try to … but S2 interrupt S1 與 S interrupt…when…以下透過範例作進一步説明：

EX I try to explain why I do so, but she interrupts me.
我試圖解釋為何這樣做的原因，但她打斷我。

→ 説話者想辯解，但對方卻不讓他一次把話説完，故應以 interrupt 來表達這種干擾。

EX We interrupt our trip when we heard that grandma breaks her leg.
祖母摔斷腿使我們得暫時擱置出遊的計畫。

→ 説話者本來要出遊，但由於祖母意外受傷，暫時無法成行，故應以 interrupt 來表達事情被迫擱置。

實作練習與解析

❶ Danny always _____ with his colleagues' affairs, so he has no friend in his office.

(A) interrupts　(B) interferes　(C) meddles

Ans: (C)。同事的事應該留給他們自己處理，但丹尼卻插手了，故應以 meddle 來表達他的干預。

❷ Mark always _____ in the issue he has little understanding.
  (A) meddles   (B) interferes   (C) interrupts
  Ans: (A)。馬克明明對某項議題不熟悉可是卻愛高談闊論，故應以
       meddle 來表達他的自以為是。

❸ Since we are not the parties involved, we have no right to __
       _____ their decision making.
  (A) meddle   (B) interfere   (C) interrupt
  Ans: (B)。當事人才有權決定接下來該怎麼做，其他人想要插手就是
       interfere。

❹ Sam tries to illustrate how he came up with this idea, but ken
       _____ him many times.
  (A) interrupts   (B) meddles   (C) interferes
  Ans: (A)。山姆想要分享概念的發想，但卻一直被中斷，故應以
       interrupt 來表達肯的不當行為。

❺ We _____ our three-day trip when we heard that John
  twists his ankle.
  (A) meddle   (B) interrupt   (C) interfere
  Ans: (B)。說話者本來要與約翰出遊，但由於約翰扭傷腳暫時無法成
       行，故應以 interrupt 來表事情的擱置。

❻ Not being the member of this association, we had better not
       _____ their internal affairs.
  (A) interfere   (B) meddle   (C) interrupt
  Ans: (A)。協會內部的事應由其成員來處理，若有外人要插手，就應
       以 interfere 來表達。

1 亂世佳人
2 傲慢與偏見
3 理性與感性
4 咆哮山莊
5 小婦人
6 簡愛

Unit 42
咆哮山莊

俏佳人怎麼說

You could come back to me rich
and take me away. Why aren't you my prince
like we said long ago? Why can't you rescue me,
Heathcliff? —Catharine Earnshaw

你可以回來然後帶我走。為何你不再是我以前的那個王子?為何你不來救我?——凱薩琳・恩肖

作品概述

　　凱薩琳雖然心裡最愛的是希斯克里夫,但礙於現實的情況與社會的觀感,還是得選擇社會地位較高的埃德加。雖然她仍激動地說出希斯克里夫為何無法像王子那樣帶她走的反問句,但其實心中早有答案,就是我無法與你遠走高飛。在這段表述向現實妥協的話語中,出現了表「救援」的單字 rescue,但由於英文中根據情況的危急程度不同,尚有 save、salvage 在語意上與之相似,故本單元特將其並列做解析說明。

文法概述

✎ *Rescue / save / salvage* ✎

★ Rescue

若以 rescue 來表救援，對救援的一方來說，通常此拯救行動通常帶有一定的「危險性」或是「風險」。對被救援的一方而言，其情況是有「急迫性」的，若不儘快使其脫離威脅，將有可能造成不可回復的傷害。其常見句型有:S rescue⋯ from⋯，以下透過範例做進一步說明:

EX The special force is sent to the dessert to rescue the hostage ' from the terrorists.

特種部隊被派往沙漠從恐怖份子手中救回人質。

→ 若不盡快前往營救，人質可能遭不測，故應以 rescue 來凸顯此救援具有急迫性與危險性。

EX The government tries to rescue the company from going bankrupt.

政府試圖營救這間瀕臨破產的公司。

→ 若政府現在不出手相救，該公司可能就此破產，故應以 rescue 來表達救援的急迫性。

★ Save

當以 save 表救援時，被救援的一方狀況可大致區分為以下三種，一是「受傷死亡」的可能性，二是「居劣勢」的可能性，三是「毀壞」或「無法運行」的可能性。其常見句型有:S save⋯from N/Ving，以下透過範例做進一步說明:

1 亂世佳人

2 傲慢與偏見

3 理性與感性

4 咆哮山莊

5 小婦人

6 簡愛

EX Wearing a seat belt can save you from serious injuries when you have a car accident.

繫安全帶可以使你在發生車禍時免於受重傷。

→ 不繫安全帶，車禍時的受傷情形一定會比有繫更嚴重，故應以 save 來描述安全帶所產生的保護效果。

★ Salvage

雖然同樣表救援，但 salvage 屬於善後處理而非當下救援，故其多用於描述如何從災難現場(例如:沉船、火水災後的建築物)裡尋找為數可能不多但尚有搶救價值的物品，或是從不利的情況中找出些許可扳回一城的機會。其常見句型有: S be able to salvage… from，以下透過範例做進一步說明：

EX The fire is extinguished, so we are able to salvage the machine that is usable.

火勢已撲滅，因此我們得以進入火場搶救尚可使用的機器。

→ 廠房火災過後機器肯定會有損壞，還堪用的才會想辦法自火場裡移出，故應以 salvage 來表達此類型的救援。

實作練習與解析

❶ The police is ready to _____ the hostage from the gangster.

(A) salvage　(B) save　(C) rescue

Ans: (C)。若警方沒攻堅制伏歹徒，人質可能會有危險，故應以 rescue 來強調此救援行動的危急性。

❷ The government refuses to _____ the company from going

bankrupt due to its bad credit record.

(A) rescue   (B) save   (C) salvage

Ans: (A)。政府不出手相救，這間公司就會破產，故應以 rescue 來
説明此救援的危急性。

❸ A little boy falls into the river, but Thomas _____ him from drowning.

(A) salvages   (B) saves   (C) rescues

Ans: (B)。溺水會導致死亡，故應以 save 來表達湯瑪仕的救援使小
男孩脱離危險。

❹ The money borrowed temporarily _____ the business from running.

(A) saves   (B) salvages   (C) rescues

Ans: (A)。公司的營運因為額外資金的挹注暫時得以繼續運行，故應
以 save 來表達此救援的目的在於使生意免於停擺。

❺ After the serious flood, there are few things worth _____ in our house.

(A) saving   (B) rescuing   (C) salvaging

Ans: (C)。洪水過後説話者的住家應是滿目瘡痍，故應以 salvage 來
表達值得再繼續使用的物品為數不多。

❻ After the scandal, Tom tries to_____ her bad reputation, but in vain.

(A) rescue   (B) salvage   (C) save

Ans: (B)。爆發醜聞後名聲肯定跟著敗壞，因此應以 salvage 來表達
湯姆想挽回但卻無濟於事的窘境。

1 亂世佳人

2 傲慢與偏見

3 理性與感性

4 咆哮山莊

5 小婦人

6 簡愛

Unit 43
咆哮山莊

俏佳人怎麼說

My love for Linton is like the foliage in the woods: time will change it, I'm well aware, as winter changes the trees. My love for Heathcliff is the eternal rock beneath: a source of little visible delight, but necessary.—Catharine Earnshaw

**我對林頓的愛像林中的葉子，會隨著時節移轉，
對希斯克里夫的愛，卻像樹下永恆不朽的堅石般不可或缺，
猶如自我的存在。——凱薩琳・恩肖**

作品概述

　　凱薩琳雖然嫁給了埃德加林頓，但心中最牽掛的還是希斯克里夫。當問起她對兩人的愛有何差別時，凱薩琳表示他對林頓的愛是會改變的，一如季節會改變植物的樣貌。但對於希斯克里夫的愛卻是堅定不移，就好像石頭那樣堅定不易改變。在這段表達內心真正感受的自白中，出現了表「知道」的單字 aware，但由於英文中尚有 conscious 與 sense 在語意上與之相似，故本單元特將其並列做解析說明。

文法概述

Aware / conscious / sense

★ Aware

若以 aware 表達「知道」，其認知層次相對屬於「形而下」。換句話說，可用 aware 來表達對其理解的事物，必須是「感受得到」的事情到或是「有形體」的物體。其常見句型有: S be/become aware of/that…，以下透過範例做進一步說明：

EX I am well aware that this job is tough.

我深知這不是件簡單的工作。

➔ 由於說話者能夠判斷此項工作是困難還是簡單，故應以 aware 來表達他對此事的理解。

★ Conscious

相較於 aware 表達對有實際形體或感受事物的理解，conscious 的認知相對「形而上」。以此差異為出發點，便可推知其對象通常是「抽象」或是「不易客觀審視」的事物。其常見句型有 S be/become conscious of/ that…，以下透過範例做進一步說明：

EX I suddenly become conscious that my first idea has the room to improve.

我突然意識到自己的第一個想法有需要修正的地方。

➔ 說話者突然間發現想法有欠周延而想加以改正，但這樣的靈光一閃，通常很難以解釋其發生原因，故應以 conscious 來表示。

1 亂世佳人

2 傲慢與偏見

3 理性與感性

4 咆哮山莊

5 小婦人

6 簡愛

★ Sense

除表達人的各種感官，例如嗅覺、味覺等，sense 也可廣泛地表達對事物的認知或理解，對於能否找出改變的原因，並無特別要求。其常見句型有: S sense that S have pp，以下透過範例做進一步說明:

EX Tom senses that he has made a big mistake.
湯姆察覺到他犯了一個大錯。

→ 說話者想表達的是湯姆突然發現自己做錯某事，故應以 sense 來表達此種不特別敘明原因的知道某事。

實作練習與解析

❶ Ben is well _____ that the promotion is the beginning of the heavier workload.
(A) conscious   (B) sense   (C) aware
Ans: (C)。班知道升官同時也意味自己的工作量將增加，故應以 aware 來表達他對此事的理解

❷ Cathy is still not _____ of having done something wrong.
(A) aware   (B) sense   (C) conscious
Ans: (A)。事情有沒有做錯可以透過客觀標準來判定，但凱西卻完全沒發現，故應以 be not aware of…來表達她的後知後覺。

❸ John suddenly becomes _____ that he is the only one who comes from Asia in this meeting.
(A) aware   (B) sense   (C) conscious
Ans: (C)。約翰一開始沒發現自己是唯一與會的亞洲人，但後來突然發現了，因此應以 conscious 來表達他對此事的理解。

❹ I am well _____ that my working philosophy has some loopholes needed to be modified.

(A) sense   (B) conscious   (C) aware

Ans: (B)。哲學本身就是抽象的，因此當發現自己原先認同的想法有
需要修正之處時，應以 conscious 來表達對抽象事物的理解。

❺ My older brother _____ that he is in a big trouble.

(A) senses   (B) conscious   (C) aware

Ans: (A)。說話者的哥哥發現自己闖大禍，至於為何察覺苗頭不對，
自己可能也說不上來，故應以 sense 來表達此種靈光一閃。

❻ Helen _____ that Jenny is somehow absent-mined today.

(A) consciouses   (B) awares   (C) senses

Ans: (C)。海倫覺得珍妮今天總是不專心，但卻也說不出原因，故應
以 sense 來表達此種憑藉第六感的理解。

1 亂世佳人

2 傲慢與偏見

3 理性與感性

4 咆哮山莊

5 小婦人

6 簡愛

Unit 44
咆哮山莊

俏佳人怎麼說

Well, if Master Edgar and
his charms and money and parties mean
Heaven to you, what's to keep you from taking
your place among the Linton angels? —Ellen

如果埃德加主人的權勢財富對你來說就是天堂,是什麼阻止你進入天堂呢?——艾倫

作品概述

　　凱薩琳深愛希斯克里夫,但礙於當時社會的種種規範,還是選擇嫁給有權有勢埃德加。女僕艾倫深知希斯克里夫在女主人心中仍據有重要地位,因此故意反問她:「如果埃德加的種種對你來說就是天堂,是什麼阻止你進入天堂呢?」,在這段反問當中,出現了表「魅力」的單字 charm,但由於英文中尚有 allure 與 attractiveness 在語意上與之相似,故本單元特將其並列做解析說明。

文法概述

Charm / allure / attractiveness

★ Charm

若以 charm 表達魅力，其表達重點在於某事物的「特質」足以吸引你的注意或是讓你感到愉悅，但不至於使你失去客觀判斷能力。其常見句型為: N is the charm of…，以下透過範例做進一步說明：

EX Always being considerate is her greatest charm.

總是對人體貼是她最大的魅力。

→ 對說話者而言，體貼能吸引她的注意，但這不會讓他無法客觀審視其他特質，故應以 charm 此人格特質。

★ Allure

就吸引程度來看，allure 算是 charm 的強化版。也因為迷戀程度較高，容易使人失去客觀判斷能力，而有離譜的行為。其常見句型為:N is the allure that Sb…，以下透過範例做進一步說明：

EX The promise of quick profit is the allure that the tricky sales representative uses to cheat unwary investors.

保證可以快速獲利是狡猾業務用來欺騙沒有警戒心的投資者的手段。

→ 投資者會因為可以快速賺到錢而忽略有無風險，故應以 allure 來表達此種募資手段所產生的吸引力。

★ Attractiveness

Attractiveness 是由 attractive 衍生而來，故其描述重點也是放在可直接觀察的「外在條件」(例如:外貌、聲響、價格等)對於某人所產

1 亂世佳人

2 傲慢與偏見

3 理性與感性

4 咆哮山莊

5 小婦人

6 簡愛

生的喜愛感。其常見句型為: N have/has attractiveness to sb 與 The…of… decrease/increase the attractiveness of N/Ving，以下透過範例作進一步説明：

EX Mary's outer beauty has great attractiveness to her classmates.

瑪莉姣好的外貌對她的同學來説很有吸引力。

→ 瑪莉的外在條件很能吸引她的同學，故應以 attractiveness 來表達此種魅力。

EX High financial load decreases the attractiveness of owing a heavy motor.

高財務負擔降低了擁有重機的吸引力。

→ 為了買重機，説話者可能會背負很大的財務壓力，故應以 attractiveness 來表達重機對説話者的吸引力。

實作練習與解析

❶ It is a small town with a lot of old time _____.
(A) allure   (B) attractiveness   (C) charm

Ans: (C)。説話者喜歡復古的氛圍，故應以 charm 來表達古色古香城鎮對他所產生的吸引力。

❷ High and quick profit is the _____ that wicked businessmen used to hook the unwary investors to become the shareholders.
(A) charm   (B) allure   (C) attractiveness

Ans: (B)。快速地賺大錢對投資者來説太有吸引力，因此可能忽略背後的風險，故應以 allure 來表達此種讓人喪失判斷力的狀況。

❸ Helen's beautiful eyes are the greatest _____ to her colleagues.
(A) allure   (B) attractiveness   (C) charm
Ans: (B)。海倫的明眸很能吸引她的同事，故應以 attractiveness 來表達此種魅力。

❹ Zero interest installment increases the _____ of owning a car to me.
(A) attractiveness   (B) allure   (C) charm
Ans: (A)。零息分期提高了説話者買車的意願，故應以 attractiveness 來表達此促銷手段所帶來的吸引力。

❺ The gentle smile is the greatest _____ of Jason.
(A) charm   (B) attractiveness   (C) allure
Ans: (A)。傑森的笑容很吸引人，故應以 charm 表達一舉動的魅力所在。

❻ Extremely low price is the _____ that businessmen use to attract consumers to buy something they may not really need.
(A) charm   (B) allure   (C) attractiveness
Ans: (B)。超低價容易讓人因為覺得賺到而忽略是否有實用性，故應以 allure 來表達此種手法對消費者所產生的吸引力。

1 亂世佳人

2 傲慢與偏見

3 理性與感性

4 咆哮山莊

5 小婦人

6 簡愛

Unit 45
咆哮山莊

俏佳人怎麼說

Proud people breed sad
sorrows for themselves. —Nelly Dean
驕傲的人終將替自己招來不幸。——奈莉・丁

作品概述

　　奈莉雖然只是咆哮山莊的僕人，但這個角色在故事劇情的發展上極為重要。奈莉認為希斯克里夫太過驕傲，深覺自己如果為凱薩琳而哭，凱薩琳同樣會為他傷心，因而說出驕傲的人最後終將承擔苦果的這段言論。在這段帶有警世意味的話語中，出現了表「孕育」的單字 breed，但由於英文中尚有 raise 與 produce 在語意上與之相近，故本單元特將其並列作解析說明。

文法概述

Breed / Raise / Produce

★ Breed

　　Breed 最初的語意是以人為控制的方式使動物不斷繁衍年輕後代，因

此若用來表達「培育」時，目的十分明確，其常見句型有:S breed… for…。此外，由於培育是因為知道某方法有效而去執行，故也隱含「導致」的語意。其常見句型有: N1 breed N2，以下透過範例做進一步說明：

EX We breed dogs for the police.

我們替警方培育警犬。

→ 說話者養狗的目的就是使其成為警犬，故應以 breed 來表達此種有目的的培育。

EX Polluted water breeds the wither of plants

汙水導致植物枯萎。

→ 當汙水流入植物的生長區域，植物就可能因為受到汙染而枯萎，故應以 breed 來表達此種因果關係。

★ Raise

若以 raise 表培育，其描述重點不在有無特定目的，而是在於個體的成長(由幼年至成年)，其對象不僅限於人，動植物亦可。其常見句型有:S be raised by…，以下透過範例作進一步說明：

EX Joe's parents work overseas, so he is raised by his grandparents.

喬的父母在國外工作，所以他是由祖父母帶大的。

→ 祖父母一路把喬拉拔到成年，故應以 raise 來描述此養育過程。

★ Produce

若以 produce 表孕育，除表示動物生育後代外，尚可用於說明某人

1 亂世佳人

2 傲慢與偏見

3 理性與感性

4 咆哮山莊

5 小婦人

6 簡愛

(物)可以產生或做出某物。其常見句型有:S produce N,以下透過範例作進一步說明:

EX My cat produced four kittens last night.

我的貓昨晚生了四隻小貓。

→ 說話者的貓昨晚生小貓,故應以 produce 來描述寵物的後代繁衍。

EX Australia produces a great deal of beef for export.

澳洲生產大量牛肉供出口。

→ 要做為出口品項,其產量須達一定程度,故說話者以 produce 表示澳洲有能力出產大量牛肉。

實作練習與解析

❶ We _____ fish for the lab to experiment.

(A) produce (B) breed (C) raise

Ans: (B)。說話者養魚的目的是讓實驗室做實驗,故應以 breed 來表達此種有目的性的培育。

❷ Pollution around the industries park _____ the disease.

(A) produce (B) raise (C) breed

Ans: (C)。汙染物足以導致疾病的產生,故應以 breed 來表達兩者間的因果關係。

❸ My parents work in other county, so I am _____ by my grandparents.

(A) raised (B) bred (C) produced

Ans: (A)。陪伴說話者長大的是他的祖父母，故應以 raise 來表達此種自年幼到成年的照顧。

❹ My dog _____ one doggy last Friday.

(A) bred (B) raised (C) produced

Ans: (C)。說話者的狗上週五生小狗，故應以 produce 來表達此依繁衍後代的事實。

❺ USA _____ a great deal of corn for export.

(A) produces (B) breeds (C) raises

Ans: (A)。要做為出口品項，其產量須達一定程度，故說話者以 produce 表示美國有能力出產大量玉米。

❻ Brown's parents got divorced when he was young, so he was _____ by his father alone.

(A) bred (B) raised (C) produced

Ans: (B)。布朗的父母在他年紀很小的時候就已離婚，而布朗的監護權歸爸爸，故應以 raise 來表達此段歷程。

1 亂世佳人

2 傲慢與偏見

3 理性與感性

4 咆哮山莊

5 小婦人

6 簡愛

Unit 46
咆哮山莊

🔍 俏佳人怎麼說

A person who has not done one half his
day's work by ten o'clock runs a chance
of leaving the other half undone.—Nelly Dean

到十點鐘前還沒完成,當天一半工作的人,
就有可能把今天剩下的工作擱置不做。——奈莉·丁

作品概述

　　宛如整個故事的旁白,奈莉的話語使劇情不停向前推展。當洛克伍德向奈莉問起過去所發生的一切時,奈莉的娓娓道來讓他聽到欲罷不能。即使奈莉用今天聽到太晚會讓你明天無法把事情好好做完當擋箭牌,依然無法使其打消念頭。在這段試圖開脫的話語中,出現了表「留下」的單字 leave,但由於英文中尚有 remain 與 keep 在語意與用法上與之相似,故本單元特將其並列做解析說明。

文法概述

✥ *Leave / remain / keep* ✥

★ Leave

若以 leave 表達留下,其描述重點大致可以分為三個面向。一是某人或某物在某處產生了「印記」,二是某事件結束後,物品被「置放」在其相關場地,三是不更動某事物發生的客觀條件,使其保持某一特定「狀態」。 其常見句型有: S leave …in/on/at …,以下透過範例做進一步說明:

EX My boots leave muddy marks on the mat.

我的靴子在地墊上留有泥印。

→ 說話者離開某地後,他的鞋子在該處留產生痕跡,故應以 leave 來描述此印記的產生過程。

EX There are many empty beer bottles left in booth after the party

派對過後包廂裡留下許多空啤酒瓶。

→ 派對後喝完的酒瓶被放在包廂內,故應以 leave 來表達物品在活動結束後未被妥善處理。

EX I have to go back to my dorm now because I think I must have left the air conditioner on.

我現在必須回宿舍一趟,因為我覺得我應該沒關冷氣。

→ 說話者覺得自己沒關冷氣就出門了,故應以 leave 來表達冷氣持續處於運轉的狀態。

1 亂世佳人

2 傲慢與偏見

3 理性與感性

4 咆哮山莊

5 小婦人

6 簡愛

★ Remain

若以 remain 來表達留下，意指除了現在所描述的部分，其他部分都已消失或毀壞。也因為是強調還剩多少，其後所接的數量通常不大，其常見句型有:Sth/sb remain in/on/at⋯，以下透過範例做進一步說明：

EX After the earthquake, only few buildings remain in this region.

地震過後此區域只剩下少數幾築物沒有倒塌。

→ 說話者想強調是地震後沒倒的建築物為數不多，故應以 remain 來表達這些受災尚稱輕微的部分。

★ keep

若以 keep 表達留下，其重點在於所有權的歸屬，故經常用於以描述是某人尚未擁有某物，因而請求擁有者轉讓。其常見句型有：Can sb keep⋯if⋯，以下透過範例做進一步說明：

EX Can I keep the photo if you agree?

如您同意的話，我可以擁有這張照片嗎？

→ 說話者尚未擁有這張照片，因而詢問擁有者是否肯轉讓，故應以 keep 來表達歸屬權變化的可能性。

實作練習與解析

❶ My shoes _____ a clear mark on the mud.
(A) leave   (B) keep   (C) remain
Ans: (A)。說話者走過泥濘之處，因而該處留下鞋印，故應以 leave 來表達印記的產生。

❷ The friction _____ a tiny mark on my helmet.
(A) keeps   (B) remains   (C) leaves
Ans: (C)。摩擦使說話者的安全帽些微受損，故應以 leave 來表達微
小印記的產生。

❸ After the party, there are much trash _____ in the booth.
(A) kept   (B) remained   (C) left
Ans: (C)。由於垃圾在活動結束後未被妥善處理，故應以 left 來表達
物品被遺留在活動場地的狀態。

❹ I have to go back to the kitchen now because I think I might
have _____ the gas burner on.
(A) left   (B) kept   (C) remained
Ans: (A)。說話者覺得自己可能沒關瓦斯就離開廚房，故應該 leave
來表達瓦斯爐一直處於開啟的狀態。

❺ After the flood, almost nothing _____ in this town.
(A) keeps   (B) remains   (C) leaves
Ans: (B)。說話者欲表達的是洪水後幾乎整個城鎮被破壞殆盡，故應
以 remain 來表達尚稱完好的部分為數不多。

❻ Can I _____ this poster if you are willing to share it to me?
(A) leave   (B) remain   (C) keep
Ans: (C)。說話者尚未擁有此張海報，因而詢問對方是否願意轉讓，
故應以 keep 來表達所有權轉移的可能性。

1 亂世佳人

2 傲慢與偏見

3 理性與感性

4 咆哮山莊

5 小婦人

6 簡愛

Unit 47
咆哮山莊

俏佳人怎麼說

Any relic of the dead is precious,
if they were valued living.—Nelly Dean

如果仍被視為活著，死者的任何遺物都很珍貴。——奈莉・丁

作品概述

　　當希斯克里夫再次回到畫眉山莊時，為了報復埃德加，他誘騙埃德加的妹妹伊莎貝拉與之私奔。在凱薩琳死後，伊莎貝拉寄回一封信給管家奈莉，信中提到她很想寫信回來，但又有所顧忌的心情。面對這種種的衝擊，奈莉不禁說出如果有被重視的話，即使死去，尚存於世的點點滴滴都彌足珍貴的感慨。在這段充滿緬懷的話語中，出現了表「珍貴」的單字 precious，但由於英文中尚有 expensive、valuable 在語意上部分與之相近，故本單元特將三者並列，針對其相同與相異之處作解析說明。

文法概述

Precious / expensive / valuable / costly

★ Precious

若就適用範圍而言，precious 為本單元三者中最大。，舉凡物品因為「稀少」、「昂貴」、「重要」等因素而使其深具價值，皆可以 precious 表示。其常見句型有：sth is precious to sb，以下透過範例做進一步說明：

EX The memory of the good old time is precious to me.

過去美好時光的記憶對我來說彌足珍貴。

→ 過去的記憶對說話者來說很重要，故應以 precious 來描述此珍貴性。

★ Expensive

若以 expensive 表有價值的，其描述重點在於取得物品或享受服務所需支付的「費用」很高。其常見句型有: S is expensive to…，以下透過範例做進一步說明：

EX Super sport car is expensive to maintain.

超跑維修保養費很高。

→ 超跑屬奢侈品，其維修保養費自然比一般車款還高，故應以 expensive 來表達所費不貲。

★ Valuable

Valuable 是由 value 一字衍生而來，除描述所需費用很多外，也可用來說明某事物對某人有所助益。其常見句型有: N is valuable to sb，以下透過範例做進一步說明：

1 亂世佳人

2 傲慢與偏見

3 理性與感性

4 咆哮山莊

5 小婦人

6 簡愛

EX This information is valuable to me.

這些資訊對我來非常有用。

→ 眼前的這些資訊能對說話者有所助益，故應以 valuable 來表達其價值所在。

★ Costly

除表所費不貲外 costly 也經常用於表述做某事必須有很大的「付出」或做很大的「犧牲」。其常見句型有: N/Ving/ To V is a costly… 以下透過範例做進一步說明:

EX Renting an office downtown is a costly decision.

在市中心租辦公室是個代價很高的決定

→ 市區的租金相對高，故應以 costly 來表達選定此地點每用所需付出的費用相對較多。

實作練習與解析

❶ Since the experiment is difficult, the time for the data we collected is _____.

(A) expensive   (B) precious   (C) valuable   (D) costly

Ans: (B)。實驗很不容易成功，本次成功收集到數據彌足珍貴，故應以 precious 來顯示其重要性。

❷ High class hotel is _____ to stay.

(A) valuable   (B) expensive   (C) precious   (D) costly

Ans: (B)。高級旅館提供高檔設施與服務，故應以 expensive 來表達所需支付費用也相對較高。

❸ Jason's suggestion is ＿＿＿＿ to me

(A) costly　(B) valuable　(C) precious　(D) expensive

Ans: (D)。說話者覺得傑森的建議對他有所幫助，故應以 valuable 來表達此建議所產生的影響。

❹ Buying a pair of hand-made leather shoes is a ＿＿＿＿ decision.

(A) costly　(B) expensive　(C) precious　(D) valuable

Ans: (A)。手工皮鞋價格遠超過一般皮鞋，故說話者以 costly 來表達決定買鞋所需支付的費用很高

❺ It is hard to find this kind of animal, so the picture you take is ＿＿＿＿.

(A) valuable　(B) costly　(C) precious　(D) expensive

Ans: (C)。由於說話者所提及的動物平時不易看見，故應以 precious 來表達所拍攝到的照片的珍貴性。

❻ The cost for earning at the high class restaurant is ＿＿＿＿ to eat.

(A) costly　(B) expensive　(C) valuable　(B) precious

Ans: (B)。吃高檔餐廳享受的可能是好的氣氛、手藝或食材，故應以 expensive 來表達需支出較多費用。

1 亂世佳人

2 傲慢與偏見

3 理性與感性

4 咆哮山莊

5 小婦人

6 簡愛

Unit 48
咆哮山莊

俏佳人怎麼說

I have such faith in Linton's love
that I believe I might kill him, and he
wouldn't wish to retaliate.—Catherine Earnshaw
我對林頓的愛有信心,我相信我可能會殺了他,且他也不想報復。
——凱薩琳・恩肖

作品概述

　　凱薩琳認為林頓對她的愛跟希斯克里夫對她的愛是幾乎相等的,而且她自認林頓會對她言聽計從。由於這段感情是女性掌握主導權,因此凱薩琳甚至敢大膽地說出,林頓的性命也是掌握在她手上這種誇張言論。在這段帶有宣示意味的話語中,出現了表「對…有信心」的單字 faith,但由於英文中尚有 confidence 與 trust 在用法上與之相似,故本單元特將其並列做解析說明。

文法概述

Faith / confidence / trust

★ Faith

若以 faith 來表達「對…有信心」，立基點是對事物的「期待」。也因為是自己所接受的信念，一般來說較不易改變。其常見句型有:S have faith…，以下透過範例做進一步說明：

EX I have great faith in you, so you can just do it.

我對你有信心，所以你就放膽去做吧!

➔ 說話者深信對方可以做到某事，所以應以 faith 來表達其支持。

★ Confidence

若以 confidence 來表達「對…有信心」，其立基點是對某事物的「知識」或「認知」。但也因為知識有修正的空間，認知可能隨客觀條件的變化做調整，故其變動性較 faith 大。其常見句型有:S have confidence in sb/ to v /that…，以下透過範例做進一步說明：

EX You are well prepared for this test, so you should have more confidence in yourself.

這次考試你準備很充分，所以要對自己有信心。

➔ 說話者認為考試前如果有準備，不應擔心自己會考不好。故應以 confidence 來表達此種認知。

EX Since I am the only applicant with working experience, I have confidence to get the permission from the graduate institute.

我是申請者中唯一有工作經驗的，所以我有信心獲得研究所的入學

許可。

→ 說話者認為工作經驗可以幫助自己會通過審核，故應以 confidence 來表達此種認知。

EX The consecutive growths in Q3 and Q4 make me feel confident that our performance will be better next year.

第三與第四季的持續成長使我有信心明年業績會告好。

→ 持續成長的銷售數字使說話者相信此趨勢能夠延續至明年，故應以 confidence 來表達此種認知。

★ Trust

若以 Trust 來表達「對…有信心」，其利基點是對於個人、組織或事物的性格、技術或安全性等的認可。換句話說，當你覺得某事物能夠完成你的交付時，就可以用 trust 來表示。其常見句型有: S have trust in…以下透過範例做進一步說明：

EX I have trust in your security system, so let's extend the contract for one more year.

我對你們的保全系統有信心，所以就再簽約一年吧!

實作練習與解析

❶ I have _____ in the future of our company.

(A) trust (B) confidence (C) faith

Ans: (C)。說話者深信公司具有發展性，故應以 faith 來表達此一信念。

❷ I have _____ in your ability, so you can start to design the new logo from tomorrow.

(A) faith　(B) trust　(C) confidence

Ans: (C)。說話者認可對方的設計能力，故應以 confidence 來表達此種認知。

❸ Since I have two professional certificate in this field, so I have _____ to get this job.

(A) confidence　(B) trust　(C) faith

Ans: (A)。說話者認為專業證照會成為他求職的優勢，故應以 confidence 來表達此種認知。

❹ What you want to do next is too challenging, so I have no _____ that you will success.

(A) faith　(B) confidence　(C) trust

Ans: (B)。說話者認為對方想做的事情難度太高不可能成功，故應以 have no confidence 來表達不認同。

❺ We have cooperated for years, so I have _____ in the quality of your products.

(A) faith　(B) trust　(C) confidence

Ans: (B)。說話者因為長期與對方合作，進而對其產品品質感到放心，故應以 trust 來表達信賴。

❻ I have great _____ in your profession, so just tell me the truth.

(A) trust　(B) confidence　(C) faith

Ans: (A)。說話者對於對方的專業能力感到放心，希望他能告訴自己到底真實情況為何，故應以 trust 來表達此種信賴。

1 亂世佳人

2 傲慢與偏見

3 理性與感性

4 咆哮山莊

5 小婦人

6 簡愛

Unit 49
咆哮山莊

俏佳人怎麼說

*I've dreamt in my life dreams that have
stayed with me ever after, and changed my
ideas; they've gone through and through
me, like wine through water, and altered the
colour of my mind.—Catherine Earnshaw.*

**我生命中做過的有些夢會在夢過之後一直留在我的身邊,
並改變我的想法:它們在我心中穿來穿去,就像酒流進水中一樣,
最後改變了我的思想的顏色。——凱薩琳·恩肖**

作品概述

　　在答應埃德加·林頓的求婚後,凱薩琳反而突然覺得迷惑,甚至希望管家奈莉給她些意見。奈莉表示既然兩情相悅,就沒什麼好擔心的。凱薩琳問奈莉是否做過什麼奇怪的夢,當奈莉回答偶爾後,凱薩琳便娓娓道來自己的想法。在這段表露心聲的話語中,出現了表「改變」的單字 alter,但由於英文中尚有 change 與 modify 在語意用法上與之相似,故本單元特將其並列做解析說明。

文法概述

✎ *Alter / Change / modify* ✎

★ **Alter**

若以 alter 表變動，通常是針對事物的某些「特點」做調整，或是修改服飾的部分設計使其更加「合身」，因此其修正幅度通常不會太大。其常見句型有：S alter… to V。以下透過範例做進一步說明：

EX I have altered the design a little bit to make the appearance brighter.

我稍微改變設計好讓表面更加光亮。

→ 說話者認為自己的設計還有些微調整空間，故應以 alter 來表達修正之意。

EX The tailor alters the pants to fit me.

裁縫師幫我把褲子改得合身。

→ 褲子原本可能不合說話者的身型，透過裁縫師的修改才得貼身，故應以 alter 來表達此種修改。

★ **Change**

相較於 alter 與 modify 的小幅更動，change 所表現的變動幅度明顯較大。Change 經常用於相似類型事物的轉換、想法的更替以及方法態度的改善。其常見句型有:S change…for… 與 S change…from…to…。以下透過範例做進一步說明：

EX I change the shoes I just bought for a bigger pair.

我把剛買的那雙鞋去換成更大尺寸。

→ 說話者更換的是鞋子的尺寸而非款式，故應以 change 來表達

1 亂世佳人

2 傲慢與偏見

3 理性與感性

4 咆哮山莊

5 小婦人

6 簡愛

此種變動。

EX After my explanation, her viewpoint changes from against to support.

經過我的解釋，她的觀點從反對轉為支持。

→ 對方因為說話者的說明而改變看法，故應以 change 來表達此種想法上的更替。

★ Modify

若以 modify 來表變動，經常用於說明對於計畫、想法、律法或是行為的些微調整，目的提高其接受度或是改善缺失。其常見句型有：S modify… to V。以下透過範例做進一步說明：

EX We modify the system to make it more suitable for the beginners.

我們修改好系統讓它更適合初學者。

→ 當前系統初學者不易上手，透過微調方可改善，故應以 modify 來表達修此類型的修正。

實作練習與解析

❶ I _____ my idea a little bit to make it more practical.
(A) change   (B) modify   (C) alter

Ans: (C)。經過些微調整後，說話者的想法更符合實際需求，故應以 alter 來表達此種變化。

❷ The tailor _____ the coat to make it shorter

(A) alters　(B) changes　(C) modifies

Ans: (A)。說話者的外套原本長度太常，裁縫師修改後才得以合身，故應以 alter 來描述此種調整。

❸ I _____my mind and join this game.

(A) modify　(B) alter　(C) change

Ans: (C)。說話者原本不想參加比賽，但後來改變心意了，故應以 change 來表達此種想法上的變動。

❹ Feeling cheated, his mood _____ from good to bad.

(A) modifies　(B) changes　(C) alters

Ans: (B)。發覺自己被騙後，說話者心情大受影響，故應以 change 來描述心情上的轉變。

❺ The enrollment system is _____ to meet most applicants' need

(A) modified　(B) changed　(C) altered

Ans: (A)。舊的註冊系統完全滿足大部分申請者的需求，因而需要做些維修，故應以 modify 來描述此種調整。

❻ The coding you use may affect the efficiency, so I strongly suggest you _____ them.

(A) alter　(B) change　(C) modify

Ans: (C)。對方現在使用的編碼方式會降低系統效能，說話者建議他稍作調整，故應以 modify 來描述此種修正。

1 亂世佳人

2 傲慢與偏見

3 理性與感性

4 咆哮山莊

5 小婦人

6 簡愛

Unit 50
咆哮山莊

俏佳人怎麼說

A good heart will help you to a bonny face, my lad", I continued, "if you were a regular black, and a bad one will turn the bonniest into something worse than ugly.—Nelly Dean

**相由心生，好心腸讓你有好氣色，我的好友。
但你如果只是一般的黑人，只要有任何壞的地方，
就可以最好的變得比醜陋還更糟。——奈莉・丁**

作品概述

　　在咆哮山莊的時空背景中，白人以外的人種，其社會地位相對低下。因此當希斯克里夫被收養時，其出身不免被放大檢視。好事可能沒人知，但只要壞事一出，便會傳遍千里。在這段語帶提醒但卻又帶有些許歧視的話語中，出現了表條件的句型 if sb were…，由於假設語氣常常困擾許多英文學習者，故本單元特選擇與現在事實相反以及與過去事實相反的假設，做進一步解析說明，讓讀者們能夠快速釐清兩者用法上的差異。

文法概述

現在事實相反的假設 / 過去事實相反的假設

★ If S Ved, S would/could/should/might

當以 if 來表達假設的情況與現在事實相反時，做為條件的句子會使用過去式，做為結果的句子會用助動詞(would/could/should/might)加上原形動詞(v)。唯一比較特別的是，當條件句的動詞為 Be 動詞時，只能用 were 來表示。更簡單來說，當某人做不到某事，或是某種條件無法形成，預期的結果就無法發生，就可以採用本句型。以下透過範例作進一步說明：

EX If I worked hard, I would buy a sport car.

如果我努力工作的話，我就可以買跑車了。

→ 若說話者沒有努力工作，想買跑車的夢想自然無法實現，故應以 If S Ved, S would /could/should/might V 句型來表示。

EX If I were you, I would buy this car.

如果我是你的話，我會買這輛車。

→ 說話者與對方是兩個不同的人，故當 If S were, S would /could/should/might V 時，表達的是說話者想買，但對方可能不買的情況。

★ If S had pp, S would /could/should/might have pp

當以 if 來表達假設的情況與過去事實相反時，做為條件的句子會使用過去完成式(have pp)。做為結果的句子會用助動詞(would/could/should/might)加上過去完成式(have pp)。更簡單來說，當某人過去做不到某事，或是某種條件無法形成，當時預期的結果就無法發生，就可以採用本句型。以下透過範例作進一步說明：

1 亂世佳人

2 傲慢與偏見

3 理性與感性

4 咆哮山莊

5 小婦人

6 簡愛

EX If I had studied hard, I could have passed the exam.

如果當時我有認真讀書，就可以通過考試了。

➔ 說話者過去沒有認真讀書，以致於當時的考試也沒考好，故應以 If S had pp, S would /could/should/might have pp 句型來表示。

EX If it had not rained, Jane would have caught the bus.

如果當時沒下雨，珍就可以趕上巴士了。

➔ 珍趕公車的那天就是有下雨，導致她沒搭到車，故應以 If S had pp, S would /could/should/might have pp 句型來表示。

實作練習與解析

❶ If Joe_____ up early, she would catch the train

(A) get (B) got (C) gotten

Ans: (B)。喬沒早起，以致於沒趕上火車，故應以 f S Ved, S would /could/should/might V 句型來表示。

❷ If I _____ you, I would not buy this watch.

(A) be (B) am (C) were

Ans: (C)。說話者跟對方是兩個不同的人，故 If S Ved, S would/ could/should/might V 句型可用來表示說話者對於是否購買此款手錶的看法。

❸ If James _____ early, he would have avoid getting hurt.

(A) had left (B) have left (C) have been left

Ans: (A)。詹姆士當時沒有提早離開，所以最後難逃受傷的命運。故
應以 If S had pp, S would /could/should/might V 句型來
表示。

❹ If it _____ that day, I would not gotten a cold.
(A) haven't rain　(B) had not rained　(C) have been not
rained

Ans: (B)。說話者所描述的過去某天有下雨，所以他感冒了。故應以
If S had pp, S would /could/should/might V 句型來表示。

❺ If I _____ hard, I would have bought a small apartment
downtown.
(A) had worked　(B) have been worked　(C) have worded

Ans: (A)。說話者沒有努力工作，所以沒有辦法在市中心買戶小公
寓。故應以 If S had pp, S would /could/should/might V 句
型來表示。

❻ If I _____ much more money, I would have bought a new
car.
(A) had　(B) have　(C) has

Ans: (A)。說話者雖然想買新車，但手邊的資金不足，故應以 If S
Ved, S would /could/should/might V 句型來表示。

1 亂世佳人

2 傲慢與偏見

3 理性與感性

4 咆哮山莊

5 小婦人

6 簡愛

Part 5

Week 5 小婦人

Unit 51
小婦人

俏佳人怎麼說

If God wants me with Him, there is none who will stop Him. I don't mind. I was never like the rest of you... making plans about the great things I'd do. I never saw myself as anything much. Not a great writer like you. —Beth

如果主要我跟隨他，就沒人可以阻止。我並不介意。我不像妳們一樣能夠替想做的事情做出好的規劃。我認為我最多就只能做到這樣，不可能像你一樣是名優秀的作家。——貝絲。

作品概述

　　貝絲是四姊妹中個性最內向膽小的，深知自己不像姐姐喬擅長寫作，也沒想替自己想做的事情加以規劃，但她對信仰非常虔誠，覺得神有賦予她一些責任，且這樣的任務是誰也無法阻止她的。在這段對自己能力與宗教信仰坦承的話語中，出現了表「停止」的單字 stop，但由於英文中尚有 finish 和 suspend 在語意與用法皆與之相似，故本單元特將三者並列做解析說明。

文法概述

❧ *stop / finish / suspend* ☙

★ Stop

若以 stop 表停止，遭終止的可能是動作、習慣、運作等，且這樣的停止可能是肇因於以下三種面向，一是難以承受或力求改變，二是要素失去作用，使事物無法正常運行，三是在某處短暫停留，之後將離開此處。其常見句型有: Stop Ving, or sb will…以及 Sb/sth will stop at… for…，以下透過範例做進一步說明：

EX Stop touching me, or I will punch you.

不要再碰我，否則我會揍你。

→ 説話者希望對方別再動手動腳，因而出言警告，故應以 stop 來表達他對此行為難以忍受。

EX The bus will stop at this place for five minutes

巴士將於此處停留五分鐘。

→ 巴士不會一直停留在説話者現在所描述的地點，故應以 stop 來表達稍後即將離開之意。

★ Finish

雖然同樣表達停止，但 finish 所強調的是「到此結束」。換句話説，當某事邁向結束，且可能不會再次進行，就可以用 finish 來表示。其常見句型有:Sth finish with…與 Sth should finish around…，以下透過範例做進一步說明：

EX The play finished with a chorus.

此劇由一首合唱曲結尾。

1 亂世佳人

2 傲慢與偏見

3 理性與感性

4 咆哮山莊

5 小婦人

6 簡愛

→ 在演員合唱完這首歌後，此劇就結束了，故應以 finish 來表達表演內容已告一段落。

EX The meeting should finish around three o'clock if there were no delay.

如無任何延誤的話，本會議應於下午三點結束。

→ 如一切順利，會議將於三點結束，故應以 finish 來描述此事件的終止。

★ Suspend

若以 suspend 表停止，通常用於描述某人因犯下錯誤而無法行使權利或參與活動。其常見句型有 S be suspended for…/ from… for Ving，以下透過範例做進一步說明：

EX The player is suspended for ten matches after punching one of the player from the rival team.

出拳毆打對方球員後，該名球員遭禁賽十場。

EX James is suspended from school for fighting.

詹姆士因為鬥毆而遭退學。

→ 詹姆士因為打架而無法保有繼續就學的權利，故應以 suspend 來表達此種權利上的中斷。

實作練習與解析

❶ _____ complaining, or I will cease our cooperation.

(A) finish   (B) suspend   (C) stop

Ans: (C)。若對方一直抱怨，說話者就會選擇不再與之合作，故應以

stop 來表達他對於此種行為的低耐受度。

❷ The train will _____ at this station for ten minutes.

(A) stop　(B) suspend　(C) finish

Ans: (A)。說話者所描述的是火車載運旅客的情況，故應以 stop 來
表達車輛的停靠。

❸ The movie_____ with the scene that the hero says that he will be back.

(A) suspends　(B) finishes　(C) stops

Ans: (B)。主角說完這句台詞後，電影就結束了，故應以 finish 來表
達影片到此完結。

❹ The seminar should _____ around four to five o'clock.

(A) finish　(B) suspend　(C) stop

Ans: (A)。研討會在四點到五點之間就會告一段落，故應以 finish 來
表達活動的結束。

❺ The hitter is _____ for two matches for arguing with the referee.

(A) stopped　(B) finished　(C) suspended

Ans: (C)。打擊者因為與裁判爭執而失去接下來兩場出賽的權利，故
應以 suspend 來描述他暫時無法參賽的情況。

❻ Helen is _____ from her company for the scandal.

(A) stopped　(B) suspended　(C) finished

Ans: (B)。海倫因身陷醜聞而遭公司停職以待調查，故應以 suspend
來表達她目前無法執行相關業務的情況。

Unit 52
小婦人

🔍 俏佳人怎麼說

❧ *Christmas won't be Christmas without any presents.—Jo* ❧
聖誕節沒禮物就不像聖誕節了。——喬

作品概述

馬區一家家境不富裕，因此四姊妹無法像有錢人家的小孩那樣要什麼有什麼。但由於聖誕節即將來臨，二姊約瑟芬認為聖誕禮物是成就整個過節氣氛的關鍵因素，因而說出沒禮物就不像過節的這段話語。在這隱含家貧以致於無法好好過節的隨口一語當中，出現了表「禮物」的單字 present，但由於禮物屬於贈送品，英文中尚有 gift、offering 與 donation 在語意上與之相似，故本單元特將其並列做解析說明。

🪭 文法概述

❧ *Present / gift / offering* ❧

★ Present

當以 present 來表達禮物之意時，其前提有二，一是受贈者未主動要

求，二是贈送目的通常是為了表現友誼或感謝。其常見句型有 S gave O as a present，以下透過範例做進一步說明：

EX I give Jason a concert ticket as a present to show my appreciation.

我送給傑森一張演唱會門票作為禮物以示感激。

→ 說話者送票的目的是為了感謝傑森的幫忙，故應以 present 來表達這樣的贈禮。

★ Gift

若要從文法面刻意區分 gift 與 present 的差異，其實並不容易。但在現代英文中，已習慣將免費獲得的「額外商品」以 gift 來表示(例如：買大送小的組合中，規格或容量較小的那個贈送品)，收到的禮品才稱作 present。其常見句型有: S get…as a/the gift，以下透過範例做進一步說明：

EX I get a belt as the gift when I buy this jeans.

我買這條牛仔褲時獲得一條皮帶做為贈品。

→ 牛仔褲是說話者花錢購買，皮帶則是額外免費獲得，故應以 gift 來描述皮帶在本次交易中的性質為何。

★ Offering

Offering 是由 offer 所衍生而來，若將其做禮物解釋，通常指的是因為「宗教」或「談判」所贈與的物品或是金錢，惟兩者在意願上有所差異。若為宗教因素，信眾是出於「自願」。若為其他因素，往往是「被迫」或基於某種考量所做出的「利益交換」。其常見句型有:S provide… as the offering for…，以下透過範例做進一步說明：

1 亂世佳人

2 傲慢與偏見

3 理性與感性

4 咆哮山莊

5 小婦人

6 簡愛

EX The side with serious casualty provides many precious jewelry as the offering for peace-seeking.

傷亡慘重的一方提供許多貴重的珠寶做為求合的禮物。

→ 此場戰爭中的其中一方為了不要再有傷亡選擇和談，故應以 offering 來描述他們為了停火所準備給予對方的物品。

實作練習與解析

❶ I give Sam a pair of boots as his birthday _____.
(A) gift　(B) offering　(C) present

Ans: (C)。說話者為了在山姆生日表達兩人之間的友誼，買了靴子送他，故應以 present 來描述此一贈禮。

❷ Hanks gets a T shirt with brand logo as the _____ when he buys the classic boots.
(A) present　(B) gift　(C) offering

Ans: (B)。漢克購買經典款靴子時，額外獲的一件免費的品牌商標 T 恤，故應以 gift 來描述此服飾屬於贈品

❸ I provide one tenth of income as the _____ for the church.
(A) gift　(B) present　(C) offering

Ans: (C)。說話者基於宗教信仰將收入的十分之一奉獻給教會，故應以 offering 來描述此種贈與。

❹ I buy Sam a new tie as his wedding _____.
(A) present　(B) gift　(C) offering

Ans: (A)。說話者為了要慶賀買山姆結婚，買一條領帶送他，故應以 present 來表達此領帶為一項賀禮。

❺ In this special sale, I buy one pair of shoes and get a backpack as the _____.
(A) offering   (B) present   (C) gift
Ans: (C)。說話者在特賣會中買了鞋子,並免費再獲得一個後背包,故應以 gift 來描述此包款為贈品。

❻ I provide a free meal in high class restaurant as the_____ for seeking the help from the one I had conflict with in the past.
(A) offering   (B) present   (C) gift
Ans: (A)。說話者因故有求於過去曾與他有過衝突的人,希望以請吃高級餐廳為誘因讓對方願意幫忙,故應以 offering 來描述此種利益交換。

1 亂世佳人

2 傲慢與偏見

3 理性與感性

4 咆哮山莊

5 小婦人

6 簡愛

Unit 53
小婦人

俏佳人怎麼說

*I don't see how you can write
and act such splendid things, Jo. You are a
regular Shakespeare. —Beth*

**我不明白為何你能寫出與表現出這麼精彩的內容，
喬你簡直就是莎士比亞。——貝絲**

作品概述

　　約瑟芬是四姊妹中最會寫作的，由於妹妹貝絲自己不擅寫作，個性也較害羞，因而更加好奇為何二姊能夠如此文思泉湧。再看過姊姊的作品後，甚至將其與大文豪莎士比亞做比擬。在這段讚揚約瑟芬的話語中，出現了表「了解」的單字 see，但由於英文中尚有 know、understand 與 comprehend 在用法上與之相似，但卻表達出理解程度與給對方觀感的差異，故本單元特將其並列做解析說明。

文法概述

★ See

若以 see 表了解，代表經由對方的解釋後，你突然明白某事的來龍去脈或是找出問題的癥結點。其常見句型有:S see what/why…，以下透過範例做進一步說明：

EX Now I finally see what you mean.

我現在終於弄懂你真的想表達的意思。

→ 說話者原本可能不清楚對方想傳達怎樣的訊息給他，但現在恍然大悟了，故應以 see 來描述此種突然想通的情況。

★ Know

雖然同樣表達了解，但 know 隱含出我已經知道，你大可不必再提醒的語意，容易讓訊息接受者覺得不悅。其常見句型有: S know that…/what…，以下透過範例做進一步說明：

EX I know what you mean, so let's stop here.

我知道你想說什麼，所以我們就此打住。

→ 對方試圖多做解釋，但說話者卻表現出我已經知道你接下來想說什麼的不耐煩態度，故應以 know 來表達此種理解。

★ Understand

若以 understand 表了解，代表你對事物的理解已有一定程度，且在語氣上也較為禮貌，其常見句型有:S understand why sth/sb…，以下透過範例做進一步說明：

1 亂世佳人

2 傲慢與偏見

3 理性與感性

4 咆哮山莊

5 小婦人

6 簡愛

EX Thanks to your explanation, now I understand why this method works.

經你解釋過後，現在我懂為何這個方法有用了。

➔ 說話者原本想不通為何此方法可行，經由對方解釋後才知其源委，故應以 understand 來表示已經理解。

★ Comprehend

若從理解程度的高低來排序，comprehend 為本單元四者中最高，因此除非是要對於某事物已有充分研究或理解，否則較不適用 comprehend。其常見句型有: S comprehended why… ，以下透過範例做進一步說明：

EX After reading the reference you provide, now I comprehend why this product can hit the market.

讀完你給的參考資料後，我現完全理解為何此產品能夠轟動市場了。

➔ 說話者可能原本對產品熱賣的原因一之半解，但讀完資料後就完全理解了，故應以 comprehend 來描述此種前後差異。

實作練習與解析

❶ When I glimpse the picture you take, I _____ what's going on now.

(A) understand (B) comprehend (C) see (D) know

Ans: (C)。說話者原本不清楚現在的狀況為何，看到對方拍的照片後突然就搞懂了，故應以 see 來表達恍然大悟的感受。

❷ I _____ you may want to explain now, but I think all of them are just excuses.

(A) comprehend   (B) understand   (C) know   (D) see

Ans: (C)。對方想解釋，但説話者卻未聽內容將其視為理由，故應以
　　 know 來描述此種極其主觀的理解。

❸ After the lecture, now I generally _____ why the model can be so popular.

(A) see   (B) understand   (C) comprehend   (D) know

Ans: (B)。説話者上課前對於此模式能風行的原因不甚理解，上課後
　　 就懂了，故應以 understand 來描述此種前後差異。

❹ After taking a 50-hour-intensive course, now I _____ the theory that makes this system works.

(A) comprehend   (B) know   (C) understand   (D) see

Ans: (A)。在密集上過課後，説話者已充分了解運作的理論基礎，故
　　 應以 comprehend 來描述他當前對此系統的理解。

❺ Your words remind me to check the sequence, so now I _____ why we fail this time.

(A) understand   (B) see   (C) comprehend   (D) know

Ans: (B)。説話者原本可能沒想到順序是影響成敗的關鍵，好在對方
　　 一語點醒夢中人，故應以 see 來描述此種突然產生的理解。

❻ I think I _____ what to do next, so I won't take any suggestion now.

(A) see   (B) comprehend   (C) understand   (D) know

Ans: (D)。説話者對下一步已有明確想法，且不願接受任何建議，故
　　 應以 know 來描述此種對未來情況的理解。

Unit 54
小婦人

俏佳人怎麼說

*You think your temper is the worst in
the world, but mine used to be just like it. ...
I've been trying to cure it for forty years, and
have only succeeded in controlling it. —Marmee March*

你覺得你脾氣是這世上最糟的，但老實說我以前也跟你一樣。
我已經花了四十年想改掉這個毛病，
但也只做到能夠控制它而已。──馬區太太

作品概述

　　當約瑟芬向媽媽表示她覺得自己的脾氣一直以不太好時，站在做母親的立場，馬區女士選擇以開導的方式來告訴她情緒的控管本來就非一蹴可幾的。她以自己做例子，告訴約瑟芬自己年輕時脾氣也很差，但隨著歲月的增長，雖無法變成好脾氣，但至少已能控制情緒的起伏。在這段母女之間的真情告白中。出現了表「實現」的單字 succeed，但由於英文中尚有 realize 與 achieve 在語意與用法上與之相似，故本單元特將其並列做解析說明。

文法概述

✑ *Succeed / achieve / realize* ✑

★ Succeed

若以 succeed 表實現，代表某人實現其所設定目標，或是計畫的發展一如預期，故其適用範圍也為本單元三者中最廣。其常見句型有: S succeed in…，以下透過範例做進一步說明：

EX This campaign has succeeded in raising the awareness of environment protection.

此活動已成功喚起環保意識。

→ 本活動的主旨是希望大眾留意環保議題，現在也確實成功引發話題，故應以 succeed 來描述目標的達成。

★ Achieve

若以 achieve 表實現，除表述目前已完成或達到的目標有哪些之外，強調的是這些成果是「努力」所換來的。其常見句型有: S have achieved…in…，以下透過範例做進一步說明：

EX I have achieved the goal of owning a coffee shop.

我已達成當咖啡店老闆的目標。

→ 說話者目標是自己開間咖啡店，現在這個在他努力過後實現了，故應以 achieve 來描述此過程。

★ Realize

Realize 是由 real 一字衍生而來，若從積極角度來看，其描述重點在於如何讓計畫或是想法「成真」。若從消極角度來看，則是擔心壞事可能「發生」。其常見句型有: Sth… be realized…，以下透過範例

1 亂世佳人

2 傲慢與偏見

3 理性與感性

4 咆哮山莊

5 小婦人

6 簡愛

做進一步說明：

EX My goal of being a writer is finally realized this year.

我當作家的目標終於在今年實現了。

→ 說話者想當作家，這個目標在今年得以成真，故應以 realize 來描述此一變化過程。

EX The shortage in raw material he worried is realized this quarter.

他所擔心的原物料短缺在本季發生。

→ 說話者擔心未來可能原物料的供應會出現問題，而這樣的情況也確實在本季發生了，故應以 realize 來描述壞事成真。

實作練習與解析

❶ The protest has _____ in drawing the attention of the media.

(A) succeeded　(B) achieved　(C) realized

Ans: (A)。抗議的目的就是希望訴求被看見，由於現在已獲得媒體的注意，故應以 succeed 來描述目標的達成。

❷ I have _____ the goal of working in the top 500 businesses in USA.

(A) achieved　(B) succeeded　(C) realized

Ans: (A)。說話者希望能夠進入全美前 500 大企業工作，現在夢想成真，故應以 achieve 來描述努力所獲得的成果。

❸ My goal of getting the professional certificate is finally _____ _ this month.

(A) succeeded　(B) achieved　(C) realized

Ans: (C)。說話者希望能拿到專業證照，現在終於通過測驗，故應以 realize 來描述目標成真。

❹ The huge raise in the vegetable price is _____ this Chinese Lunar New Year.

(A) succeeded　(B) realized　(C) achieved

Ans: (B)。菜價可能就蠢蠢欲動，一到過年價格馬上攀升，故應以 realize 來表達壞事的發生。

❺ The controversial advertisement has _____ in creating the buzz among the audience.

(A) succeeded　(B) realized　(C) achieved

Ans: (A)。爭議話題容易引起討論，廣告商善用此點來創造話題，故應以 succeed 來表達此手段的效果極佳。

❻ The goal of getting 5 percent more in the market share is _ _____ this year.

(A) realized　(B) succeed　(C) achieved

Ans: (A)。說話者希望能夠再增加百分之五的市佔率，此一成長於今年達成，故應以 realize 來描述目標的完成。

1 亂世佳人

2 傲慢與偏見

3 理性與感性

4 咆哮山莊

5 小婦人

6 簡愛

Unit 55
小婦人

俏佳人怎麼說

I love my gallant captain with all my heart and soul and might, and never will desert him, while God lets us be together. Oh, Mother, I never knew how much like heaven this world could be, when two people love and live for one another! —Amy

當主讓我倆在一起，我將全心全意愛我英勇的勞里，絕不遺棄他。母親，當兩個人相愛且為彼此而活，我從不知道這會這麼像置身天堂。——艾美

作品概述

　　原本四姊妹的好友勞理喜歡的是二姊約瑟芬，但無奈約瑟芬拒絕了他，他轉而追求小妹艾美。當艾美接受這段感情後，也深覺她自己遇到了真命天子，兩人能夠相戀，讓她彷彿置身天堂。在這段艾美對於感情的自白中，出現了表「遺棄」的單字 desert，但由於英文中尚有 abandon 與 forsake 在語意與用法上與之相似，故本單元特將其並列做解析說明。

文法概述

❧ *Desert / abandon / forsake* ❧

★ **Desert**

若以 desert 表遺棄，通常指某人在對方遭遇困難或需要幫助時，不僅袖手旁觀並自此離開不再返回。也因為是有能力做某事但故意不做，故 desert 同時也傳達出對責任或義務的逃避或不履行。其常見句型有: S desert…for…，以下透過範例作進一步說明:

EX The man deserts his wife and daughter for another young lady.

這位男士為了另一名年輕女性而拋家棄子。

→ 這名男士，不顧妻小可能頓失依靠，選擇與其他女人交往，故應以 desert 來描述此種行為。

★ **Abandon**

雖然同樣表遺棄，abandon 多用於表述某人自此離開某地或某人這個「行為」，其原因可能出於自願，但也可能是情勢所逼。另當某人覺得某種想法已無發展價值，或是無法從某種負面情緒中抽離，也可以用 abandon 表示。其常見句型有: S abandon sth/sb 與 S abandon oneself to…，以下透過範例作進一步說明:

EX We have to abandon the car and move to the higher place if it keeps raining heavily.

如果還一直下大雨的話，我們必須棄車逃往高處。

→ 若持續下大雨，說話者目前身處的位置安全性堪慮，故應以 abandon 來描述必要時所需的撤離。

1 亂世佳人

2 傲慢與偏見

3 理性與感性

4 咆哮山莊

5 小婦人

6 簡愛

EX Leo abandons himself to sorrow.

里歐陷入哀傷之中。

→ 里歐常處於哀傷情緒，且無法自我調適，故應以 abandon 來描述他對自己情緒的放任。

★ Forsake

若以 forsake 表遺棄，斷絕的是心理或生理上的依賴，故經常用於表達放棄自己所喜愛的人事物或改掉壞習慣。其常見句型有: S forsake …與 S forsake N1 to V N2，以下透過範例做進一步說明：

EX George forsakes electric engineering to study physics because of the scholarship.

喬治因為獎學金的緣故選擇放棄電機去讀物理。

→ 喬治對電機跟物理可能都有興趣，但由於物理系提供獎學金，使他選擇進入該系，故應以 forsake 來描述他放棄電機的原因。

實作練習與解析

❶ The rich businessman _____ his wife who lives with him for 30 years for another his young secretary.

(A) forsake   (B) deserts   (C) abandons

Ans: (B)。富商為了年輕秘書，不顧與之生活三十年的妻子的感情，毅然將其拋棄，故應以 desert 來描述此一行為。

❷ When the enemy arrives, the village have been _____.

(A) abandoned   (B) deserted   (C) forsaken

Ans: (A)。由於敵軍來襲，村民只好棄村逃離，故應以 abandon 來
描述此種放棄居所的行為。

❸ Fanny often _____ herself to melancholy.
(A) deserts   (B) forsakes   (C) abandons

Ans: (C)。芬妮經常處於憂鬱，且她難以自我調適，故應以
abandon 來描述她對自己情緒的放任。

❹ My uncle finally _____ his drinking habit.
(A) forsakes   (B) deserts   (C) abandons

Ans: (A)。說話者的叔叔過去很愛喝酒，現在戒酒了，故應以
forsake 來描述壞習慣的戒除。

❺ Peter _____ finance to study literature because being a
writer is his dream for a long time.
(A) deserts   (B) forsakes   (C) abandons

Ans: (B)。由於彼得想當作家，所以在財金與文學兩個系所終選擇後
者就讀，故應以 forsake 來解釋他捨棄財金的原因

❻ The irresponsible father _____ his wife and young daughter
for his mistress.
(A) deserts   (B) abandons   (C) forsakes

Ans: (A)。不負責任的父親為了情婦選擇拋家棄子，故應以 desert
來描述他的惡意行為。

1 亂世佳人

2 傲慢與偏見

3 理性與感性

4 咆哮山莊

5 小婦人

6 簡愛

Unit 56
小婦人

🔍 俏佳人怎麼說

*If you feel your value lies in being merely
decorative, I fear that someday you might find
yourself believing that's all that you really are.
Time erodes all such beauty, but what it cannot
diminish... is the wonderful workings of your mind.
Your humor, your kindness... and your moral courage.*
— Marmee March

**如果你覺得自己的價值就只是裝飾而已,我擔心某天你會覺得自己就
真的如此。時間可以吞噬一切,但它絲毫不能減少的是你偉大的思想,
你的幽默,你的善良,還有你的勇氣。——珍**

作品概述

　　雖然在經濟上處於弱勢,馬區太太對於女兒的教育並未因此而馬虎,
她告訴女兒們女性絕對不是像裝飾品那樣華而不實。外在的美貌會隨時間
逝去,內在的充實反而因為歲月的歷練更顯風華。在這段母親對女兒的諄
諄教誨中,出現表「減少」的單字 diminish,但由於英文中尚有 lessen
與 curtail 在語意上與之相似,故本單元特將其並列做解析說明。

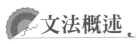文法概述

Diminish / lesson / curtail

★ Diminish

若以 diminish 表減少,若以之描述物品,多用於說明其尺寸的縮小、價格下跌與總量的減少;若以之描述人或是事件,則多指稱形象變差或觀感不佳。其常見句型有:N diminish one's … ,以下透過範例做進一步說明:

EX The medical expense diminishes most of Joan savings.

醫療支出耗掉了喬安大半的積蓄。

→ 喬安的積蓄因為需要支付大筆的醫藥費而大幅減少,故應以 diminish 來描述此種總量的下降。

EX Allen's improper statement diminishes his good reputation.

艾倫的不當發言損害了他的好名聲。

→ 不當的發言影響他人對的艾倫觀感,故應以 diminish 來描述他形象的受損。

★ Lessen

若以 lessen 表減少,針對未來可能發生的事件,降低的是其發生的機率。對於已經發生的事件,則是減低強度。其常見句型有: N can lessen the…of… ,以下透過範例做進一步說明:

EX A light diet can lessen the risk of the heart disease.

清淡飲食可以降低得到心臟病的可能性。

→ 說話者欲表達是飲食保持清淡就能比較不會得心臟病,故應以 lessen 來表達可能性的降低。

1 亂世佳人

2 傲慢與偏見

3 理性與感性

4 咆哮山莊

5 小婦人

6 簡愛

★ Curtail

若以 curtail 表減少，通常是針對總量做控管、對權力做限縮以及提早結束某事件或動作。其常見句型有: S curtail the N of…to…，以下透過範例做進一步說明:

EX The government curtails the spending of education to buy more weapon.

政府削減教育支出以購買更多軍火。

→ 國家預算有限，當要增加某項目的支出，勢必排擠其他項目，故應以 curtail 來表達此種削減。

EX When other colleagues go back to the office, we curtail our conversation concerning the policy of our company.

當其他同事回到辦公室時，我們提早結束關於公司政策的這個話題。

→ 兩人因為不想談話內容被其他人知道，當同事都回來後，就暫時不繼續討論此話題，故應以 curtail 來描述此種提早結束。

實作練習與解析

❶ The house _____ sharply in value in the past few months.
(A) diminished (B) curtailed (C) lessened

Ans: (A)。由於是在描述房屋價格的下跌，故應以 diminish 來表達此類型的縮減。

❷ Andy's controversial statement _____ his good image built a long time ago.

(A) curtails　(B) diminishes　(C) lessens

Ans: (B)。爭議性的言論使安迪的好形象受到影響，故應以 diminish
　　來描述其名聲受損

❸ Regular exercise can _____ the risk of getting many diseases.

(A) diminish　(B) curtail　(C) lessen

Ans: (C)。規律運動使人較不易生病，故應以 lessen 來描述患病可
　　能性的降低。

❹ The new general manager _____ the expense of personnel to buy more machines.

(A) lessens　(B) curtails　(C) diminishes

Ans: (B)。新任總經理為了購買新機具選擇刪減人事費，故應以
　　curtail 來描述此種經費上的縮減。

❺ We _____ our talk when the colleague who likes to gossip comes back.

(A) curtail　(B) lessen　(C) diminish

Ans: (A)。談話的兩人有名愛八卦的同事，因此當他出現了，兩人就
　　結束閒聊，故應以 curtail 來描述此種中斷。

❻ The round table meeting can _____ the tense among all parties involved.

(A) diminish　(B) curtail　(C) lessen

Ans: (C)。本次會議可望使原本緊繃的情勢轉為和緩，故應以
　　diminish 來表達緊張程度的下降。

1 亂世佳人

2 傲慢與偏見

3 理性與感性

4 咆哮山莊

5 小婦人

6 簡愛

Unit 57
小婦人

俏佳人怎麼說

For, with eyes made clear by
many tears, and a heart softened by
the tenderest sorrow —Marmee March

眼因流多淚水而愈益清明，心因飽經憂患而愈益溫厚。——馬區太太

作品概述

　　眼見女兒們為了不同的事情而煩惱，馬區太太試圖以自己的人生經驗開導她們。她以母親的身分告訴女兒們，流淚是難免的，但這些淚不會白流，淚水能讓你們更明辨是非。傷心也是無法避免的，但這些心傷會使你們的心靈更加成長。在這段母親對女兒的教誨中，出現了表哀傷的單字 sorrow，但由於英文中尚有 grief 與 sadness，此篇就以 sorrow、grief，sadness 此三字來作為解說。

文法概述

❧ *Sorrow / grief / sadness* ❧

★ Sorrow

若以 sorrow 表傷心，其情緒強度雖然高，但可以透過與人分享而逐漸抹平，故經常用於表達對於某事的悔恨或是對某人感到抱歉，其常見句型有:S feel sorrow at/for⋯，以下透過範例做進一步說明:

EX I feel sorrow at the wrong decision I have made in this project.

我對自己在此專案所做出的錯誤決定感到悔恨。

→ 說話者過去做了一些錯誤決策，現在對此感到懊悔，故應以 sorrow 此種混合後悔與傷心的情緒。

★ Grief

若以 grief 表傷心，其哀痛程度極高，故多用於是描述某人的過世或是對於困境無能為力所引發的悲傷情緒。其常見句型有: S V with grief 與 Sth is a grief to⋯，以下透過範例做進一步說明:

EX Ken cries with grief when he knows one of his best friend is killed in a car accident.

當得知其中一個好友因車禍過世，肯哀痛地大哭。

→ 讓肯情緒潰堤的原因是朋友因意外過世，故應以 grief 來描述此種哀痛。

EX Betty's drug-addicted husband is a grief to her.

貝蒂吸毒成癮的丈夫讓她萬分痛心。

→ 丈夫有毒癮無法戒除，貝蒂對此卻也無能為力，故應以 grief 來

1 亂世佳人

2 傲慢與偏見

3 理性與感性

4 咆哮山莊

5 小婦人

6 簡愛

描述她心中的哀痛。

★ Sadness

若以 sadness 表傷心，此種負面情緒與 sorrow 最大差異在於其宣洩僅可由本人為之，他人無法為之分勞解憂。有此限制原因在於人悲傷可以沒有理由，因此若要走出這樣的情緒，只能靠自己。其常見句型為: When…, S feel sadness at…，以下透過範例做進一步說明：

EX When I review the picture I took, I feel sadness at one thing I have done.

在回顧自己過去拍的照片時，我對過去所做過的某事感到哀傷。

→ 說話者感傷的原因其他人可能無法理解，更遑論解憂，故應以 sadness 來描述此種哀傷。

實作練習與解析

❶ I feel _____ at the bad attitude I had toward you in past one year.

(A) grief (B) sorrow (C) sadness

Ans: (B)。說話者過去對於對方態度極差，現在對此感到抱歉，故應以 sorrow 來描述此種後悔的態度。

❷ Sam sobs with _____ when knowing his father is murdered.

(A) grief (B) sadness (C) sorrow

Ans: (A)。山姆聽聞父親遭到謀殺，淚水已無法完全宣洩心中的痛，故應以 grief 來表達此哀痛。

❸ Mark's drinking habit is the _____ to his wife.

(A) sorrow　(B) sadness　(C) grief

Ans: (C)。馬克愛喝酒，他太太無法使其戒酒，故應以 grief 來表達馬克太太帶有無助的悲傷情緒。

❹ When looking back to my school day, I feel _____ at the ridiculous things I have done.

(A) sadness　(B) sorrow　(C) grief

Ans: (A)。說話者求學時做過很多荒唐事，現在回想起來很後悔，故應以 sadness 來描述此種懊悔情緒。

❺ Tom feels _____ for misunderstanding what Linda and blame her for bringing the wrong message to him.

(A) grief　(B) sadness　(C) sorrow

Ans: (C)。說話者對於誤解琳達深感抱歉，故應以 sorrow 來表達此種愧疚。

❻ When finding the toy he played in his youth, William feels the _____ at his wasteful attitude at that time.

(A) sadness　(B) grief　(C) sorrow

Ans: (A)。當威廉長大後再看到兒時玩具時，他對於自己那時浪費的態度感到懊悔，故應以 sadness 來描述此種混合後悔與哀傷的情緒。

Unit 58
小婦人

俏佳人怎麼說

Love is the only thing that we can carry with us when we go, and it makes the end so easy. —Beth

愛是我們去世時唯一能夠帶走的東西，
它使得死亡變得如此從容。——貝絲

作品概述

　　在故事的末段，老三貝絲因染上猩紅熱而健康情況日益下滑。貝絲雖然還只是個十幾歲的小女孩，但對生死卻看得很開。眼見家人因為自己可能將不久於人世而感到哀傷，她反而鼓勵大家說，愛讓自己已深感此生無憾，死亡並不會斷開一家人的聯繫，要大家繼續好好生活。在這段看透生死的話語中，出現了表攜帶的單字 carry，但由於英文中尚有 take 與 drag 在語意上與之相近，故本單元特將其並列做解析說明。

文法概述

✎ *Carry / take / drag* ✎

★ **Carry**

若以 carry 表帶走，主要用於描述物體或人移動位置這個「過程」。另當某裝置或建物能將訊號、能源從某一端送至另一端，就概念上也是一種移動，故也可以 carry 來描述此種傳送。其常見句型有:S carry sth from… to…/onto，以下透過範例做進一步說明：

EX I carry a small backpack onto the plane.

我拿了一個小後背包登機。

➔ 說話者把後背包從家裡或是公司帶上飛機，故應以 carry 來描述行李位置的移動。

EX The cables carry the electricity from the city to the mountain.

電纜將電力從城市送往山區。

➔ 電纜的作用就是將電力得以從甲地傳送至乙地，故應以 carry 來描述此種能源的傳輸。

★ **Take**

若以 take 表帶走，經常用於表述在「未經允許」的情況下拿走某物或佔領(佔領可解釋為奪走控制權)。也因為其描述重點在於被誰拿走，故多採用被動式。其常見句型有 S be taken from… by… : ，以下透過範例做進一步說明：

EX The military airport is taken from our army by the enemy.

我軍的軍事機場被敵軍佔領。

1 亂世佳人

2 傲慢與偏見

3 理性與感性

4 咆哮山莊

5 小婦人

6 簡愛

→ 軍事機場的控制權本為我軍所有，但現在遭敵軍奪走，故應以 take 來描述主控權的喪失。

★ Drag

若以 drag 表帶走，所需耗費的精力較多，在手段上較本單元其他兩者激烈。若移動對象是物體，代表移動不易。若移動對象是人，代表被移動的一方可能不願離開。其常見句型有：S drag sth/sb away from…to…，以下透過範例做進一步說明：

EX I drag the heavy wood desk away from the living room to the guest room.

我把笨重的木桌從客廳搬到客房。

→ 說話者必須花很大的力氣才能搬動此木桌，故應以 drag 來描述此移動得困難性。

EX Nancy drags her daughter away from the toy shop.

南希把她的小孩從玩具店硬拉出來。

→ 南希的小孩進入玩具店後可能就賴著不走了，故應以 drag 來描述將小孩帶離的困難度。

實作練習與解析

❶ Ricky _____ a suitcase onto the high speed railway.
(A) takes (B) drags (C) carries
Ans: (C)。瑞奇將把公事包從家裡或公司一路帶上高鐵，故應以 carry 來描述此行李位置的變化情形。

❷ The bridge _____ the traffic across the river from the city to the forest areas.

(A) carries (B) drags (C) takes

Ans: (A)。橋梁聯結的是河流兩岸的交通，故應以 carry 來描述此種車輛來回移動的情況。

❸ My phone which I put in the pocket of my jeans is _____ by the thief.

(A) carried (B) taken (C) dragged

Ans: (B)。偷竊是在未獲當事人許可的情況下強行取走某物，故應以 take 來描述此種不法的拿取。

❹ All of Frank's belongings are _____ by the gangsters.

(A) dragged (B) carried (C) taken

Ans: (C)。匪徒未獲法蘭克的同意，就拿走他所有的行李，故應以 take 來表達此種不法的拿取。

❺ Owen _____ his canoe from the warehouse to his SUV.

(A) drags (B) carries (C) takes

Ans: (A)。獨木舟體積大又重，故應以 drag 來描述奇搬運不易。

❻ I have to _____ my wife away from the shopping mall now in case she buys too many items.

(A) carry (B) drag (C) take

Ans: (B)。說話者的太太愛購物，一旦開始購物就不可能馬上離開，故應以 drag 來描述將其帶離的困難性。

1 亂世佳人

2 傲慢與偏見

3 理性與感性

4 咆哮山莊

5 小婦人

6 簡愛

Unit 59
小婦人

俏佳人怎麼說

I find it poor logic to say that because women are good, women should vote. Men do not vote because they are good; they vote because they are male, and women should vote, not because we are angels and men are animals, but because we are human beings and citizens of this country. —Jo

我覺得這樣的邏輯非常有問題,好的女性就應該順從,男性不順服於人因為他們夠好。當願意順服於人,是因為他們是男性。女性願意順服不是因為女性是天使而男性是動物,而是因為我們都是人類也是這個國家的公民。——喬

作品概念

　　四姐妹中,應屬二姐喬最有想法,因此當有人提出性別足以決定社會地位高低時,她深表不認同。喬認為這個社會是以男性為尊,所謂的好女性就應該順從男性,而男性被尊崇卻不是因為他好,而只是因為他是男性。喬認為不論男性或女性,都是國家的一份子,所以不應有地位之分。在這段清晰的立場表述中,出現了表居民的單字 citizen,但由於英文中

尚 inhabitant、occupant 以及 dweller 在語意上與之相近，故單元特將其並列做解析說明。

文法概述

∽ *Citizen / inhabitant / occupant / tenant* ∾

★ **Citizen**

若以 citizen 表居民，描述是居住者在法律與政治上的狀態。代表某人生於某地(國)或是居住於此多年，因而享有對應的權利。其常見句型有:Sb is the citizen of…，以下透過範例做進一步說明：

EX Tom is the citizen of USA, so he can vote for the President election.

湯姆是美國公民，所以可以參與總統大選。

→ 美國公民都可以投票，故應以 citizen 來描述湯姆在政治與法律上所享有的權利。

★ **Inhabitant**

若以 inhabitant 表居民，強調的是目前正居住在某地的「事實」，故其對象可以為人與動物。其常見句型有: S be the inhabitant of…，以下透過範例做進一步說明：

EX Thomas is the inhabitant of this city.

湯瑪士是該市的居民。

→ 說話者描述的是湯瑪士目前居住於某地的事實，故應以 inhabitant 來描述此種身分。

1 亂世佳人

2 傲慢與偏見

3 理性與感性

4 咆哮山莊

5 小婦人

6 簡愛

★ Occupant

Occupant 是由 occupy 衍生而來，因此若以 occupant 表居民，強調的是空間上的「佔有」，但由於一個人所能佔據的範圍有限，故當以 occupant 表居民時，多意指某一建物或是某一房間內的居住者。其常見句型有: The N's occupant be…，以下透過範例做進一步說明：

EX Nick and Ben are the only two male occupants in this floor.

尼克跟班是本樓層唯二的男性房客。

→ 由於班與尼克所能佔據的空間有限，故應以 occupant 來描述兩人的身分。

★ Tenant

若以 tenant 表居民，在性質在上與本單元其他三者最大不同在於 tenant 需要支付租金才能居住於某建物內。其常見句型有: S be the tenant of …，以下透過範例做進一步說明：

EX I am the tenant of David, so I pay him 500 USD per month.

我是大衛的房客，所以我每月付給他 500 美金的房租。

→ 大衛是房東，說話者付租金才能使用其房子，故應以 tenant 來描述說話者的身分。

實作練習與解析

❶ I am the _____ of this country, so I have the right to enjoy the social welfare.

(A) citizen　(B) inhabitant　(C) tenant　(D) occupant

Ans: (A)。公民才能享有對應的社會福利，故應以 citizen 來描述說話者的身分的特性。

❷ Richard is the _____ of this small town.
(A) tenant　(B) citizen　(C) occupant　(D) inhabitant

Ans: (D)。說話者描述的是理查目前居住於某地的事實，故應以 inhabitant 來描述他的身分。

❸ I am the only female _____ in this apartment.
(A) citizen　(B) tenant　(C) inhabitant　(D) occupant

Ans: (D)。說話者僅佔據公寓中一小部分的使用空間，故應以 occupant 來描述其身分。

❹ Linda is the _____ of mine, so she pays me 300 USD as the rent.
(A) tenant　(B) inhabitant　(C) occupant　(D) citizen

Ans: (A)。琳達雖是空間的使用者，但說話者才是所有權擁有者，故應以 tenant 來描述琳達的身分。

❺ Though the house is extremely old, there are still few _____ .
(A) occupants　(B) inhabitant　(C) citizens　(D) tenants

Ans: (A)。由於是在描述建物中有住那些人，故應以 occupant 來說明這些房客的身分特性。

1 亂世佳人

2 傲慢與偏見

3 理性與感性

4 咆哮山莊

5 小婦人

6 簡愛

Unit 60
小婦人

俏佳人怎麼說

I would rather Meg marry for love and
be a poor man's wife than marry for riches
and lose her self-respect. —Marmee March

我寧願瑪格妳嫁妳所愛，成為窮人的太太，
也不願妳為了財富而結婚，最後失去了自尊。——馬區太太

作品概述

　　正所謂人窮志不窮，馬區一家雖然不富有，但馬區太太要女兒們千萬別為了財富而犧牲了愛情。她寧願女兒嫁給一名窮人，但兩人彼此相愛，也不願女兒嫁給有錢人，但卻因此失去自尊。在這段母親勉勵女兒的話語中，出現了表尊嚴的單字 self-respcet，在英文中尚有 dignity majesty 在語意上與之相似，故本單元特將其並列做解析說明。

文法概述

Self-respect / dignity / majesty

★ **Self-respect**

若以 self-respect 表尊嚴，尤其字構 self 與 respect 二字來看，是以「自我尊重」為出發點。也因為是自己檢視自己，故 self-respect 無需考慮別人是否認同。其常見句型有:S could/might keep/lose one's self-respect if…，以下透過範例做進一步說明：

EX You could keep your self-respect if you confess now, or you will lose your face face in public

如果現在坦白的話，你還可保有自尊，否則就準備在眾人面前丟臉。

→ 說話者給對方一次說實話的機會，若對方不肯，就不再給予尊重，故應以 self-respect 來描述對方尚存的尊嚴。

★ **Dignity**

若以 dignity 表尊嚴，贏得此種尊重的原因是能夠冷靜、嚴肅地讓一切事情得到控制。而正所謂術業有專攻，且隔行如隔山，故 dignity 也經常用於描述對於某種職業執行其專業時，我們應該給予的基本尊重。其常見句型有:S should … with dignity 以下透過範例做進一步說明：

EX Everyone should work with dignity.

每個人都應有尊嚴地工作。

→ 工作沒有貴賤之分，故說話者以 dignity 來描述各種職務都有其值得尊重之處。

1 亂世佳人

2 傲慢與偏見

3 理性與感性

4 咆哮山莊

5 小婦人

6 簡愛

★ Esteem

若以 esteem 表尊嚴，是因為對某人「敬重」或「欽佩」，進而給予好評。也因為有關價值上的認同，esteem 就無法像 self-respect 那樣不在乎他人之意見，須接受公評。其常見句型有: S have esteem for⋯，以下透過範例做進一步說明:

EX The society has great esteem for lawyers.
社會對於律師相當尊崇。

→ 說話者認為律師享有極高社會評價，故應以 esteem 來描述大眾對此職業的敬重。

實作練習與解析

❶ You might lose your _____ soon if you refuse to cooperate with us to continue the investigation.
(A) self-respect   (B) dignity   (C) esteem
Ans: (A)。說話者給予對方一次配合的機會，若不從則不再替其保留顏面，故應以 self-respect 來描述對方尚餘的尊嚴。

❷ Men are born equal, so all walks of life in our country should work with _____
(A) esteem   (B) dignity   (C) self-respect
Ans: (B)。各行各業都有值得被尊敬的專業之處，故應以 dignity 來描述此種尊重。

❸ I have great _____ for firefighters because they always take risk to save people in danger.

(A) dignity   (B) esteem   (C) self-respect

Ans: (B)。說話者對於消防人員冒險救人感到敬佩，故應以 esteem 來表達說話者心中的正面評價。

❹ You can keep your _____ if you tell me the truth, or I will let you pay for not doing so.

(A) dignity   (B) esteem   (C) self-respect

Ans: (C)。說話者要對方說實話，否則走著瞧，故應以 self-respect 來描述對方尚存的尊嚴。

❺ Everyone works as a tiny screw of this society, so he or she should live with _____.

(A) self-respect   (B) dignity   (C) esteem

Ans: (B)。每個人對於社會都有其貢獻，故應以 dignity 來描述此種基本尊重。

❻ We should have great ___ for the police because they keep the society in an order.

(A) dignity   (B) self-respect   (C) esteem

Ans: (C)。說話者認為警察維持社會秩序貢獻卓著，故應以 esteem 來描述他心中對警察的尊敬。

1 亂世佳人

2 傲慢與偏見

3 理性與感性

4 咆哮山莊

5 小婦人

6 簡愛

Unit 61
小婦人

俏佳人怎麼說

Oh, Jo. Jo, you have so many extraordinary gifts; how can you expect to lead an ordinary life? You're ready to go out and - and find a good use for your talent. Tho' I don't know what I shall do without my Jo. Go, and embrace your liberty. And see what wonderful things come of it.—Marmee March

噢!喬!喬!你有如此出眾的天賦,怎能甘於過著一般的生活呢!你應該出去闖闖,善用自己的才能。雖然我不知道沒有你在身邊我該怎麼辦,但你還是該走,去用擁抱屬於你的自由,去看看這世界有多美。——馬區太太

作品概念

　　雖然馬區太太非常希望女兒們可以一直陪在自己身邊,但也深知她們終將長大成人,嫁作人婦或是追尋理想,終有必須放手的一天。特別是針對約瑟芬,馬區太太知道她天資聰穎,所以不該只過著平凡的人生,應當出去闖盪,才不枉費這些才能。在這段望女成鳳的殷殷期盼中,出現了表

「平凡」的單字 ordinary，但由於英文中尚有 common、normal、usual 在語意與用法上近似，故本單元特將其並列做解析說明。

文法概述

Ordinary / common / normal / usual

★ **Ordinary**

若以 ordinary 來表一般，代表我們將事物大致分成三大區塊:好的、一般的與壞的，而 ordinary 指的就是一般的。其常見句型有: S… in an ordinary way 與 S be ordinary 以下透過範例做進一步說明:

EX Without your reminding, I will do it in ordinary way.

如果沒有你提醒，我就會照一般的方法去做。

→ 多虧對方的提醒，否則說話者會按多數人採用的方式去做某事，故應以 ordinary 來表達此種方法的特性。

★ **Common**

若以 common 來表一般，代表所描述的事物隨處可見或是稀鬆平常，或是已經成為某種共識或習慣。其常見句型有:It is common to…，以下透過範例做進一步說明:

EX It is common to see people wear sunglasses in the beach.

海邊看到有人戴太陽眼鏡是很稀鬆平常的。

→ 海邊通常太陽很大，戴太陽眼睛遮陽實屬正常，故應以 common 來描述使用此種配件的普遍性。

1 亂世佳人

2 傲慢與偏見

3 理性與感性

4 咆哮山莊

5 小婦人

6 簡愛

★ Normal

若以 normal 來表一般，表示所描述的事物有其標準可供對照，而現在所描述的狀態正好符合此標準。其常見句型有:It is normal for…to…，以下透過範例做進一步說明：

EX It is normal for consumers to return the product when they find that they buy the wrong items.

當消費者發現自己買錯東西時，拿去退貨很正常。

→ 除非商家有特別規定，否則買錯東西都可以退，故應以 normal 來描述此種規範的一般性。

★ Usual

若以 usual 來表一般，但表示所描述的事物不會跟著時間變動。更簡單來說，就是過去這樣，現在這樣，到未來也還是這樣。其常見句型有: S V, as usual，以下透過範例做進一步說明：

EX They go to that restaurant for dinner, as usual.

他們一如往常的前往那間餐廳吃晚飯。

→ 說話者描述的對象經常至該餐廳用餐，今日也如此，故應以 usual 來描述此種重複性。

實作練習與解析

❶ I write my report in a(n) _____ way to get an acceptable score.

(A) normal (B) usual (C) ordinary (D) common

Ans: (C)。說話者只求能夠拿到一個可接受的分數，故報告也就中規中矩地寫，故應以 ordinary 來描述其手法的一般性。

❷ His performance is no _____ as a freshman in a professional baseball league.

(A) ordinary   (B) common   (C) usual   (D) normal

Ans: (A)。說話者認為這位職棒新秀雖然初入聯盟但毫不生澀,故應
以 no ordinary 來描述其不凡。

❸ It is a(n) _____ sense that you should not touch any electricity appliance when your hands are wet.

(A) normal   (B) ordinary   (C) usual   (D) common

Ans: (D)。多數人都知道雙手潮濕再去觸碰電器容易觸電,故應以
common來表示此概念的普遍性。

❹ It is _____ for us to find some reference when we are writing papers, but we have to note the source to respect others' intellectual property.

(A) common   (B) ordinary   (C) usual   (D) normal

Ans: (D)。寫文章參考別人的想法很正常,但要註明出處以示尊重。
故應以 normal 來描述此原則已獲廣泛認可。

❺ Jack donates the clothing he doesn't put on for long this year to the charity, as _____ .

(A) usual   (B) common   (C) normal   (D) ordinary

Ans: (A)。傑克每年都會今年很少穿衣物捐給慈善機構,今年也如
此,故應以 usual 來描述此舉的重複性。

1 亂世佳人

2 傲慢與偏見

3 理性與感性

4 咆哮山莊

5 小婦人

6 簡愛

Unit 62
小婦人

If I weren't going to be a writer I'd go to New York and pursue the stage. Are you shocked?—Jo

如果我沒成為作家的話，我想會去紐約尋找屬於我的舞台。
我這樣說有讓你覺得驚訝嗎？——喬

作品概述

　　熱愛寫作的二姊約瑟芬一直以來都想成為作家，因此當這個夢想無法在家鄉實現時，她想到外地闖看看。但追夢等同必須離鄉背井，離開家人也離開她的好友勞里，因此喬特地問勞里在知道自己的計畫後，是否感到驚訝。在這段喬所提出的人生規劃中，出現了表「追尋」的單字 pursue，但由於英文中尚有 chase 與 seek 在語意及用法上與之相似，故本單元特將其並列做解析說明。

文法概述

✎ *Pursue / chase / seek* ✎

★ Pursue

若以 pursue 表追尋，其目的大致分為三種，一是抓住或是殺掉其鎖定目標，二是無法擺脫某事物，三是朝設定的目標努力。其常見句型有:S be pursued by…與 S pursue the…of…，以下透過範例做解析說明：

EX The suspicious is pursued by the police.

警方在追緝可疑車輛。

➜ 警方緊追該車的目的就是要使其停車受檢，故應以 pursue 來描述此類型的跟隨。

EX Joseph has been pursued by misfortune for weeks.

喬瑟夫近幾週來運勢不佳。

➜ 喬瑟夫過去幾週都厄運纏身，故應以 chase 來描述壞運的難以擺脫。

EX He decides to pursue the goal of perfection in his drawing skills.

他決定追求繪畫技巧上的完美。

➜ 說話者所描述的對象希望自己的繪畫技巧可以越來越好，故應以 pursue 來描述其所付出的努力。

★ Chase

若以 chase 表追尋，代表這樣的跟隨有其急迫性，目的是要抓住所追趕的目標或是找出所需的事物。其常見句型有 S chase after…

1 亂世佳人

2 傲慢與偏見

3 理性與感性

4 咆哮山莊

5 小婦人

6 簡愛

to…:，以下透過範例做解析說明：

EX The police chase after the gangster to make him drop the weapon to surrender.

警方緊追歹徒好使其棄械投降。

→ 警察追緝歹徒的目的就是要將其繩之以法，故應以 chase 此種執法時的緊追不捨。

★ seek

若以 seek 表追尋，目的是尋找或取得某事物。一般來說，seek 所搜尋的目標，又以無形事物居多，例如保護、認同等。其常見句型有: S be seeking for…，以下透過範例做解析說明：

EX The refugees are seeking for the political asylum.

難民們正尋求政治庇護。

→ 難民由於流離失所，需要人保護，故應以 seek 來描述對無形事物的追求。

實作練習與解析

❶ The wild goose is _____ by hunters

(A) pursued   (B) chased   (C) sought

Ans: (A)。獵人追趕獵物的目的是要將其擊殺，故應以 pursue 來描述此種緊追不捨。

❷ Hank is _____ by the bad luck today.

(A) sought   (B) pursued   (C) chased

Ans: (B)。漢克今天總是與好運沾不上邊，故應以 pursue 來描述他的壞運纏身。

❸ I decide to go abroad to ＿＿＿＿ my further study.
(A) chase　(B) seek　(C) pursue

Ans: (C)。說話者決定要進修，故應以 pursue 來表達對目標的追求。

❹ Mary ＿＿＿＿ around the city to find the parts she needs in urgent.
(A) pursued　(B) chased　(C) seeked

Ans: (B)。瑪莉急需某個零件，因而四處奔波。故應以 chase 來表達四處奔走之意。

❺ Since Ryder underestimates the demand of the manpower, now he has no choice but to ＿＿＿＿ for help.
(A) chase　(B) pursre　(C) seek

Ans: (C)。萊德低估人力需求，導致需要協助，故應以 seek 來描述此種非具體事物的尋求。

❻ The helicopter and police car are ＿＿＿＿ after the gangster who just commits the bank robbery.
(A) chased　(B) pursued　(C) sought

Ans: (A)。警方派出警車與警用直升機的目的是要抓到搶匪，故應以 chase 來描述此種窮追不捨。

Part **6**

Week 6 簡愛

Unit 63
簡愛

俏佳人怎麼說

I am glad you are no relation of mine.
I will never call you aunt as long as I live.
I will never come to see you when I am grown up;
and if any asks me how I liked you, and how you
treated me, I will say the very thought of
you makes me sick.—Jane Eyre

我很高興你跟我互不相干。只要我活著,我就不會在叫你一聲舅媽。我長大後也絕對不會來探望你。如果有人問起我說我喜不喜歡你,以及你如何對待我,我會說你讓我感到反感。——簡愛

作品概念

女主角簡愛是個孤兒,因此自幼就被舅媽里德太太收養。簡愛看似不再孤單,但事實上舅媽對她卻是百般虐待,因此當簡愛得知自己能夠離開此處時,心中是帶有喜悅的,也因此說出自己很慶幸從此不在與舅媽有牽連,即使後來長大成人了,也絕對不會回來探望她,最後甚至以我對你感到反感來總結幾年下來對於舅媽的評價。在這段宣洩心中不滿的話語中,出現了表「反感」的單字 sick,但由於英文中尚有 antipathy 與

disfavou\r 在語意上與之相似，故本單元特將其並列做解析說明。

文法概述

～ *Sick / antipathy / disfavour* ～

★ Sick

除表因疾病所導致的身心理不適外，sick 也經常用於表達無法忍受對方的行為或視言論，導致心理上有芥蒂，以致於無法與之好好相處。其常見句型有: S be sick with sb /of N，以下透過範例做進一步說明：

EX I am sick with my colleague Green for always being impolite to me.

我對同事格林反感，因為他總是對我不禮貌。

→ 說話者無法忍受有人對他不禮貌，但偏偏格林就觸碰此底限，故應以 sick 來描述說話者的憤怒。

EX I am sick of your nonsense.

我對你的胡說八道反感。

→ 說話者討厭別人跟他講一堆沒意義的話，故應以 sick 來表達當對方在胡說八道時說話者心中的不悅。

★ Antipathy

Antipathy 是 sympathy(同情)的反意詞，anti 為反對的字首，pathy 意為心理狀態，兩者相加，即為反感之意，用於表達對某事物的強烈厭惡或惱怒。其常見句型有: S feel antipathy toward/against/between…，以下透過範例做進一步說明：

1 亂世佳人

2 傲慢與偏見

3 理性與感性

4 咆哮山莊

5 小婦人

6 簡愛

EX Joe is the person who likes to work alone, so he has strong antipathy to teamwork.

喬喜歡獨立作業，因此他對於團隊合作反感。

→ 喬凡事喜歡自己來，與人共事反而不自在，故應以 antipathy 來表達他對合作的不適應。

★ Disfavor

Favor 代表支持或贊同某事物，但若在加上 dis 這個不…的字首，語意上就變成不支持，故也可廣意解釋為反感。其常見句型有: S … with disfavor 與 S fall into disfavor，以下透過範例做進一步說明:

EX He sits down and looks the food on the table with disfavor.

他坐下來並且以嫌惡的眼神看著桌上的食物。。

→ 桌上的食物不為說話者描述的對象所喜愛，故應以 disfavor 來描述其好惡。

EX Since your idea is too modern to the conservative, it falls into disfavor in the long run in the meeting.

你的想法對保守派來說太過前衛，因此最終未於會議中獲得支持。

→ 保守人士往往無法接受較新穎的想法，故應以 disfavor 來描述此種想法上的不認同。

實作練習與解析

❶ I am _____ with my roommate for always being selfish.
(A) disfavor   (B) sick   (C) antipathy

Ans: (B)。說話者無法忍受室友的自私，故應以 sick 來描述他心中的反感。

❷ Though Evans is a famous singer, he has _____ to the press.

(A) antipathy (B) sick (C) disfavor

Ans: (A)。雖然伊凡斯是有名的歌手，但卻不喜歡接受採訪，故應以 antipathy 來描述他對媒體的厭惡。

❸ Even though we try our best to meet his needs, him still looks our staff with _____

(A) sick (B) disfavor (C) antipathy

Ans: (B)。雖然說話者盡力想滿足對方需求，但對方始終不滿意，故應以 disfavor 來描述對方所表現出的嫌惡。

❹ Your idea is somehow unrealistic, so I am not surprised it falls into _____ in the final decision making.

(A) disfavor (B) sick (C) antipathy

Ans: (A)。對方所提出的想法最後因為有些許的不切實際而遭否決，故應以 disfavor 來描述此種否定。

❺ I am a person who likes teamwork, so I have _____ toward working alone.

(A) sick (B) disfavor (C) antipathy

Ans: (C)。說話者喜歡團隊合作更勝於單打獨鬥，故應以 disfavor 來描述他對獨立作業的排斥。

1 亂世佳人

2 傲慢與偏見

3 理性與感性

4 咆哮山莊

5 小婦人

6 簡愛

Unit 64
簡愛

俏佳人怎麼說

If people were always kind and obedient
to those who are cruel and unjust; the wicked
people would have it all their own way: they
would never feel afraid, and so they would never alter,
but would grow worse and worse.—Jane Eyre

如果人們能那些對他們殘忍不公正的人仁慈,這些壞蛋就會恣意橫
行。他們將有恃無恐,死性不改,最後變本加厲。——簡愛。

作品概述

　　簡愛生為孤女,自幼便命運多舛,不論是在舅媽家,或是到了寄養學
校,皆遭百般虐待。這樣不平順的成長歷程,使她覺得遭受不公平待遇就
應反抗,默默承受只會使壞人變本加厲。在這段簡愛向好友海倫吐露的心
聲中,出現了表順從的單字 obedient,但由於英文中尚有
submissive、 yielding 在語意與用法上與之相似,故本單元特將其並
列做解析説明。

文法概述

Obedient / Submissive / yielding

★ Obedient

若以 obedient 表順服，代表願意接受目前掌握權力的某人指揮，依其指示去行事。另由於當人訓練動物時，動物也是依照我們的指示行動，故 obedient 也可用來描述寵物或牲畜對人類的服從。其常見句型有: S be obedient to⋯，以下透過範例做進一步說明：

EX Students should be obedient to their teachers in the classroom.

在教室裡學生應服從老師。

→ 做為教導者，老師在教室內掌握一定的權力，故說話者以 obedient 來描述學生應服從指揮。

EX My dog is obedient to my order.

我的狗很聽從我的指揮。

→ 動物受過訓練後，會聽從主人的指揮，故應以 obedient 來描述寵物對主人的服從。

★ Submissive

Submissive 是由 submit(屈服)衍生而來，因此若以之表達順服，不論是出於自願或是被迫，服從者皆願意接受指揮者發號施令。的其常見句型有:S be submissive to⋯，以下透過範例做進一步說明：

EX He is submissive to practical suggestions from his peers.

他願意接受同儕所提出具建設性的建議。

→ 若對方提出的建議具有可行性，說話者願意照做，故應以

1 亂世佳人

2 傲慢與偏見

3 理性與感性

4 咆哮山莊

5 小婦人

6 簡愛

submissive 來表達願意接受指教。

★ Yielding

若以 yielding 表屈服，經常用於表達願意犧牲或是貢獻某項事物，以達到自己所期望的目地。做其常見句型有 S …in yielding to…，以下透過範例做進一步說明：

EX The sordid businessman sell out the principle in yielding to the domination of the market.

市儈的商人出賣原則只為獨佔市場。

➜ 有些商人覺得賺錢最重要，因此即使要違背誠信原則，他也願意。故應以 yielding 來描述他的不擇手段。

實作練習與解析

❶ Before you finish the training, you should be _____ to the trainer.

(A) yielding   (B) submissive   (C) obedient

Ans: (C)。參與訓練時，學員聽從指揮方可完成訓練，故應以 obedient 來表達服從。

❷ Since the dog is _____ to the trainer in the training, the trainer gives it some fresh meat as the reward.

(A) obedient   (B) submissive   (C) yielding

Ans: (A)。在訓練動物時，當動物願意依指令動作，訓練員通常會給予獎勵，故應以 obedient 來表達狗對訓練員的服從。

❸ Though I am your supervisor, I am _____ to the practical suggestion.

(A) yielding (B) submissive (C) obedient

Ans: (B)。雖然身為主管，但如果下屬的建議是有建設性的，說話者願意照辦。故應以 submissive 來表達他願對事不對人。

❹ The broker smuggles the weapon the rebel army in _____ to the great commission.

(A) submissive (B) obedient (C) yielding

Ans: (C)。掮客匯了賺取大筆傭金，願意替叛軍走私軍火，故應以 yielding 來表達只要有錢賺，殺頭的生意也有人會做。

❺ After your presentation, now I am _____ to the modification you propose.

(A) obedient (B) submissive (C) yielding

Ans: (B)。聽取簡報過後，說話者願意接受對方所提出的修正，故應以 submissive 來描述願意認同。

❻ The greedy double spy sells the information to the both sides in_____ to get more commission.

(A) yielding (B) obedient (C) submissive

Ans: (A)。雙面間諜把情報同時透露給對立的雙方，以便賺取更多傭金，故應以 yielding 來描述他願意為了錢承擔巨大風險。

1 亂世佳人
2 傲慢與偏見
3 理性與感性
4 咆哮山莊
5 小婦人
6 簡愛

Unit 65
簡愛

俏佳人怎麼說

I can so clearly distinguish between the criminal and his crime; I can so sincerely forgive the first while I abhor the last. —Helen Burns

我能清楚地區分罪犯與其所犯的罪,我能夠真心的原諒前者,但卻厭惡後者。——海倫・柏恩斯

作品概念

　　海倫跟簡愛雖然是好友,但兩人的個性卻是天差地遠。簡愛認為人生在世就該為自己討公道,但海倫卻認為死後世界的救贖才是重點。海倫認為靈魂與肉體是可獨立的,因而説出她能夠原諒犯罪的那個人,但卻不能原諒罪本身。在這段海倫表述其信仰的話語中,出現了表「區分」的單字distinguish,但由於英文中尚有 differentiate 與 discriminate 在語意與用法上與之相似,故本單元特將其並列做解析説明。

文法概述

Distinguish / differentiate / discriminate

★ **Distinguish**

若以 distinguish 表區分，代表某人能夠從正面角度發現或是理解具「相似性」或「對立性」的兩個事物的不同處為何。或是希望自己能夠與眾不同，進而為人所羨慕或景仰。其常見句型有：S can distinguish… between/from…與 S distinguish oneself in…，以下透過範例做進一步說明：

EX I can distinguish the difference between British English and American English.

我能夠分辨美式英語跟英式英語的差別。

→ 雖同為英語，說話者知道美式英語與英式英語的差異處在哪，故應以 distinguish 來表示他能有效辨別。

EX Jason distinguishes himself in the field of performance.

傑森讓他自己在表演領域出類拔萃。

→ 傑森現在已成為出色的表演者，故應以 distinguish 來表達他比一般表演者更加傑出。

★ **Differentiate**

由於 differentiate 是由 different 衍生而來，若以之表區別，代表可由此分辨出兩相比較事物的差異點為何，且其比較的切入角度比較為中性。其常見句型有：S differentiate between … and …，以下透過範例做進一步說明：

EX We can differentiate the quality between excellent ones and standard ones by their colors.

我們能夠由顏色分辨高級與一般品質的差別為何。

→ 物品等級不同，其品質自然也不同，故應以 differentiate 來表達能夠分辨當中差異。

★ Discriminate

若以 discriminate 表區分，被比較的事物通常在群體中遭到不好的對待，也形成許多人所最熟悉的語意「歧視」，故本單字所表達的區別，其切入角度在本單元三者中屬於負面，其常見句型有：S discriminate against/in favor of…，以下透過範例做進一步說明：

EX The new law discriminates against the foreign labors.

新法歧視外籍勞工。

→ 若依此法案行事，外籍勞工的權益未獲得保障，故應以 discriminate 來描述此種不平等對待。

實作練習與解析

❶ You can easily _____ between traditional Chinese character and simplified Chinese character

(A) differentiate (B) discriminate (C) distinguish

Ans: (C)。繁體中文字與簡體中文字有相同也有相異之處，故說話者以 distinguish 來表達能夠找出當中差異。

❷ Can you _____ between the classic Jazz and new Jazz?

(A) distinguish (B) discriminate (C) differentiate

Ans: (A)。傳統爵士與新爵士有相似性，但在某些方面又大相逕庭，故應以 distinguish 來表達能夠找出當中差異。

❸ To _____ herself in this field, Mandy practices more than 14 hours a day.

(A) discriminate　(B) differentiate　(C) distinguish

Ans: (C)。蔓蒂每天練習超過 14 小時，目地是要在該領域終有一席之地，故應以 distinguish 來解釋她為何如此努力。

❹ Though we are not experts, we still can _____ the quality between good and normal by the texture.

(A) differentiate　(B) distinguish　(C) discriminate

Ans: (A)。說話者表示自己雖然非專家，但可從東西的質地分出好與普通，故應以 differentiate 來描述此種辨別能力。

❺ Since this park is a place for all, its facility should not _____ against any group.

(A) differentiate　(B) discriminate　(C) distinguish

Ans: (B)。公園屬於全民皆可使用的空間，若其設施造成任何族群不便，應以 discriminate 來描述。

❻ This regulation _____ in favor of the wealth.

(A) discriminates　(B) distinguish　(C) differentiate

Ans: (A)。此規定對於有錢人較有利，故應以 discriminate 來描述其他族群遭受不平等對待。

Unit 66
簡愛

俏佳人怎麼說

If all the world hated you, and believed
you wicked, while your own conscience approved
you, and absolved you from guilt, you would
not be without friends. —Helen Burns

如果整個世界都討厭你，還覺得你很壞，但你的良心過得去，並赦免
你的罪，你就不用擔心自己沒有朋友。——海倫・柏恩斯

作品概述

　　簡愛一直認為教育可以改變她的一生，但偏偏最後成就她的卻不是教育，她在舅媽家所學的，並未獲得學校的認同，面對這樣的落差，好友海倫鼓勵她，只要自己對得起自己的良心，就算覺得整個世界都不認同你，你還是找得到跟你志同道合的人。在這段朋友的鼓勵話語中，出現了表「壞的」的單字 wicked，但由於在英文中尚有 evil、sinful、vicious 在語意與用法皆與之相似，故本單元特將其並列作解析說明。

文法概述

❧ *Wicked / evil / sinful / vicious* ❧

★ Wicked

若以 wicked 表壞的，經常用於表達企圖傷害某人，或是用明知不好但卻很吸引人的方式來對待別人。其常見句型有:It is a wicked N to…與 S wicked N….，以下透過範例做進一步說明：

EX You wicked child—finish your meal soon or you will get no candy.
你這個愛搗蛋的小朋友!快把飯吃完，否則你就沒糖果了!

→ 小朋友打鬧不乖乖吃飯，說話者明知這不對，但也沒生氣，故應以 wicked 來描述小朋友的調皮。

★ Evil

若以 evil 表壞的，代表此種行為「違反道德紀律」或是非常「殘忍」，故最終往往也會被制裁。其常見句型有: S be Ved for one's evil…，以下透過範例做進一步說明：

EX The cunning businessman is punished for his evil conspiracy in the long run
狡猾的商人最終還是因為其邪惡陰謀受到懲罰。

→ 商場上雖然利益掛帥，帶還是有其道德底限，故應以 evil 來描述超過此限應受懲罰。

★ Sinful

罪惡大致分為「觸犯規定」行為與「有違道德」兩類，若以 sinful 來表達「壞的」，傳達的就是此事不符合規定，或是做了讓人充滿罪惡感。

其常見句型有: N be a sinful…of…，以下透過範例做進一步說明：

EX Buying a famous brand watch is a sinful consumption of money for me.

花大錢買名錶讓我充滿罪惡感。

→ 花大錢買名牌讓說話者渾身不自在，故應以 sinful 來描述他當前的心理狀態。

★ Vicious

若以 vicious 表壞的，多指稱有意對某事物造成嚴重傷害或破壞，以及某種情況或話語會造成身心理上的不適。其常見句型有: N be the most vicious N …have pp 與 S have got a vicious…，以下透過範例做進一步說明：

EX This terrorist attack is the most vicious one that the police have seen in the past few years.

本次恐怖攻擊為警方過去幾年來所見最殘暴的一次。

→ 警方過去處理過不只一次的恐攻，但這次最殘忍，故應以 vicious 來強調其嚴重性。

實作練習與解析

❶ It is a _____thing for my brother to do, so I can tell you now he will reject this cooperation.

(A) wicked   (B) sinful   (C) vicious   (D) evil

Ans: (A)。說話者知道自己兄弟的處事原則，故應以 wicked 來強調傷天害理之事他兄弟絕對敬謝不敏。

❷ You _____ little boy— finish your homework first and then I will take you to the shopping mall.
(A) sinful (B) evil (C) wicked (D) vicious
Ans: (C)。小男孩貪玩不想寫作業,但説話者並沒生氣,只是要他快點做完,故應以 wicked 來描述男孩的調皮。

❸ Don't try to cheat consumers, or you will be punished for your _____ tricks.
(A) sinful (B) wicked (C) vicious (D) evil
Ans: (D)。做壞事最終一定難逃懲罰,故應以 evil 來描述商人唬弄消費者的手段實屬惡劣。

❹ Buying a fancy jewelry is a _____ waste of money.
(A) evil (B) wicked (C) vicious (D) sinful
Ans: (D)。花錢買昂貴珠寶是浪費錢的,故應以 sinful 來描述她當下帶有罪惡感的心情。

❺ The _____ terrorist attack cause hundreds of injuries, so the hospital nearby is filled with the patient of this disaster.
(A) sinful (B) vicious (C) wicked (D) evil
Ans: (B)。恐怖攻擊造成上百人受傷,塞滿鄰近醫院,故應以 vicious 來描述此攻擊的殘忍。

❻ Tom has got a _____ cold, so he takes a sick leave today.
(A) vicious (B) sinful (C) evil (D) wicked
Ans: (A)。湯姆因重感冒到讓他無法來上班,故應以 vicious 來表達病症的嚴重性。

1 亂世佳人

2 傲慢與偏見

3 理性與感性

4 咆哮山莊

5 小婦人

6 簡愛

Unit 67
簡愛

🔍 俏佳人怎麼說

It is in vain to say human beings ought to
be satisfied with tranquility: they must have
action; and they will make it if they cannot find it. —Jane Eyre
勸人應滿足平靜是徒勞無功的。因為他們必須有所行動,且如果他們
無法獲得平靜,就會想辦法找到。——簡愛

作品概述

對簡愛來說,人生就是場奮鬥。秉持這樣的想法,簡愛認為勸人安於現狀,基本上是徒勞無功的。人只要覺得現況不如預期,就會汲汲營營地追求改變。在這段簡愛表達其人生哲學的話語中,出現了表「平靜」的單字 tranquility,但由於英文中尚有 peace 與 serenity 在用法上與之相似,故本單元特將其並列做解析說明。

文法概述

✎ *Tranquility / peace / serenity* ✎

★ **Tranquility**

若以 tranquility 表平靜，描述的是一種安靜祥和的狀態。在此狀態下，沒有噪音、暴力、擔憂等負面因子存在。其常見句型有 S V in tranquility，以下透過範例做進一步說明：

EX I live in tranquility in rural area, so moving back to the big city won't be the option for me now.

住在鄉下讓我覺得平靜，所以現在我不可能再搬回大都市。

➔ 鄉下的生活環境帶給說話者一種平和的氛圍，故應以 tranquility 來描述此種狀態。

★ **Peace**

若以 peace 表平靜，描述的是一種在無需簽定任何條款或合約的前提下，但能免於戰爭或暴力威脅的狀態。其常見句型有: S V in peace，以下透過範例做進一步說明：

EX After a long talk, now we final live in peace with our neighbors.

在與鄰居們長談後，我們現在終於能和平共處。

➔ 說話者原本與鄰居可能有衝突，但釐清原因後，彼此已握手言和，故應以 peace 來描述此狀態。

★ **Serenity**

若以 serenity 表平靜，雖同表安靜祥和的狀態，但卻多了一種無需擔心任何事情的氛圍。其常見句型有: S remain one's serenity in…，

1 亂世佳人

2 傲慢與偏見

3 理性與感性

4 咆哮山莊

5 小婦人

6 簡愛

以下透過範例做進一步說明：

EX Even everything is in a mess, James still remains his serenity.

雖然一切亂糟糟，但詹姆士仍能保持平靜。

→ 雖然狀況混亂，但詹姆士並未因此亂了手腳，故應以 serenity 來描述他的沉著。

實作練習與解析

❶ I live in _____ in my small apartment now, so I decide not to move in the coming few years.
(A) tranquility　(B) peace　(C) serenity

Ans: (A)。說話者很滿意現在所住的公寓，未來暫無搬家計畫，故應以 tranquility 來描述現況所帶來的平靜。

❷ My neighbors often make noises in the midnight, so I can't live in_____ in the room I rent.
(A) serenity　(B) tranquility　(C) peace

Ans: (B)。說話者的鄰居經常製造噪音，令其難以忍受，故應以 can't live in tranquility 來描述他的不堪其擾。

❸ After a three-month war, the two countries finally cease the fire to live in _____.
(A) tranquility　(B) serenity　(C) peace

Ans: (C)。兩國原本處於戰爭狀態，現在終於停火，故應以 peace 來描述其和平相處。

❹ After a long talk, Tom and I can work in _____now.

(A) peace   (B) tranquility   (C) serenity

Ans: (A)。湯姆跟說話者之前可能有過節，但現在盡釋前嫌，故應以 peace 來描述兩人又可和平共處。

❺ Though everything is in chaos, Tim remains his _____ in such a circumstance.

(A) tranquility   (B) peace   (C) serenity

Ans: (C)。雖然情況一團亂，但提姆未因此自亂手腳，故應以 serenity 來描述他的沉著冷靜。

❻ This problem is too complicated, so I think I can't keep my ___ _____ in dealing with it.

(A) serenity   (B) tranquility   (C) peace

Ans: (A)。由於問題太過複雜，說話者自認無法冷靜處理，故應以 can't keep my serenity 來描述他的手忙腳亂。

1 亂世佳人 2 傲慢與偏見 3 理性與感性 4 咆哮山莊 5 小婦人 6 簡愛

Unit 68
簡愛

俏佳人怎麼說

It is not violence that best
overcomes hate — nor vengeance that
most certainly heals injury. —Helen Burns

暴力不能消除仇恨，一如報仇絕對無法抹滅傷害。——海倫・柏恩斯

作品概述

　　做為一名虔誠的基督徒，海倫的宗教信仰深深影響的做人處事。不同於簡愛人的有仇必報，海倫認為暴力無法化解仇恨，報仇更無法讓已受到的傷害得以撫平。在這段表現基督教以德報怨的思想話語中，出現了表戰勝的單字 overcome，但由於英文中尚有 conquer 與 overpower 在用法上與之相似，故本單元特將其並列做解析說明。

文法概述

Overcome / conquer / overpower

★ Overcome

　　若以 overcome 表戰勝，代表已成功擊敗某人，或是讓一切在掌控之

中。其常見句型有: S overcome … in…與 S overcome one's … in…，以下透過範例做進一步說明：

EX I overcome my main competitor Sam in the final and win the champion of this tennis match.
我打敗最大的對手山姆贏得本次網球賽的冠軍。
→ 要打敗對手才能奪冠，故應以 overcome 來描述說話者已成功達標。

EX Tom overcomes his anxiety to deliver a speech in public.
湯姆克服自己的焦慮成功公開發表演說。
→ 湯姆原本無法在眾人前演說，但後來他突破自我了，故應用 overcome 來表達終於克服困難。

★ **Conquer**
若以 conquer 表戰勝，通常代表已成功佔據既有領土、使某族群屈服於你，或是成功解決問題，消弭恐懼。其常見句型有: The N conquer…與 S conquer one's…of… ，以下透過範例做進一步說明：

EX The Mongolian conquered almost the whole Europe in 13 th century.
蒙古大軍於 13 世紀時橫掃幾乎整個歐陸。
→ 蒙古人占領了原本屬於歐洲各國的土地，故應以 conquer 來描述其戰無不勝。

EX I finally conquer my fear of eating fried insects.
我終於克服對於吃炸昆蟲的恐懼。

→ 說話者原本不敢吃炸昆蟲，但現在敢了，故應以 conquer 來描述終於突破此心理障礙。

★ Overpower

若以 overpower 表戰勝，代表是以更大的力氣或權力壓制對方，或是某種的氣味或感覺非常強烈，以致於讓人覺得不適。其常見句型有：S be overpowered by… 與 The feeling/smell of… overpower…，以下透過範例做進一步說明：

EX The gangster is soon overpowered by the police
歹徒很快被警方制服。

→ 警察需以更大的力量才能限制歹徒行動，故應以 overpower 來描述此種力量上的優勢。

EX The smell of rotten fruit overpowers me when I enter the kitchen. 我一踏進廚房，一陣腐敗水果的味道向我襲來。

→ 腐敗食物的味道令人作嘔，故應以 overpower 來表達對此種氣味的無法忍受。

實作練習與解析

❶ As most soccer fans expected, Brazil _____ Germany in the final and wins the champion in the World Cup.
(A) conquers (B) overcomes (C) overpowers
Ans: (B)。在世足賽中，巴西在決賽打敗德國，故應以 overcome 來表達在比賽中取勝。

❷ Bob _____ his nervousness to sing on the stage.

(A) overcomes (B) overpowers (C) conquers

Ans: (A)。鮑伯原本上台唱歌就會緊張，但現在克服了，故應以 overcome 來表達他心理素質的提升。

❸ The Spanish _____ almost the whole New World in 16th century

(A) overpowered (B) overcame (C) conquered

Ans: (C)。16 世紀時西班牙海軍可謂所向披靡，故應以 conquer 來描述其戰無不勝。

❹ Now Mary final_____ the fear of eating stinky Tofu.

(A) conquers (B) overpowers (C) overcomes

Ans: (A)。瑪麗之前不敢吃臭豆腐，但現在敢了，故應以 conquer 來描述她成功克服心理障礙。

❺ Three securities _____ the drunk man who waved a broken wine bottle for fear that he might hurt other consumers.

(A) overpower (B) overcome (C) conquer

Ans: (A)。保全人員基於安全考量將醉漢制服，故應以 overpower 來描述保全在力量上握有優勢。

❻ The feeling of sadness _____ me when I see the picture of my dead friend.

(A) overcomes (B) conquers (C) overpowers

Ans: (C)。當說話者看到過世友人的相片時，強烈的哀傷感湧上心頭，故應以 overpower 來描述情緒上的難以承受。

1 亂世佳人

2 傲慢與偏見

3 理性與感性

4 咆哮山莊

5 小婦人

6 簡愛

Unit 69
簡愛

俏佳人怎麼說

I care for myself. The more solitary,
the more friendless, the more unsustained I am,
the more I will respect myself. I will keep the law given
by God; sanctioned by man. I will hold to the
principles received by me when I was sane,
not mad—as I am now.!—Jane Eyre

我在意我自己。越獨立就越沒朋友、越不受限制，就越尊敬自己。我會遵守主所給予，人所許可的法。只要我神智清楚沒有發瘋，我就會恪守我所接收到的規則。——簡愛

作品概述

做為一名重視自身權益的女性，受了委屈簡愛必會討回公道。即便是面對自己的愛情，也不會亂了方寸。在得知未婚夫羅徹斯特其實早已結婚後，她冷靜地告訴對方，她不會做出有違信仰的事，更不會去觸犯法律上所不容的通姦罪。在這段強調凡事應合理方可為之的話語中，出現了表「許可」的單字 sanction，但由於英文中尚有 approve、permit、authorize 在語意與用法上皆與之相似，故本單元特將其並列做解析説明。

文法概述

Sanction / approve / permit / authorize

★ Sanction

一提到 Sanction，「制裁」是最為人所熟知的語意，但由於此舉需有法源依據，故當 sanction 做「許可」解時，強調的也是依法核予通過。其常見句型有: S be ready to sanction…，以下透過範例做進一步說明：

EX The government is ready to sanction the use of force to cease the turmoil.

政府已準備好動用武力平息動亂。

→ 若要動用武力，須符合相關法規，故應 sanction 來描述政府此舉的正當性。

★ Approve

若以 approve 表許可，代表某人對於某人或某事物抱持正面看法，而當某人恰為政府或是有官方機構時，概念上則與 sanction 相近。其常見句型有:S do(do not) approve of N/ving，以下透過範例做進一步說明：

EX My parents don't approve of my friends.

我的爸媽不喜歡我的朋友。

→ 說話者的雙親對其友人抱持負面觀感，故應以 don't approve of 來表達他們的好惡。

EX The government doesn't approve of reforming the existing financial act.

政府反對修改既有財金法案。

293

→ 政府對於修改現行法案持反對態度，故應以 don't approve of 來表達其立場。

★ Permit

若以 permit 表許可，代表某人允許某事，或是使事變得可能。其常見句型有:S permit Ving/ O to V，以下透過範例做進一步說明:

EX The police permit her to leave after the investigation.
完成調查後，警方同意讓她離開。

→ 案件的關係人配合調查後方可離開，故應以 permit 來描述人身自由限制的解除。

★ Authorize

若以 authorize 表許可，代表此項權力是由別人所授予，請其代為執行或是允許某事的進行。其常見句型有:S authorize O to …，以下透過範例做進一步說明:

EX My supervisor authorizes me to be responsible for this project.
主管授權我負責此專案。

→ 說話者原本非專案負責人，但現在主管給予權限，故應以 authorize 來描述此種權力上的取得。

實作練習與解析

❶ The government is ready to _____ the funding.
(A) approve (B) sanction (C) authorize (D) permit

Ans: (B)。政府將依法擴大融資，故應以 sanction 來表達此舉在法理上的正當性。

❷ Though Mandy's father doesn't _____ of her boyfriend, she still wants to marry him.

(A) approve　(B) permit　(C) sanction　(D) authorize.

Ans: (A)。蔓蒂的父母對她的男朋友印象不佳，故應以 don't approve of 來描述其觀感。

❸ We don't _____ smoking in all areas of our restaurant.

(A) authorize　(B) approve　(C) permit　(D) sanction

Ans: (C)。由於餐廳內的所有區域都是禁菸區，故應以 don't permit 來描述此項行為的受限 。

❹ The commander _____ the sniper to shoot the terrorist when the hostages are threatened.

(A) authorizes　(B) sanctions　(C) permits　(D) approves

Ans: (A)。只要覺得人質受到威脅，狙擊手可無須請示直接開槍，故應以 authorize 來描述指揮官將判斷的權力交給狙擊手執行。

❺ To finalize this deal soon, my boss _____ me to provide discount to this client.

(A) sanctions　(B) permits　(C) approves　(D) aythorizes

Ans: (D)。說話者原本無權決定折扣，但現在老闆給予他此權力，故應以 authorize 來描述降價已獲許可。

Unit 70
簡愛

俏佳人怎麼說

Do you think I am an automaton? —
a machine without feelings? and can bear to
have my morsel of bread snatched from my lips,
and my drop of living water dashed from my cup?
Do you think, because I am poor, obscure, plain,
and little, I am soulless and heartless? You think wrong!
— I have as much soul as you — and full as much heart!
And if God had gifted me with some beauty and
much wealth, I should have made it as hard for
you to leave me, as it is now for me to leave you. —Jane Eyre

你以為我是一架機器？— 一架沒有感情的機器？能夠容忍別人把一口麵包從我嘴裡搶走，把一滴生命之水從我杯子裡潑掉？難道就因為我一貧如洗、默默無聞、長相平庸、個子瘦小，就沒有靈魂，沒有心腸了？—你不是想錯了嗎？—我的心靈跟你一樣豐富，我的心胸跟你一樣充實！要是上帝賜予我一點姿色和充足的財富，我會使你同我現在一樣難分難捨。——簡愛

作品概述

　　做為一個凡事為自己爭取權益的女性，即使討價還價的對象是自己的愛人，簡愛也不會心軟。因此當她發現羅徹斯特嘴上說愛她要與之共結連理，事實上卻早已另有家室時，毅然決然地斬斷這份情，說出如果對方把自己當成沒有感情的機器，那他就大錯特錯。她強調自己或許不富有，外貌條件也不出色，但這不代表她就沒靈魂，就該受到不平等待遇。在這段充滿憤怒的話語中，出現了表「潑灑」的單字 dash，但由於英文中尚有 sprinkle、spray、spill 在語意與用法與之相似，故本單元特將其並列做解析說明。

文法概述

Dash / sprinkle / spray / spill

★ **Dash**

　　若以 dash 表潑灑，除力道十分強大外，由於是朝特定目標而去，故此類型的液體噴濺多具有針對性。其常見句型有 S dash…on/in…，以下透過範例做進一步說明：

EX David dashes a glass of wine in my face.

　　大衛拿了杯酒朝我臉上猛潑。

　　→ 由於是對著臉大力潑灑液體，故應以 dash 來強調此舉出於故意。

★ **Sprinkle**

　　若以 sprinkle 表潑灑，由於潑灑的量不多，力道也較輕，故此字也經常用於描述加入少量液體調料以增加食物風味。其常見句型有:S sprinkle…on…，以下透過範例做進一步說明：

1 亂世佳人　2 傲慢與偏見　3 理性與感性　4 咆哮山莊　5 小婦人　6 簡愛

EX The chef sprinkles some lemon juice on the fried fish fillet to make it taste better.

主廚在炸魚柳上加了點檸檬汁使其風味更佳。

➔ 檸檬汁的作用是要提味，故應以 sprinkle 來描述加入份量並不多。

★ Spray

若以 spray 表潑灑，代表此液體是裝在某種容器內，透過加壓的方式，使其噴濺的形式趨向霧狀。其常見句型有:S spray… on…，以下透過範例做進一步說明：

EX He sprays water on the flowers in the morning.

他早上替花澆水。

➔ 替花朵澆水不宜一次大量，故應以 spray 來描述此種少量霧狀灌溉方式。

★ Spill

若以 spill 表潑灑，意指因為移動、流動、擴散等原因，使液體超出容器的邊緣而流出。其常見句型有:S spill…down/on …，以下透過範例做進一步說明：

EX I spill coffee on my white shirt.

我把咖啡灑到我的白襯衫上了。

➔ 說話者可能因不留神而把杯內的咖啡濺出，因而弄髒衣服，故應以 spill 來描述此類的液體潑灑。

實作練習與解析

❶ Why you _____ the water in my face?

(A) sprinkle　(B) spray　(C) spill　(D) dash

Ans: (D)。一般來說，朝人潑水多為故意，故應以 dash 來強調潑灑的力道很強，且有針對性。

❷ My mom _____ some wine on the steamed fish to improve flavor.

(A) dashes　(B) sprinkles　(C) spills　(D) sprays

Ans: (B)。說話者的母親加酒是要去腥，故應以 sprinkle 來描述添加的分量不多。

❸ The farmer _____ his roses periodically to make sure them can grow well.

(A) spills　(B) dashes　(C) sprays　(D) sprinkles

Ans: (C)。花朵依此不宜用大量的水來灌溉，故應以 spray 來描述其少量的液體噴灑。

❹ I _____ red wine on my white jacket, so I have to clean it soon in case some spot left.

(A) spill　(B) spray　(C) sprinkle　(D) dash

Ans: (A)。說話者不小心將紅酒灑到白外套上，故應以 sprinkle 來表達此類的液體噴濺。

❺ To make the meat more tasty, I _____ some ginger on it.

(A) spray　(B) dash　(C) sprinkle　(D) spill

Ans: (C)。說話者加醋是要使食物更加美味，故應以 sprinkle 來強調是少量添加。

右側標籤：

1 亂世佳人

2 傲慢與偏見

3 理性與感性

4 咆哮山莊

5 小婦人

6 簡愛

Unit 71
簡愛

俏佳人怎麼說

What a singularly deep impression her injustice seems to have made on your heart... Would you not be happier if you tried to forget her severity, together with the passionate emotions it excited? Life appears to me too short to be spent in nursing animosity, or registering wrongs. —Helen Burns

她的不公平已在你的心中留下深刻印象。如果試著忘記她的嚴厲,以及那些讓人激動的強烈情緒,你會不會更快樂呢?對我來說,人生苦短,所以不該花在懷恨與計較不公平上。——海倫‧柏恩斯

作品概念

　　海倫的人生觀,大概可以用「人生苦短,何須計較」來概括。當簡愛受到老師的不當對待跟她大吐苦水時,她並未附和,而是要簡愛學會放下,因為海倫認為人生短暫,如果再把這有限的時間浪費在記仇上,實在不值。在這段強調淡然的話語中,出現了表「激動」的單字 passionate,但由於英文中尚有 ardent、zealous 在語意及用法上與之相似,故本單元特將其並列做解析說明。

文法概述

Passionate / ardent / zealous / intense

★ **Passionate**

若以 passionate 表激動的，代表某人對某事非常喜愛或抱持信念。其常見句型有:S be passionate about…與 S be a passionate N，以下透過範例做進一步說明：

EX I am passionate about soccer.

我很愛踢足球。

→ 說話者非常喜歡踢足球，故應以 passionate 來強調其喜愛程度。

EX I am a passionate fan of Los Angeles Clippers

我是洛杉磯快艇隊的忠實球迷。

→ 說話者愛看快艇隊球員打球，故應以 passionate 來描述他對這支球隊的喜愛。

★ **Ardent**

若以 ardent 表激動的，其情緒強度為本單元四者中最強，故通常用於表達對於某人或某事物的極度喜愛或強烈信念。其常見句型有: S be an ardent N of…，以下透過範例做進一步說明：

EX She is an ardent supporter of feminism.

她是女權主義的深度支持者。

→ 說話者對於女權主義高度認同，故應以 ardent 來強調其立場的堅定。

1 亂世佳人

2 傲慢與偏見

3 理性與感性

4 咆哮山莊

5 小婦人

6 簡愛

★ Zealous

若以 zealous 表激動的，多代表某人因對於政治、宗教或慈善活動抱持熱忱與渴望，故願意投入大量心力與時間於其中。其常見句型有:S be a zealous N of⋯，以下透過範例做進一步說明:

EX David is a zealous worker of charitable activities.
大衛對於投入慈善活動充滿熱忱。

→ 大衛對於行善非常有熱忱，故應以 zealous 來強調他願意投入時間心力於其中。

實作練習與解析

❶ I am _____ about basketball, so I practice my dribbling skill almost everyday

(A) zealous   (B) passionate   (C) ardent

Ans: (B)。說話者因為愛打籃球而幾乎天天練習運球，故應以 passionate 描述他對此項運動的熱愛。

❷ I am a _____ fan of Robert Downey Jr..

(A) ardent   (B) zealous   (C) passionate

Ans: (C)。說話者非常喜歡小勞伯道尼這位演員，故應以 passionate 來凸顯其喜愛程度。

❸ Mark is an _____ believer of parallel universes.

(A) ardent   (B) zealous   (C) passionate

Ans: (A)。馬可深信平行時空的確存在，故應以 ardent 來描述他對此想法的深信不疑。

❹ Frank is a _____ political reformer.

(A) passionate　(B) zealous　(C) ardent

Ans: (B)。法蘭克對於政治改革有即大熱忱，故應以 zealous 來描述其全心投入。

❺ Being a _____ believer of Gravitational wave theory, I am so excited to know that scientists have found some evidence to prove its existence.

(A) zealous　(B) passionate　(C) ardent

Ans: (C)。說話者深切相信重力波確實存在，故應以 ardent 來描述他對理論的深信不疑。

❻ Peter is a _____ supporter of taxation reformation.

(A) ardent　(B) zealous　(C) passionate

Ans: (B)。彼得非常支持政府對稅制進行改革，故應以 zealous 來凸顯其立場堅定。

1 亂世佳人

2 傲慢與偏見

3 理性與感性

4 咆哮山莊

5 小婦人

6 簡愛

Unit 72
簡愛

🔍 俏佳人怎麼說

By dying young, I shall escape great
sufferings. I had not qualities or talents
to make my way very well in the world:
I should have been continually at fault. —Helen Burns
由於我的人生提早謝幕，使我可免受許多苦難。我沒有本事或才能讓
我出人頭地，我應該只會一直出錯。——海倫·柏恩斯

作品概述

　　進入寄宿學校後，簡愛結交了一名好友海倫，但由於學校的飲食衛生條件都不好，海倫染上斑疹傷寒，最後因該病而過世。面對死亡，海倫雖年紀尚輕，但卻看得很開。她覺得自己一無是處，留在人世會多受磨難，死亡反而是種提早解脫。在這段參透生死的話語中，出現了表「遠離」的單字 escape，但由於英文中尚有 evade、flee、abscond 在語意與用法上與之相似，故本單元特將其並列做解析說明。

📃 文法概述

☙ *Escape / evade / flee / abscond* ❧

★ Escape

若以 escape 表遠離,代表擺脫限制離開某處或是避免某事的發生。其常見句型有:S escape from…與 S narrowly escape…,以下透過範例做進一步說明:

EX Several lions just escaped from its cage, so all tourists are evacuated.
好幾隻獅子剛從欄舍中逃脫,所以園方疏散所有遊客。

➔ 欄舍的功用在侷限獅子的活動範圍,故應以 escape 來描述當前限制功能的喪失。

EX I narrowly escape a huge fine.
我差點就要繳交鉅額罰款了。

➔ 說話者差點就讓受罰這件事發生,故應以 narrowly escape 來表現出千鈞一髮的語境。

★ Evade

若以 evade 表遠離,經常用於描述不想與某人有所接觸、不想做某事,以及閃躲某些話題,有其常見句型有: S evade Ving 與 S evade O by…,以下透過範例做進一步說明:

EX As the male citizen of our country, you can't evade doing your military service.
做為本國的男性公民,你不能逃避服兵役。

➔ 服兵役雖為公民義務,但仍有人想閃躲,故應以 escape 來表

305

1 亂世佳人
2 傲慢與偏見
3 理性與感性
4 咆哮山莊
5 小婦人
6 簡愛

達少數人對此事的抗拒。

EX Sam evades his ex-girlfriend by moving to other place.
山姆搬家以躲避前女友。

→ 山姆不想與前女友有所接觸，故應以 evade 來表達他刻意隱藏
行蹤。

★ Flee

若以 flee 表遠離，通常是因為遭遇危險或是心生恐懼而離開某處。其
常見句型有:S flee from⋯，以下透過範例做進一步說明:

EX Sandy flees from the building with fear.
姍蒂一臉驚恐地自大樓中逃離。

→ 姍蒂因恐懼而選擇離開大樓，故應以 flee 點出她逃跑的原因。

★ Abscond

若以 abscond 表遠離，通常是臨時起意或是秘密進行，獨自或團體
行動都有可能，也可能攜帶某些物品，但目的都是希望不為人所察
覺。其常見句型有:S abscond from⋯with⋯，以下透過範例做進一
步說明:

EX The thief absconded from the billionaire's house with all
the luxury jewelry.
竊賊從億萬富翁家中偷走所有貴重珠寶後逃離。

→ 竊賊在未被察覺的情況下偷走珠寶，故應以 abscond 來描述
此種計畫性的逃跑。

實作練習與解析

❶ Two criminals are found _____ from the prison, so the police is chasing them.

(A) absconding (B) escaping (C) fleeing (D) evading

Ans: (B)。監獄目的在限縮罪犯的活動範圍，故應 escape 來說明脫逃的兩人突破此限制。

❷ I narrowly _____ a car accident.

(A) escape (B) flee (C) evade (D) abscond

Ans: (A)。說話者差點就發生車禍，故應以 narrowly escape 來強調其千鈞一髮。

❸ The dishonest businessman try to _____ paying tax.

(A) flee (B) abscond (C) escape (D) evade

Ans: (B)。有收入就應繳稅，故應以 evade 表達少數人試圖不履行此舉。

❹ Parker _____ her ex-girlfriend by changing a job.

(A) flees (B) escapes (C) evades (D) absconds

Ans: (C)。帕克不想再與前女友有所接觸而選擇換工作，故應以 evade 來描述他對此人的躲避。

❺ I _____ from my room with fear when a serious earthquake happens.

(A) evade (B) abscond (C) escape (D) flee

Ans: (D)。地震的發生讓說話者非常驚恐，故應以 flee 來描述他帶有恐懼地逃離。

1 亂世佳人

2 傲慢與偏見

3 理性與感性

4 咆哮山莊

5 小婦人

6 簡愛

Unit 73
簡愛

🔍 俏佳人怎麼說

School-rules, school-duties, school-habits
and notions, and voices, and faces, and phrases,
and costumes, and preferences, and antipathies —
such was what I knew of existence. —Jane Eyre

學校規定與職責、學校生活習慣和觀念、聲音，面孔和用語，以及服
飾、喜好、厭惡─我就只知道有這些。──簡愛

作品概述

　　來到寄宿學校後，簡愛原本以為一切生活會更好，可以學到更多，可以多看看這個世界。但無奈天不從人願，學校能給她很有限，簡愛覺得每天就好像活在象牙塔裡，外頭的世界是怎樣，她完全一無所知。在這段簡愛對於學校生活的抱怨裡，出現了表「責任」的單字 duty，但由於英文中尚有 liability、responsibility、obligation 在語意及用法皆與知相似，故本單元特將其並列做解析說明。

文法概述

Duty / responsibility / liability / obligation

★ Duty

若以 duty 表責任，除代表某事為某人工作的一部分，或是法律上所規定之義務。但當與 out of 連用時，由於既不是工作也不是義務，代表完全出於自願。其常見句型有：S have the duty to…與 S V out of duty，以下透過範例做進一步說明：

EX You have the duty to finish the case by this Friday.

你有責任於本週五完成此案件。

→ 被提醒的一方有責任如期完成案件，故應以 duty 來表達此案為其工作的一部分。

★ Responsibility

若以 responsibility 表責任，若表達此為工作的一部分，多代表某人要替成敗負責。但更多時候用於說明自發性地做某事。其常見句型有：It is one's responsibility to…與 S have the responsibility for Ving，以下透過範例做進一步說明：

EX Sally has the responsibility for checking the document before shipping.

莎莉有責任在出貨前確認文件的正確性。

→ 如果出貨後文件有錯誤，莎莉需負責，故應以 responsibility 來描述她所承擔的責任。

★ Liability

若以 liability 表責任，側重的是法律上的權力與義務的對應關係，尤

1 亂世佳人

2 傲慢與偏見

3 理性與感性

4 咆哮山莊

5 小婦人

6 簡愛

其是關於「金錢」的部分。其常見句型有:S have liability for…，以下透過範例做進一步說明：

EX According to the contract, sellers have legal liability for any lost cause by the delay of the shipment to buyer.

根據合約，賣方有責任賠償任何因出貨延遲所衍生的損失給買方。

→ 出貨延遲可能造成買方金錢上的損失，故應以 liability 來描述賣方所承擔的責任。

★ Obligation

若以 obligation 表責任，強調的是在法律的基礎上，某人應於某個時段內完成某事。其常見句型有:S have obligation to…，以下透過範例做進一步說明：

EX Since the purchase amount is huge, buyers have the obligation to pay 30 percent as the deposit before shipment.

由於採購量極大，買方需先支付百分之三十的訂金。

→ 賣方要收到訂金才出貨，故應以 obligation 來描述買方所需負擔的責任。

實作練習與解析

❶ I have the _____ to send the document before 15:00 today.
(A) liability　(B) obligation　(C) responsibility　(D) duty
Ans: (D)。今天三點前把文件寄出是說話者工作的一小部分，故應以 duty 來描述此種責任。

❷ I have the _____ to pack the good well before shipment.

(A) obligation   (B) duty   (C) responsibility   (D) liability

Ans: (C)。出貨後如果包裝不完善，說話者必須負責，故應以 responsibility 來描述其所承擔的責任。

❸ It is son and daughter's _____ to make their parents free from worry when they grow up.

(A) duty   (B) responsibility   (C) obligation   (D) liability

Ans: (B)。子女長大成人後，本就應當照顧好自己不讓父母擔心，故應以 responsibility 來描述做到此點乃理所當然。

❹ If you fail to send me the parts in time, you have the _____ to compensate my lost.

(A) responsibility   (B) duty   (C) obligation   (D) liability

Ans: (D)。說話者保是對方如無法及時寄出零件給他，就需負擔相關損失，故應以 liability 來描述此種有關金錢的責任。

❺ According to the agreement, you have the _____ to pay the down payment within five working days after the arrival of the product.

(A) obligation   (B) liability   (C) duty   (D) responsibility

Ans: (A)。依照合約，收到貨品後五個工作天內買方要匯尾款給賣方，故應以 obligation 來描述此種需於一定時間內完成的責任。

1 亂世佳人

2 傲慢與偏見

3 理性與感性

4 咆哮山莊

5 小婦人

6 簡愛

Unit 74
簡愛

🔍 俏佳人怎麼說

Women are supposed to be very calm generally; but women feel just as men feel; they need exercise for their faculties and a field for their efforts as much as their brothers do; they suffer from too rigid a restraint, too absolute a stagnation, precisely as men would suffer; and it is narrow-minded in their more privileged fellow-creatures to say that they ought to confine themselves to making puddings and knitting stockings, to playing on the piano and embroidering bags. —Jane Eyre

一般來說，女人也應該是很冷靜的;但女人其實跟男人一樣;也需要練習自己的才能，向她們的兄弟那樣做很多努力;她們遭到嚴格限制，這無疑地是一種停滯，一如男人所會遭受的那樣;但如果享有特權的男性認為，女人應當只做做布丁、針織襪子，彈彈鋼琴和縫製繡花袋，這樣就非常心胸狹隘了。——簡愛

作品概念

當簡愛離開寄宿學校來到桑費爾德莊園，她以為這次終於可以過著快

樂的日子，但是事實上，現實的種種依舊讓她焦躁不安，她也在腦中思考這世界上有哪些事情是可能成立的，例如男女的地位。簡愛覺得男女不該是不平等的，女性的才能與努力都不輸男性，但卻因為重男輕女的觀念，而有刻板印象。在這段強調男女平權的話語中，出現了表「能力」的單字 facility，但由於英文中尚有 ability 與 capability 在語意及用法上與之相似，故本單元特將其並列做解析說明。

文法概述

Facility / ability / capability

★ Facility

若以 facility 表能力，代表某人可以輕易完成或做到某事。其常見句型有: One's facility for …is…，以下透過範例做進一步說明：

EX My facility for English is good.

我的英文能力很好。

→ 說話者可以輕易地用英文與人溝通，故應以 facility 來描述他所擁有的能力。

★ Ability

若以 ability 表能力，表達的是做某事所需具備的「聰明才智」與「相關技能」有哪些。其常見句型有:S have the ability to…，以下透過範例做進一步說明：

EX Mary is an experienced sales, so she has the ability to finish this project alone.

瑪莉是很有經驗的業務，所以她有能力獨自完成此專案。

1 亂世佳人

2 傲慢與偏見

3 理性與感性

4 咆哮山莊

5 小婦人

6 簡愛

→ 瑪莉過去的實務經驗使她寧願獨立作業的，故應以 ability 來描述所具備的才能。

★ Capability

若以 capability 表能力，代表某人達到做某事所需的條件或標準。其常見句型有:S have the capability to，若要表達某事超過某人的能力所及，則常以…is beyond one's capability of…來表示，以下透過範例做進一步說明：

EX Though Tim is a five-year-old child, he has the capability to solve senior high school math questions.

提姆雖然才五歲，但他能夠算出高中數學問題的答案。

→ 五歲的提姆的數學能力達到高中的水準，故應以 capability 來表達他所數學能力的水平。

EX This math test is far beyond the capability of elementary school students.

本次數學考試的難度遠超小學生的程度。

→ 本次數學考試對小學生來說太難，故應以 beyond the capability of 來表達其解題能力尚未達此水準。

實作練習與解析

❶ Jason's _____ of Japanese is astonishing, so many people think he is a native speaker.

(A) capability (B) ability (C) facility

Ans: (C)。傑森的日文非常好，好到有人以為他是母語人士，故應以 facility 來描述他語言能力的傑出。

❷ Amy has the _____ to introduce our product in a neat but attractive way.
(A) facility   (B) ability   (C) capability
Ans: (B)。艾咪介紹產品簡潔有力且引人注意，故應以 ability 來表達她具備優秀的行銷能力。

❸ The physics exam is beyond the _____ of most students, so the average score is only 32.
(A) capability   (B) facility   (C) ability
Ans: (A)。本次物理考試對多數學生來說太難，故應以 beyond the capability of 來表達知識吸收上的不足。

❹ Ivan's _____ of Spanish is good, so he almost has no language barrier when he travel in South America.
(A) capability   (B) ability   (C) facility
Ans: (C)。艾文的西班牙語很好，在南美洲旅遊幾乎不會有語言障礙，故應以 facility 來描述他語言能力的傑出。

❺ David has the _____ to settle down the conflict, so you don't have to worry.
(A) facility   (B) ability   (C) capability
Ans: (B)。大衛可以把事情都處理好，故應以 ability 來表達他優秀的危機處理能力。

1 亂世佳人
2 傲慢與偏見
3 理性與感性
4 咆哮山莊
5 小婦人
6 簡愛

Unit 75
簡愛

🔍 俏佳人怎麼說

I don't think, sir, you have a right to command me,
merely because you are older than I, or because
you have seen more of the world than I have;
your claim to superiority depends on the use you
have made of your time and experience. —Jane Eyre

我不認為只因為你比我年長一些，或是你比我多了解這世界一些，你就有權命令我。你所主張的優越不過就是你比我多活一些時日與多些社會經驗罷了。——簡愛

作品概念

　　當發現遭受不公平對待或是受了委屈，不管對象是誰，簡愛絕對不會默默承受。因此，當她的愛人羅徹斯特以他較年長為由，要簡愛凡事聽他的時，簡愛馬上出言反擊，男女相處應平等相待，用年紀與社會經驗來強迫對方聽你指揮實屬不該。在這段強調男女平權的話語中，出現了表「優越」的單字 superiority，但由於英文中尚有 ascendancy、precedency 在語意即用法上與之相似，故本單元特將其並列做解析說明。

文法概述

Superiority / ascendancy / precedency

★ Superiority

若以 superiority 表優越，代表某一方在競爭或是衝突中因設備較佳、人數較多或是表現較好等因速而掌握優勢。在其常見句型有:S enjoy superiority over/in… by/with…，以下透過範例做進一步說明：

EX The home team enjoys superiority (over the guest team) in last second of the match with a three-point shot.
主隊在最後一秒一記三分球在比賽中(對客隊)取得優勢。

→ 主隊在因為一次三分球出手而在比數上取得領先，故應以 superiority 來描述主隊保有的優勢。

★ Ascendancy

若以 ascendancy 表優越，代表某人或某群體獲得較大的權力或影響力，而想有主導地位。其他其常見句型有:S gain/lose the ascendancy in…，以下透過範例做進一步說明：

EX The left wings gain the ascendancy in this meeting.
本次會議中左派取得優勢。

→ 再開會過程中，通常會有一方的看法取得多數人同意，故應以 ascendancy 來表達左派獲得較多認同。

★ Precedency

若以 precedency 表優越，通常描述以下兩種情況，一是某人在特定組織、機構或團體內的重要程度較高。二是某特定情況下，應優先

1 亂世佳人

2 傲慢與偏見

3 理性與感性

4 咆哮山莊

5 小婦人

6 簡愛

執行的事項。其常見句型有:The precedency of…in…is/are…，以下透過範例做進一步說明：

EX The precedency in this team is director, deputy director, specialist, and assistant.

此團隊的職位由高至低為組長、副組長、專員及助理。

→ 就位階來看，組長最高，助理最低。故應以 precedency 來表達此種重要程度的排序。

EX The precedency of medical aid in evacuation plan is the unconscious, the conscious but serious injured, and the injured.

疏散計畫中優先給予醫療協助的順序是失去意識的、有意識但重傷的，最後才是輕傷的。

→ 疏散人群時，無意識的傷患應優先救治，最後才是輕傷的。故應以 precedency 來描述給予醫療協助的先後順序。

實作練習與解析

❶ The guest team enjoys the _____ with a homerun in 9th inning.

(A) precedency (B) ascendancy (C) superiority

Ans: (C)。客隊在第九局靠全壘打取的分數上的優勢，故應以 superiority 來描述鎖定戰局的機會極高。

❷ The conservative gain the _____ in the direction of the investment plan.

(A) ascendancy　(B) precedency　(C) superiority

Ans: (A)。開會本來就會有的意見被否決，而有的被接受，故應以 ascendancy 來描述保守派這次獲得較多支持。

❸ The ＿＿＿＿ of this team is project manager, sales representative, and assistant.

(A) precedency　(B) superiority　(C) ascendancy

Ans: (A)。這個團隊的以專案經理為主管，底下設置業務與助理，故應以 precedency 來描述其位階有高低之分。

❹ For many business people, the ＿＿＿＿ of good business English is often fluency, commotion, and grammar.

(A) superiority　(B) ascendancy　(C) precedency

Ans: (C)。商界人士心中的好商業英文要流利且能溝通，文法上有沒有瑕疵相對次之，故應以 precedency 來描述此種排序。

❺ The team I love gain the ＿＿＿＿ with a free kick.

(A) superiority　(B) precedency　(C) ascendancy

Ans: (A)。說話者所支持的球隊因為自由球而取得分數上的領先，故應以 superiority 來描述此種優勢。

❻ Though most shareholders expect more investment, the right wing still gains the ＿＿＿＿ in this board meeting.

(A) precedency　(B) ascendancy　(C) superiority

Ans: (B)。雖然股東覺得公司要有更多投資，但董事會上右翼還是獲得認同，故應以 ascendancy 來描述保守作為還是較被接受。

1 亂世佳人
2 傲慢與偏見
3 理性與感性
4 咆哮山莊
5 小婦人
6 簡愛

Leader 047

文法俏佳人

作　　者	邱佳翔
發 行 人	周瑞德
執行總監	齊心瑀
企劃編輯	陳韋佑
校　　對	編輯部
封面構成	高鍾琪

內頁構成	菩薩蠻數位文化有限公司
印　　製	大亞彩色印刷製版股份有限公司
初　　版	2016 年 7 月
定　　價	新台幣 360 元
出　　版	力得文化
電　　話	(02) 2351-2007
傳　　真	(02) 2351-0887
地　　址	100 台北市中正區福州街 1 號 10 樓之 2
E-mail	best.books.service@gmail.com
網　　址	www.bestbookstw.com

港澳地區總經銷	泛華發行代理有限公司
地　　址	香港新界將軍澳工業邨駿昌街 7 號 2 樓
電　　話	(852) 2798-2323
傳　　真	(852) 2796-5471

國家圖書館出版品預行編目資料

文法俏佳人 / 邱佳翔著. -- 初版. -
臺北市 : 力得文化, 2016.07 面 ;
公分. - (Leader ; 47)
ISBN 978-986-92856-6-7(平裝)
1.英語 2.語法
　805.16　　　　　　　　　　105010258